Copyright © 2022 Olivia Hayle

All rights reserved. No part of this publication may be distributed or transmitted without the prior consent of the publisher, except in case of brief quotations embodied in articles or reviews.

All characters and events depicted in this book are entirely fictitious. Any similarity to actual events or persons, living or dead, is purely coincidental.

The following story contains mature themes, strong language and explicit scenes, and is intended for mature readers.

Cover by Ana Grigoriu-Voicu, books-design.com.
Edited by Stephanie Parent
www.oliviahayle.com

OLIVIA HAYLE

ONE

Audrey

It's the waiting I hate the most. Nerves grow until they're so thick in my stomach that I feel nauseous, my palms turning slick around my glass. Why had I ordered a Cosmo? I've never had one before in my life.

Brian's late. How late is acceptable before I'm entitled to leave? Leaving would be the easier option. A quick text. *Let's rain check.* But that would be fleeing, and I'd promised myself I would face my fears.

Idiot, I think. I should have started with something smaller. Confined spaces, spiders, the concept of infinity.

Just not blind dating.

I can't handle the awkwardness. To see how he looks down at his phone, or worse, to look down at my own in search of an excuse. What if he's visibly disappointed by me? Or worse, what if he wants to grab a nightcap and I don't?

I take a fortifying sip of my pink drink. One drink. That's all we have to share, and then I can say I have to get back home because I have work tomorrow. I'll order some food on the way home to celebrate surviving.

The bar looks good, at least. He'd been the one to suggest it after a week of awkward text exchanges. Dim lighting and patrons in fancy clothes. Music at just the right volume. Not too loud, not too quiet. The prices are just shy of fortune-ruining, which is good for Manhattan.

My phone vibrates against the table with a text. Brian's late, which I already know, and he apologizes profusely.

He actually uses the word *profusely*.

I put the phone down and take five steadying breaths. Maybe I should have eaten something after my job interview before coming here. Maybe scheduling a blind date and an interview for my dream job on the same day was too much. But I'd been caught up in a rush of adrenaline and bravery, and I'd done it.

And now I'm paying the price.

"It's just a date," I murmur to myself. The ball of nerves in my stomach doesn't listen, continuing to spin in nausea-inducing patterns. "Just a date. I can leave if I don't like it. Just leave."

I don't feel better, so I try another argument. One that Nina had said over and over again last night as she talked me back from the ledge of cancelling.

The only way to get more comfortable with it is exposure.

But exposure doesn't seem so harmless tonight, and not when Brian just gave me another fifteen minutes to sit alone and look like a dork while my nerves rise from innocent butterflies to Hitchcock-like birds in my stomach.

I need a glass of cold water.

I leave my Cosmo on the table and head for the bar. It's mostly empty, a few businessmen leaning against it in smarmy suits. Standing up feels good. Moving about feels good.

I lean against the bar and tap my fingers against the glass counter.

The bartender spots me. "Yes?"

"A cold glass of water, please," I say. "Lots of ice."

"Still or sparkling?"

"Still."

"Sure thing." He turns, but stops. "Would you like some lemon in that?"

"Just water. Please." Why is dating horribly, awfully nerve-wracking for me? Everyone else seems to have a breeze doing it. They dance from one date to the next like it's a game.

The bartender sets a tall glass of water in front of me. I drain it, every last drop, until there's nothing but clinking ice left.

A voice speaks to my left. "You doing okay?"

I catch the sleeve of a suit jacket beside me, a large hand curled around a glass of scotch, but I keep my eye on my own. My chest is heaving. "Yes. Just fine, thank you."

"Need another glass of water?" The voice is male, smooth and deep.

I shake my head and close my eyes. The last thing I need is someone to waste all my pent-up small-talk energy on. "Nope. All good."

A small bowl of complimentary peanuts is pushed into my field of vision. "Just in case."

The gesture makes me chuckle. It comes out like a nervous squeak, but it releases some of the tension rising up inside of me like a teapot.

"Thank you," I say, turning toward him.

Light, tawny eyes meet mine. I've never seen eyes like that on a man before. Hair a dark shade of auburn is pushed back over his forehead, rising over a square face. "If you're planning on having a panic attack," he says, "I can think of better places than this bar."

"I'm not having a panic attack. Besides, who *plans* on having one?"

"It's just a figure of speech."

"It's a stupid one," I say, and smooth my hands over my dress. Then I realize what I've just said. "Sorry. I didn't mean to insult you."

He turns toward me, his lips curling at the corner. He's

tall, now that's he's stretched to his full height. "I'm not insulted."

"Good. Well… thank you for the peanuts."

"You're welcome, although I have a confession to make. They were already here."

I snort again. Perhaps this is good. I can blow off steam with this Wall Street banker. "I suspected. Nice gesture, though."

He waves a hand at the bartender, who turns mid-stride to listen to whatever peanut guy has to say. I glance at his suit. He looks like money. It's there in the well-fitting fabric, glossy beneath the dim lights. I don't trust guys who look like him. Too charming to be real, and too rich to be humble.

"Another water for the lady," he says. "Lots of ice, no lemon. You know the drill."

The bartender nods. "Coming right up."

He disappears down the bar and peanut guy turns back to me.

I frown at him. "You didn't say please."

His eyebrows rise. "I'm sorry?"

"To the bartender." I'm speaking more frankly than usual, especially to a stranger, but my nerves have me turned upside down. My cheeks heat up. "I mean, it's just more polite to say please."

"Noted," peanut guy says. He leans against the bar, lips still quirked. "Although, I'm sure that bartender has seen people far ruder than me in his days."

"That's not an excuse to be rude going forward."

"I tip generously," he says. "Always have."

"Flinging money around doesn't make up for a lack of manners."

"So now I'm lacking manners? Interesting."

I shake my head. "That's not what I'm implying. Gosh, can we ignore where I tried to correct you? I'm sorry. That was rude of me."

He doesn't look the least bit offended. "Not particularly."

The bartender returns with a full glass of ice water and puts it down in front of me. I open my mouth to say thank you, but peanut guy beats me to it.

"Thank you," he says, voice dropping. "We really appreciate your help here tonight."

The bartender doesn't stop moving down the bar. "Anytime," he tosses over his shoulder.

Peanut guy turns to me with a triumphant smile. "Am I back in your good graces now?"

"Yes. Sorry."

He rests his suit-clad arms on the bar counter. "So what's got you so bent out of shape?"

"Bent out of shape," I repeat, reaching for my ice water. I drain half of it before confessing. "I'm actually waiting for someone."

"I figured. Is he late?"

"He is, yeah. Is it obvious?"

"Well, you're here and he's not, so yes. Boyfriend?"

"Just a date." I twirl my glass around. "A first date, actually."

"And he's late? That's not a good sign." Peanut guy reaches for an actual peanut, his hand cutting across my vision. It's broad and lightly dusted with dark brown hair. A masculine hand, with long fingers. "How late is too late?"

"I don't know. I don't have a hard and fast rule about it."

"Do you have hard and fast rules about a lot of things?"

I look over at him. It's a bad idea, because he's stupidly good-looking. Square jaw and eyes that meet mine with steady charm. Oddly enough, I'm not nervous talking to him. We're so obviously not suited. He's amusing himself, I'm distracting myself.

Exposure, I think.

"About some things, I guess. I have criteria."

"Let's hear them," he says.

"Well, he has to be a nonsmoker."

Peanut guy gives a nod. "Right."

"I'd like it if he could cook me dinner once in a while."

"So he needs to be a renowned chef," he says. "Got it."

I chuckle at that. "Right. Oh, and he has to subscribe to a newspaper or magazine. *At least* one, preferably more, and they can't just be digital subscriptions."

"Oddly specific," he says. Long fingers curl around his glass, eyes the color of whiskey. "Is that a literacy test? Because I think you can reliably assume a guy your age would be able to read."

"No, I'm a journalist."

"Is that so?"

"Yes. I need someone who appreciates the written word, you know? I want to spend my Sunday mornings arguing over who has what portion of the newspaper." Hearing myself, my cheeks flare up again. "I know how I sound. Like a hopeless romantic."

"Are you one?"

"I'm a realistic romantic," I say. "Which is why I'm on a first date with a stranger."

He lifts an eyebrow again. "This is a blind date?"

"Yes."

"And he's late. Really not off to a good start."

I shrug, feeling the nerves settle into a current in my stomach. Talking to this guy helps. "Well, I'll give him a shot. Something might have happened to him on the way here, you know." I look over his shoulder, but the businessmen down the end of the bar counter are talking amongst themselves, paying him no mind. "Why are you here? Waiting for your own blind date?" I can't say it without smiling. As if.

"No," he says, swirling the amber liquid in his glass around. "I've met her before."

That makes me roll my eyes. "Of course. She's late too?"

"Yes. Often is, as a matter of fact."

"I guess that's not on your list of criteria, then."

"No. Come to think of it, I don't know if she subscribes to a newspaper."

"You should ask her that tonight," I say. "I've heard it's a dealbreaker for some."

His smile stretches wide. "So have I, kid," he says. "Tell me why dating makes you this nervous."

"Kid? We're practically the same age!"

He's still smiling. "Are we? I can't remember the last time I was as nervous as you waiting for someone to show up."

This guy is a roller coaster. "That doesn't define my maturity. I'm twenty-six," I say. Honesty makes me add the rest. "Well, I will be in four months' time. How old are you?"

"Thirty-two," he says.

That's when my phone vibrates in my pocket again. Ice shoots through my veins, freezing me to the spot. Brian's probably here. Has it already been fifteen minutes? God, I hate this. Hate it hate it hate it.

A glance down at my phone confirms it. *I'm outside. Did you grab a table?*

"Is that him?" Peanut guy says.

"Yes," I murmur. "It's showtime."

"For him, not for you," he says. "Just be yourself."

"Right." My fingers fly over my phone. *I have a table inside.*

"Good luck, kid. I'll be over here if you need me."

"Stop calling me a kid," I say. My nerves are flaring up again, making me lash out. "And don't look at me the whole date. That's weird."

He smiles wide, and I catch a hint of a dimple beneath the dark five-o'clock shadow coating his jaw. "Just signal and I'll give you a plausible excuse."

"Um, thanks. Have a nice evening," I say and head toward my table. My disgusting drink stands there, forgotten. I sit down and smooth my hands over my dress. *I can do this.* When I look up, I cast my eyes about for a man striding my way.

Instead I meet peanut guy's gaze.

He's leaning against the bar, glass in hand, and gives me the smallest of nods. There's a hint of a smile on his face.

The arrogant bastard.

But he's quickly eclipsed by the man who approaches me. This has to be Brian. Nina set me up with him, a guy from her old job. She promised he would be nice. That was the word she used. *Nice.*

He looks nice, I think, in a friendly sort of way. He's wearing a beanie that sits low on top of dark curls. He shrugs out of his denim jacket.

"Hey," he says. "Sorry I'm late."

"No worries."

He looks down at my drink, and a frown mars his face. "You've already ordered?"

Yeah, dude. I was waiting here alone for twenty minutes. "I did, yes. I hope that's okay."

He shrugs and sits down opposite me. "Sure, sure. So Nina told me you're a journalist."

"I am, yes. I'd love to work in investigative reporting someday," I say. Hopefully sooner than just *one day*, if the interview today had gone as well as it felt. I'd spent over two hours today at the *New York Globe*'s offices.

"So you write, like, these exposing pieces about government corruption and scandals?" He slouches in his chair, but his eyes glow with enthusiasm. This is promising.

I spin my disgusting drink around and nod. "I'd like to, at least."

"You know, I have a lot of opinions about the press."

"You do?"

He raises a finger. Almost like he's lecturing me. "You guys need to start reporting more on facts, and less with your emotions."

Um... "Yes. Well, reporting on the facts as they are is the hallmark of good journalistic integrity."

"Sure, but so often they don't. You know, I haven't subscribed to a newspaper in years. The facts I care about are all online. I can find them with the press of a button."

I rub a hand over my neck. "Well, a lot of people do that nowadays. Print media is struggling for that very reason."

"It's dying, more like it. But if you reported more on facts, you'd be doing better." He raises a hand, signaling to the waitress. "Over here!"

Oh, dude. That's not okay. My nerves turn to irritation instead. "Say please," I mutter. He doesn't hear me.

"I'll have a beer," he tells the waitress. "Easy on the head, all right? And not a wheat beer. Anything but a wheat beer." He turns back to me, like our conversation was never interrupted. "That's why a lot of people don't trust journalists anymore. It's not that hard of a job, right? Reporting the facts. Not like working in manual labor or, like, working at a brewery."

"Not as hard as your job, you mean?" I say. My hand is tight around my glass.

He shrugs and gives me a smile, like we're sharing a joke. "You said it, not me. Hey, I have a few stories you should write about. I'm sure everyone says that, but I'm serious. I think this could be good for you."

Oh boy. "Really?" I ask. "What are they?"

"I'm a member of an online community. We don't really tell people about it, but we share updates the regular media won't report on. I know exactly how you'll react—but listen with an open mind. Sasquatch was sighted recently, just upstate. Farmers in the area have been covering it up, and a friend of mine online has seen the FBI vehicles." His eyes widen. "This goes all the way to the very top."

I take a long, hard sip of my disgusting drink. *Oh Christ*, I think.

Over Brian's shoulder, I see peanut guy talking to a leggy blonde. Her hair falls in a wave over her shoulder and she has a hand on his arm. He says something and she tosses her head back to laugh.

At least someone's having a good time.

"This is a scoop," Brian says. "Could be really good for your career. I mean, if you want the help."

―――――

An hour later, I've still not found a way to escape. Brian just won't stop talking. About how my career could go in a different direction if only I had the guts to report the *actual* facts. His ten-minute monologue would be charming, if it wasn't such a blatant example of mansplaining.

He adjusts his clear-rim glasses—I'm starting to wonder if he's only wearing them for aesthetic reasons—and leans back in his chair. "So that's why," he says, "I had to quit that job."

"Because they didn't respect your initiatives."

"Exactly," he says. He looks like he's actually enjoying himself.

Probably because *his* date has mainly been listening to himself talk.

"But strong people like others who take charge. They recognize themselves," he says. His voice has gone weird and soft, and my stomach tightens up in nerves again. No, no, no. This is what I don't like. Turning someone down or having to rebuff them. Conflict-averse to the max, that's me. "Especially women," he continues. "They really like someone who knows how to show them a good time."

"I don't—"

He lunges across the table and presses his lips to mine. It's so unexpected I jerk back, but he follows along, his mouth like a leech.

And oh God, is that his tongue?

I don't kiss him back. I sit there, hands balled on the table, for two long seconds before I push against his chest. He leans back with eyes that are warm.

"Well," he says. "You're a good kisser, at least."

At least? *At least?* This man is unbelievable.

"Thank you for tonight," I say, because I can't find it in

myself to stop being polite. "But I think I'm ready to head out."

"Back to mine?" he asks. "Or yours?"

I reach for my clutch. "Uh, I have work early in the morning. I don't think I'll be able to do that."

"Tomorrow's a Saturday" he says.

Oh, so it is. Shoot.

My gaze travels over his shoulder and locks eyes with the man from earlier. Peanut guy, who called me *kid*, but who'd also promised he would help. He's standing alone by the bar, no blonde in sight. And he catches my gaze.

He raises an eyebrow. *You need me?*

I give a teeny, tiny nod.

"Audrey?" Brian says. "Come on, have a nightcap with me. At least let me take you home. I'll even let you pick my brain for more stories."

The only thing worse than picking this guy's brain would be having him try to suck mine out again through my teeth.

"Oh," I say. "Goody. But, I don't think—"

The peanut guy has reached us. He puts a hand on the back of my chair, his tall form shadowing our table. "There you are," he tells me. His face is serious, no dimple or charming smile in sight. "We've been looking all over for you."

"You have?"

"Yes. Your mom is beside herself. Come on, we have to get going."

"Right now?" I squeak, looking from him to Brian. His eyes are wide on my suit-wearing savior.

"Yes," peanut guy says. "I have a car outside. If we go now, we can still get there in time. Come on." He turns to Brian. "You understand, I'm sure."

"Yes," he says weakly. "Go on, Audrey."

I stand up and peanut guy holds up my thin jacket. I slide into the arms. "I'm sorry. Thanks for tonight."

He nods, and doesn't even say it back. The jerk. Maybe

11

he's upset he can't keep explaining someone's profession back to them.

"Hurry," peanut guy says by my side. I try to match his long strides through the bar and toward the front door.

"My tab," I whisper to him. "I need to—"

"I've cleared it," he says. "Come on, he's watching."

We emerge into the warm New York air and he lets go of my wrist. My skin tingles where he's held it. "Oh my God," I say, looking over my shoulder at the closed bar door. "That was *awful*."

"It didn't look great," he says, but he looks mightily pleased with himself. He's even taller out here than he'd been hunched over the bar. Towering over me.

A burst of nerves flitters through my stomach.

"So, what did he do wrong?" he says. "Talk about his mother too much? Compare you to his past dates? Ask you to come back to his and check out his herb garden?"

My nerves die and I laugh. "That would arguably have been worse. No, he didn't do that. He gave me advice about my career."

"That's a bad thing?" peanut guy asks, a raised eyebrow.

"Yes! He knows nothing about it!"

"Ah. Talking out of his ass, then."

"Yes. It was so patronizing I forgot to be nervous. I can't believe I got all dressed up for this," I say, looking down at my uncomfortable shoes. "It looked like you had better luck."

He rubs a hand over his neck, almost as if he's embarrassed, and gestures toward the street. "We should walk. He might leave any minute."

"Oh. And I'm not on my way to my... What was it? My sickly mother?"

"I kept it vague," he says. "Lies usually work better that way."

"You're an expert at it?"

He snorts. "Unfortunately, yeah."

"So?" I press on, shoving my hands into the pockets of my jacket. "How was your date?"

He shrugs. "It went all right."

"I'm sorry if I interrupted it, by needing... assistance," I say.

"Oh, it was already over. I told her I didn't want to see her anymore."

I stop and stare at him. He notices and rolls his eyes. Auburn hair has fallen over his square forehead and his jawline is sharp from this angle.

"Don't look at me that way," he says. "She knew it wasn't going anywhere either."

I think back on the excited blonde he'd chatted to at the bar. "Right," I say.

"At least I didn't lecture her about how to do her job," he says, smiling crookedly. "I know better than to do that."

I rub a hand over my mouth. "God, he kissed me, too. More like lunged at me."

"I saw that," he says, and there's sympathy in his voice. "Didn't look good."

"Definitely wasn't." We've reached my subway stop and I pause, digging through my purse for my card. I doubt he's heading downstairs too. "Thank you for helping out back there," I say.

He nods, eyes on me. "Anytime, kid."

I groan. "Not that again."

"Riling you up is fun."

"You should get a hobby." It's another rude thing to say, but somehow, it feels fun with him. Knowing he can take it and dish it back just in kind.

He leans against a streetlamp, cool and collected and seemingly oblivious to the people passing us. "Oh, this is my hobby," he says. "Rescuing damsels in distress at bars who go on bad blind dates."

"Happens a lot, does it?"

"More than you'd think," he says. "Where do you find these guys, anyway? Dating apps?"

"I've tried a few of those," I admit. "They're not my favorite, but... you get dates, at least."

"I'm sure you do," he says.

I brush past the enigmatic compliment. "But this guy was actually someone my friend set me up with."

"Renouncing that friendship?"

"I really should," I say. "Anyway, this was... nice. I mean, not the date. But the before and after."

He grins. "Happy to help."

"I should probably head home. Had a full day, and all. I actually had a job interview today. For my dream job."

"Is that so?"

"Yes," I say, probably rambling. I inch toward the subway steps. "I never got your name, actually?"

He reaches inside his jacket and pulls out a small notepad and pen. It's a slick move, matching his suit, his demeanor, the moneyed air. I don't trust guys like him. Never have, not since my childhood. But something about him makes me feel energized.

Alive.

"Carter," he says, scribbling something. "I've enjoyed talking to you. Don't see this as having any strings. But if you need to pick a guy's brain or be rescued from awful blind dates again..."

I stare at the paper he's extending toward me. *Carter*, it says. And beneath it are seven digits.

"Your phone number?"

"The very one," he says.

I take it, and wonder why I'm not nervous. He's a man. An exceedingly handsome one, even. But I'd seen the woman he turned down tonight, and she could easily have passed for a model. Looked happy and smiling, too.

This thing, him and me, is so clearly a friendship thing. So I don't feel nervous at all, accepting the piece of paper.

"Thanks," I say. "Might be good to get a guy's perspective on things."

"Anytime," he says, and nods to me. Like an old-time gentleman seeing off a lady. "Get home safe."

"Thanks," I murmur again, and walk down the steps. It isn't until I'm halfway home, dizzy from all the impressions of the day, that I realize I never gave him my name. With shaking fingers, I add his number to my phone and give him the glorious name *Carter Peanuts*.

Then I send him a single text.

My name is Audrey. Thanks for the peanuts.

His response comes just as I've unlocked the room I'm renting on the second floor of a brownstone. I rest against the closed door and read it, feeling endless possibilities stirring around me.

Carter: Anytime, kiddo. Pleasure to meet you.

TWO

> Audrey

Carter: When's your next date with hyperventilation?

Audrey: I didn't hyperventilate, not fully. And I've been talking to someone new, actually.

Carter: Tell me about this guy.

Audrey: It's just someone I matched with on an app. The conversation is meh, but he seems cute and he has a dog.

Carter: Good thing conversation isn't a big part of relationships.

Audrey: Funny. Not every guy is talkative, you know. Just willing to strike up a conversation with a perfect stranger at a bar.

Carter: I get that. I'd never do that, for example.

Audrey: Me neither. What if the other person was a weirdo?

Carter: Or worse. Serial killers abound.

Audrey: That's why I never tasted any of the peanuts you offered. Had you laced them before?

Carter: You're on to me. I always carry a vial of arsenic around.

Audrey: I figured. You gave me those vibes. But, tell me. What do you do on a first date?

Carter: Beyond hyperventilate, you mean?

Audrey: Yeah. Tell me how a guy prepares.

Carter: What a question. Tells me everything I need to know.

Audrey: How so??

Carter: You prepare, do you? And work yourself into a state through it all. The trick is to not prepare at all. I don't.

Audrey: So just… show up?

Carter: Yes. He's there to date you, not the dress you spent four hours picking out. Just show up with a good attitude. That's the only prep you should do.

Audrey: This is such a guy's advice.

Carter: Isn't that what you wanted? A guy's perspective?

Audrey: Yes. But wow, is it a guy's. Please continue though. Worst mistakes a girl can make?

Carter: That's gonna vary from man to man, kid. I can only tell you what would turn me off.

Audrey: Lay it on me. I can take it, I promise. Is it aggressively eating free peanuts? Was your arsenic-laced gift actually a test?

Carter: I don't think charming a man on your first date is your problem, not judging by the other night.

Audrey: He was definitely a weirdo though. Come on. Share something.

Carter: Fine. Someone who wants to change everything about their order annoys me. I mean, if you're lactose intolerant, fair. But when a date wants to combine two dishes, have them served due north, and could they please get some sesame seeds on top? That bothers me.

Audrey: Oh I get that. I would never. So, I already know punctuality isn't important to you. But what is?

Carter: You forgot rudeness. Apparently I love being rude to waiting staff.

Audrey: Oh my god. I'm still sorry I said that. I want to blame it on my nerves but maybe I'm just awful. Sorry!!

Carter: That text right there proves you're not.

Carter: So. What's important. That she can laugh. If I can't make a woman laugh, it's game over for me.

Audrey: Your ego can't take it?

Carter: Kid, it's my one superpower. If I don't exercise it regularly I'll die.

Audrey: Aren't you also pretty successful?

Carter: I'd take issue with the word "pretty" if we hadn't just met.

Audrey: Lol. Alright. So you're very successful, and funny. Dating has to be a game to you, and one you always win.

Audrey: This is great. I'll spam you with guy questions. You'll regret ever giving me your number.

Carter: Haven't regretted it so far. You're funny, kid.

Audrey: Still only a few years younger than you.

Carter: Ah, but you're coming to me for advice. I'm clearly the mentor here.

Audrey: Aaaand now you're obnoxious again.

Carter: It'll keep happening. Might as well get used to it.

Audrey: I'll consider myself warned.

Carter: When are you meeting guy-with-dog?

Audrey: Next Thursday. I got a new job, so I want a few days to settle in before I throw myself into the fire again.

Carter: Congrats. And it won't be that bad. Debrief with me after.

Audrey: I will. Thanks for this. Weird as it sounds I'm glad I was freaking out at that bar.

Carter: Me too, kid.

THREE

> Audrey

My faucet is leaking again.

"Crap." I bang on it, hoisting my bag up on my shoulder to avoid the spray, but it doesn't help the slow and steady drip. My little duct-tape fix from last night isn't holding up. It's soaked through.

Shit, I'm going to be late... and on my second week at the *Globe*. I crouch down low and open the cabinet. Where is it... aha! I grab the duct tape and start wrapping it around the pipe. Hopefully it'll last another twelve hours. Then I shove a clean towel under the cabinet and hope it won't be soaked through when I get back home.

I make it out of the tiny room I rent, past the closed door of my never-awake, constantly weed-smoking neighbor, and downstairs.

There's mail on the stoop. Of course there's mail.

I grab it and rush back in to my landlord's door on the first floor. Pierce owns this brownstone, and rents the converted bedrooms upstairs out to students or penniless young professionals.

"Mr. Pierce?" I half-scream. He's hard of hearing. "You've got mail! I'll put it outside your door!"

There's a thud inside. "Is that you, Audrey?"

"Yes!"

"Noted," he calls back. His voice is rusty, like always, and his choice of words makes me smile. The old man barely says thank you.

Time for the tough conversation. "My faucet is leaking again! Any news on the plumber?"

Another thud inside, and then his heavy footfalls. "Yes, yes, I called him yesterday. He's on it," Pierce says.

Which, if I know my landlord, means he forgot and is about to call the plumber right now.

"Thank you!"

Then I have to race to the subway.

I make it to the *Globe* with a few minutes to spare. Walking through the prestigious lobby, past the gold-framed articles of legend, the sleek logo behind reception, and pulling out my employee keycard… even now, two weeks in, it makes me feel giddy. This job is like winning the lottery, and not even the paltry salary can make me think otherwise.

I ride the elevator up to my floor with a smile on my face. Ridiculous, perhaps, and I'm sure the stressed journalists and department heads who ride with me think I'm nuts. But I'm just a junior investigative reporter at the *Globe* who just got the greenlight to investigate my first story. And probably a little bit nuts too.

My phone buzzes in my pocket, and my smile widens. It's past eight thirty, when he drinks his first cup.

Carter: You're wrong. Flavored creamer makes it worse, not better, and I'll fight anyone who tells me otherwise.

I type my reply as I walk through the long hallway on my floor.

Audrey: I told you to only do one-and-a-half pumps. Did you put two? It ruins it if you put two.

Carter: Do you think I have time to measure out a half-pump?

Audrey: You have time to text me, so yes.

Carter: Touché.

Over the past weeks, our texting has grown from tentative hellos to a frenzy of banter. Never about anything serious, and rarely about our own lives.

But we have differing opinions on almost everything.

I sit down at my desk in the open landscape, and while my computer turns on, I send him another one.

Audrey: You know, I still don't know what you do for a living. Is that weird?

Carter: I've told you. I rescue women from bad blind dates.

Audrey: No, you said that's your hobby. Not so good at remembering all your lies, are you?

Carter: It's the number-one problem for superheroes, actually. Trouble keeping up with multiple identities. Leads to a lot of early retirements.

I grin down at my phone. He never says what I expect him to say. Always thinks of something different, something unexpected, doesn't like the way I take my coffee, disagreed with my choice of date location last weekend.

We haven't seen each other again since the bad date.

I don't know if I want to, either. This, our texting friendship, is… perfect. Exactly what I need.

Someone to shake me out of my rut. Exposure therapy.

"You look happy," a voice says to my left. "Too happy. Do you remember what story you're supposed to be working on?"

I turn toward Declan. He's my deskmate and he's always, *always*, in the newsroom early. He looks over at me with a vaguely disapproving frown, his round glasses low on his nose.

Like me, Declan is a junior reporter. He carries a leather satchel to work and yesterday he rocked a sweater vest. I think he fancies himself a journalist in the '40s, but I hope to one day win a Pulitzer, so Lord knows we both have journalistic dreams.

"I remember," I tell him. "How's your piece coming along?"

He pushes his glasses up. "Great. I'm going out after lunch to interview members of the church."

"They agreed to your request?"

He hesitates, but then he turns his chin up. "They will."

I smile at his resolve and set about opening my email inbox. I start the day by reading through all the official memos from the editor-in-chief and from the executive team.

Today's is short. It mentions the acquisition of *The New York Globe* by Acture Capital. It's a hands-off venture capital firm. The announcement is phrased in pretty terms, but I read it with a sinking pit of despair.

Print media is being sold to investor funds, one after one, and we all know how the worst of them treat newspapers. They lay off employees, rack up subscription prices, and bleed the company into bankruptcy.

Declan breaks through my mid-morning read-through. "Booker read through the draft of the Johnson article you helped with yesterday."

"She did?!"

He nods, but he looks pleased with himself. "Yes."

"Did you see her read it?"

"Yep."

"Declan," I say, "please. How did she seem?"

He finally relents and turns toward me with a shrug. "She said it was decent."

"Decent," I breathe. "Really?"

"Yes."

It might not seem like a lot, but decent is basically *great* in Booker's terminology. Tara Booker is the editor of investigative journalism and my direct boss, although she usually concerns herself with the reporters who don't have *junior* in front of their names.

"Did you get statements from the victim's family?" Declan asks.

I nod. "Yes. I'm going to write it up today."

"Should make for a good piece," he says, and that's the most friendliness I've gotten out of Declan so far.

What is this? My birthday?

I allocate an hour to my solo project. It's a story I've been following for months, about a bodega in Queens that's being illegally shut down because of rising rent prices. The owners had tried to take it to court, but because they didn't have the right paperwork—and no money to pay for an attorney to help them with it—they didn't get past the initial hurdle. So the construction company who wants them out will get away with it.

It's the type of David-and-Goliath story that makes my blood boil. I work straight through lunch, the words flowing, and I barely notice when a shape leans against my desk.

"Audrey," a sharp, feminine voice says. "Take a break."

I look up at Booker. She has her arms crossed over a peach blouse, the color accentuating her dark-brown skin. Brown eyes that regularly skewer seasoned reporters meet mine.

"Right," I say. "I will, just as soon as I've typed up the transcript from my interviews."

"Take a break now," she says, in a voice that brokers no dispute. "I need to talk to you."

"Oh." I close the lid to my work laptop and turn in my chair.

"Bad news," she says. "Your solo beat is put on hold."

"I'm... sorry?"

She inclines her head, and her voice sounds strained. "Wish I could say otherwise, but those are the new orders coming from management. The *Globe* has been bought. Seems like there's a different tune coming from the top."

"I just read about that... but surely it's a quiet owner? Someone who sits on the board?"

"No. They've changed management. As of two days ago, we have a new CEO."

I sink back into my chair. My article, lost. To another Goliath. "Why would they cut my article?"

"They don't know about you," Booker says. "But all solo-initiative reporting has been put on pause while management enacts some structural changes."

She says the last two words like they're sour on her tongue. There's quiet panic in her eyes.

"This is bad," I guess.

"It might be," she agrees, and it's her candor more than anything that makes me worry. Booker has always seemed like a queen on her throne, ahead of the curve, doling out the story beats in the newsroom like a commander with her legions.

She sighs. "Anyway, we won't know more for a while. There's talk of whole departments being cut, major buyouts, but nothing confirmed yet."

"Whole departments," I repeat. "Surely they can't do that?"

"Acture Capital has bought the majority stake," she says. "They can do anything with the *Globe* they feel like."

I open my mouth to say something, but her gaze has locked on a spot beyond my shoulder. I turn to see, and watch a man walk through the hallway with a box. A picture frame sticks up over the edge.

"Oh my god," I whisper. He's been fired.

"Shit," Booker says. "That's Phil, our music correspondent."

"They're already firing people?"

"Seems like it. He worked here for decades." Her voice sounds like it's coming from far away, and she stares at the door where Phil disappeared. "I have another job for you, Audrey."

"You do?"

"It's not fancy, and I won't pretend to you that it is," she says. No-nonsense, just as always. "Someone needs to interview the new CEO for the corporate newsletter."

"The person responsible for all of this," I say. "Right?"

Her tone is hard. "Yes. The interview order is coming from management itself. Something about introducing the CEO to the staff. No doubt it'll be a puff piece, Audrey. You'll probably speak to an assistant. You might even get pre-recorded answers."

I nod. It's grunt work, as opposed to my solo article, but I'm a junior reporter. I'll do it. I'll do anything, any journalistic writing they'll allow me.

But I don't have to enjoy it.

"I'll get on it right away," I say.

"Good. I've been told they're expecting you up on the fifteenth floor."

"Now?"

"Now," she repeats grimly. She shakes her head and strides off, and I get the feeling she has a lot more thoughts about the new management than she's letting on.

They'd let Phil go. They'd cut my article, and so many others, without even knowing what they were about. Just a halt on all employee-driven initiative.

Departments might get slashed. Whole groups of people, just like Phil.

I grab my notepad and head toward the elevators. They might want a puff piece, but I'll be damned if I don't ask the new CEO at least one question about what's going on. I make it up to the fifteenth floor with my heart hammering in my chest. This is what I like doing. Asking tough questions, getting real answers. But I'll also come face-to-face with someone who now owns the company I work for.

The reality of that sets in.

One wrong word, and I might be the one to collect my things from my desk and leave. Not that I have many things to collect yet. And if they're planning on gutting the newsroom, slashing the *Globe*, junior reporters won't be high on the list. This whole thing, my dream job, the beginning of my career, could all be over before it's even started.

I'm greeted by a soft-spoken assistant in an atrium. His name is Timothy, according to the name tag on his desk, and he's an executive receptionist.

"My name is Audrey Ford," I say. "I'm here for an interview with the new CEO for the company's newsletter?"

"Ah, yes. Thanks for coming so quickly," Timothy says. "Mr. Kingsley is waiting for you just inside here."

It takes me a moment to process his words. I really will come face-to-face with the CEO. No fast-talking assistant, no pre-recorded answers.

I clutch my notepad like a shield and walk toward the closed door. Knocking twice, I announce myself.

"Audrey Ford here, from Investigative, for an interview!"

"Come in," a voice calls.

I push the heavy door open and step into an office flooded with light. The CEO has the best office, I think. *How typical.*

Then I register who's sitting behind the glass desk.

Auburn hair pushed back over a square forehead. A mouth that looks like it's always quick to charm, a smile hiding in the corner. And familiar tawny eyes that lock on mine.

"Carter?" I ask.

FOUR

Carter

Audrey is standing in the doorway to my office, clutching a notepad to her chest like it's armor. She looks different than that night, three weeks ago, when she'd been hyperventilating inside a dark bar.

Her dark brown curls are swept back in a low ponytail and the dress she'd worn is long gone. In her place is a woman in slacks and a blouse, professional, her attention fully focused on me.

Her eyes are wide. "Carter?"

"Audrey?" I stand. "What are you doing here?"

"I work here."

"Here? At the *Globe*?"

"Yes," she says. Then she looks out at the hallway, as if my assistant might hear. She pushes the door closed. "I told you I was a journalist!"

"I never thought you'd work here," I say.

"Started two weeks ago, actually."

That makes me smile. "Which is why they're sending you up to interview me for the company newsletter."

She frowns at me, like I've just offended her. Like we haven't given each other much worse punches over text.

"You're the CEO," she says, voice tense. "You work for Acture Capital?"

"I'm one of the co-owners, yes," I say. "We acquired the *Globe* a few weeks ago, though negotiations have been ongoing for over a year."

She takes a seat in the chair opposite my desk and demonstratively opens her notebook. I sit back down. Despite the irritation etched on her face, her features shine more without the makeup she'd worn in the bar. A smatter of freckles dance across her nose.

An old phrase my mother likes to say flashes through my brain. *The kind of woman you earn, not charm.*

"So," Audrey says, picking up her pen. "What made you want to acquire the *Globe*?" Then, before I can respond, she puts her pen down again. "How can you be the new boss of the company I work for? How did this *never* come up in text?"

"We never spoke about our jobs."

"We should've," she says. "I can't believe this."

I rub the back of my hand over my mouth to hide my amusement. She's not impressed by this, then. Weirdly enough, it makes me like this sarcastic, funny, intelligent enigma of a woman even more.

A lot of women like what I do. Never for what it entails, and they never want to hear the details, but they seem turned on by the SparkNotes version.

I open my mouth, but she cuts in with an irritated sigh. "I guess this means I can't ask you for advice anymore."

"Of course you can," I say. "Excited for your date on Friday?"

"I can't talk to you about that, you're my boss! My boss's boss's boss, probably. It would be wrong."

"We're the same people."

"No, we really aren't," she says, and opens her notepad again. This time, it seems like she's determined to keep it open, because she starts jotting down notes.

"I haven't said anything yet," I say.

"You've said plenty," she mutters. This time I don't try to hide my smile.

"What questions have you prepared?"

"None," she says. "I was told to head up as soon as I got the task, and that there'd likely be pre-prepared talking points."

Technically, there are. I have them in front of me on the desk, a set of bullet points the editor-in-chief, Wesley, had given me. Aspects of my leadership he thought would be good for company morale.

I don't look at the paper.

"It's better if you conduct the interview," I say. "You're the journalist, right?"

She shoots me a look that's dark with irritation. So she's annoyed that she can't keep texting me, then, or else she wouldn't have reacted this way. Oddly enough, that makes me glad. Talking to her had become one of the highlights of my day.

Odd, and unexpected, sure. At times a distraction from work.

But fun in a way I hadn't had with a woman in years. Fun without expectations or pretense.

"Fine," Audrey says. "I'll repeat my first question, then. Why did you want to acquire the *Globe*?"

I lean back in the chair. I'll have to give her an honest, professional answer, even if the only thing I want is to keep riling her up. "Acture Capital has been looking for an opportunity in the media sphere for years. The *Globe* fit the bill. It's a paper with a strong history, solid human capital, and prospects. It was also struggling in areas that Acture felt could be amended."

Audrey nods, her head bent over her notepad. "Has Acture Capital, or yourself, worked with the media industry before?"

She knows what questions to ask. "It's a new foray for

us," I admit, "but my partners and I are confident that the knowledge and capital we bring are up for the task."

"Right," Audrey murmurs, her pen working. "Why were you the one elected to become CEO of the *Globe*? If you have partners?"

I put my hands on the edge of the glass desk. "I'm interested in the industry. It's worth preserving and protecting."

Audrey looks up from her notepad. I meet her gaze, seeing hesitation in hers. "You believe that?" she asks.

"I do."

"So you're not just here to turn a profit?"

"A good journalist knows how to make their subject feel at ease," I say with a grin. "I'm feeling a bit attacked right now."

"Attacked," she mutters, shaking her head. "You don't feel attacked at all."

"Honestly? I want to turn a profit," I say. "Of course Acture Capital wants that. So does the *Globe*, in fact. It hasn't for a long time, which is no secret to any of the employees who might read this newsletter. Feel free to put it in there."

"But you're slashing departments," she says. "Aren't you?"

I pause. "Where did you hear that?"

"Co-workers talk."

"No decisions have been made," I say.

"But you are firing people," Audrey challenges. Her eyes are blazing on mine. "I saw Phil from the music section just earlier."

Ah.

We're on tricky ground, here. I could explain my decision, but I won't do it if there's a chance it will be blasted to a company where the employees number in the hundreds.

"Tough decisions have been made," I say. "More will have to be in the future. Acture isn't here to decimate the *Globe*, though. We're not picking it apart. We have no plans to sell it for parts. The end goal is to make the *Globe* slimmer, more efficient, and equipped to handle the ever-changing media landscape. That's something I want you to put in the interview."

Dutifully, she notes it down. "Is that something Acture does a lot? When you acquire companies?"

"Make them better? Yes."

The look she shoots me isn't impressed. "Layoffs."

"If necessary, yes," I say honestly. "It's not a part of the process we enjoy, but organizations often have vestiges of previous takeovers, projects, re-organizations. Often times those can be a drain on a company's potential growth."

Audrey cocks her head. "Did you know? When we met at that bar?"

"Know what?"

"That I'd just been at the *Globe* for an interview that very day?"

This time, I can't hide my smile. "Do you think I personally vet every person this company hires? Because I can assure you, I don't have that kind of time."

It echoes the text I'd jokingly sent her earlier, after I'd tried coffee the way she'd pestered me to, saying it was the best. It wasn't. Like so many things, we disagreed.

She must hear it too, because her cheeks flush with color. "Right. Of course you don't."

"Go on," I say. "Ask me anything else for the newsletter."

Her eyes meet mine. Flustered, challenged, annoyed. And intrigued. Try as she may to act aloof, she's interested, just as she'd been standing next to me at the bar.

I know what she says next will surprise me. She always does.

"What's your exit strategy?" she asks.

Both my eyebrows rise. "We've just bought the company. We're not thinking of selling it anytime soon."

"But you will, one day," she says. "That's the strategy of venture capitalist firms, if I understand them correctly, Mr. Kingsley."

"Mr. Kingsley?"

"We should be professional," she says.

"We should," I agree. "I will lodge a formal complaint with HR about your atrocious taste in coffee."

Her eyes flare. "You should have used one and *a half* pumps. But don't deflect. What's your exit strategy?"

"Is that really a question on that little sheet of yours?"

"Mr. Kingsley," she warns.

"You've got the stamina to be a journalist," I mutter, but I lean back in my chair and consider her question. It's a fair one. Perhaps not something I want to have announced to the world yet, though. "There is one," I say. "Suffice it to say that Acture is committed to seeing the *Globe* as a booming, one-stop source for news, a place that has as solid a future as it has a renowned past, before we consider letting go of the reins."

"Cashing in on your profits," she translates. "Right?"

I smile at her. She knows I can't answer that.

Reluctantly, she sighs, looking down at her notepad. "This interview doesn't contain much substance."

"That's okay," I say. "That's not what your co-workers are looking for right now."

She taps her pen against the notepad. "They want reassurance, and information, and I don't have either of those things yet."

"Yes, you do," I correct her. "Not in the way you want it, perhaps. But you can tell them that there is someone at the top who has a vision and a plan. They're bound to be nervous after hearing about people getting fired."

Audrey pauses in her writing, eyes meeting mine. I can't decipher what's in hers. "Wow," she says. "You really mean that, don't you?"

"Yes. Why wouldn't I?"

She shakes her head and keeps writing, and my fingers tap annoyedly at the glass desk. It had been a standard answer for me.

"You're young to be this successful," she says, head still bowed. "Only thirty-two and CEO of this company."

"You remembered?"

"Unless it was a lie," she says. "You can't keep track of them all."

The reference to our earlier text conversation doesn't make me smile. I don't want to lose that. Being ridiculous with her, sending her texts designed to make her laugh…

"Wasn't a lie," I say. "And you're twenty-six."

"In four months' time," she adds. "But that's not relevant for this interview."

"Is my age?"

"Of course. I'm introducing Carter Kingsley, thirty-two-year-old partner of Acture Capital and newly appointed CEO of the *Globe*, to all of your employees. Very few of whom, I should say, have ever seen your face."

"I haven't called an all-hands meeting yet," I admit, running a hand over my jaw. "But I will."

Audrey purses her lips. They're without lip gloss today, I see, a warm, dusky pink that looks natural and soft. "Will you be accessible to your employees?"

"Accessible?"

"If any should have questions, concerns or… complaints about the way the changes are being implemented. Where should they go?"

"Ah. Well, they're always free to email me or Wesley, and we will do our best to answer their questions."

Audrey looks down at her notepad again. Probably surveying what she has, but judging from the faint crease in her brow, she's not happy. "What are the odds of me getting an actual response from you about any future plans? What you're going to implement next?"

"Zero," I say.

"Like I suspected." She rises from her seat and smooths a hand over her slacks. "Thank you for your time, Mr. Kingsley."

"Anytime, Audrey."

She pauses, hand on the back of the chair. "Miss Ford."

"Miss Ford," I repeat.

"I will send the interview to you, with your assistant in copy, as soon as it's done," she says. Her eyes aren't on me, but on the emblazoned name plate on my desk. *Carter Kingsley, CEO, The New York Globe.* Wesley had it made for me when I arrived. It had been an over-the-top gift from a suck-up, and I'd known it. Now I wish I hadn't put it here on display. Somehow, it didn't seem quite so ironic when she was looking at it.

"Thank you," I say. "I'm sure I'll be pleased with it."

Audrey is halfway to the door before she turns around. Her eyes aren't challenging this time. They're hesitant.

"Yes?"

"This won't affect my job in any way," she says. "Will it?"

Something inside me sinks at the question. Of course she'd wonder. And with that, the most normal interaction I'd had with someone, the most casual, no strings-attached conversation, is gone for good. Nail in the coffin.

She might not expect the same things my exes did, but she sure expects something. It's just not flattering.

"No," I say. "It won't. You never have to worry about that."

She breathes out a sigh. "Right. Okay, well… thank you, then. Mr. Kingsley."

"No, thank you… Miss Ford."

Kid had been on the tip of my tongue. Not that it suits her, but because it harkens back to the first time I'd called her that in teasing. She'd hated it. I'd used it liberally in texting since.

Audrey gives me a last nod and closes the door behind her. Leaving me alone in the too-big, too-bright office. I reach for the gold plaque with my name on it and shove it in the bottom drawer of my desk.

The phone on my desk blinks and I press it down. "Yes?"

"Colt Whittaker is here for you, sir. Should I send him in?"

I close my eyes. That's another person I need to fire, and I hate it every single time. But I'll be damned if I'll make the decision and then send in someone else to make the kill for me. If there's one thing I've learned in this business, it's that integrity matters.

My father taught me that, by having absolutely none at all himself.

"Send him in," I say.

FIVE

Audrey

I leave my tiny apartment and the leaky sink—Old Man Pierce hadn't called a plumber after all. He'd called one of his old friends from the post office, who had come and installed a temporary fix.

So temporary, in fact, that it only lasted two days.

He's gotten mail again, although by the looks of it, it's just coupons. I shove them under his door and race toward the subway.

My phone has been as good as dead this week. Not a text from Carter since the scene in his office, and I haven't reached out either. That avenue is closed.

I can't believe the man I joked with is the same person who'd sent three members of the junior trainee programme out the door yesterday. The decision had baffled everyone, including Booker, who told the entire newsroom not to overreact. But she'd worn a tight look about the mouth that made me think she's as nervous as the rest of us.

Is this the beginning of the end for the *Globe*?

Declan has been frazzled all week, like he suspects he might be next. But he's been there for a year, and while he still has *junior* in his job title, there are reporters who are more junior than him.

Like me, for example.

There's a painful victory in it all. Carter had really been the slick, suit-wearing, profit-seeking businessman I'd thought he was at first glance. Now that I've seen him in his element, he reminds me too much of the man who'd ripped off my father many years ago. That conman had worn polished suits and charming smiles too, his native tongue double-talk. And he'd left my dad with empty college and retirement funds and broken pride.

By the time I make it into the office, Booker is already handing out story beats. But she's doing it earlier than usual.

"What's going on?" I whisper to Declan beside me.

"I don't know," he whispers back. "But all the higher-ups are on edge today."

I meet his worried gaze with one of my own. Is this our last day at the *Globe*?

The shoe drops a quarter past eleven, when the announcement comes through an email blast.

There's an all-hands meeting in fifteen minutes.

The news goes through the office like a shot. People turn to one another in speculation, while others turn a ghostly white at their desks. I hate it. I hate what it means, what it looks like, and most of all I *hate* how the Goliath in this situation is someone I know.

Though I don't really know him at all, do I?

There's only one spot large enough to house the *Globe*'s entire staff, and it's the newsroom with the accompanying soundstage. It's where interviews are conducted in a studio setting before they go on our website.

It's empty now.

Wesley arrives first. As the editor-in-chief, he's Carter's right-hand man. "Look at him smiling," Declan mutters at my side. It's the type of comment I've heard several times about Wesley. People don't seem to trust him.

Carter follows him into the room and the small talk quiets down.

He looks like usual. Polished suit, no tie, hair pushed back. But there's no smile lurking in the corner of his mouth this time.

He stops in front of the anxious group. "Hello, everyone. I appreciate you taking time out of your day for this meeting."

Not like we had a choice, I think.

"I understand there have been significant changes made at the *Globe* over the past few weeks. I want you all to know that while there will be more changes to come, I, as well as the entire executive team, will always strive to be clear and direct with you about the decisions we take."

In the brief silence, the entire room holds its breath.

"Unfortunately, the reason I asked you all here today is because we have to offer a number of employees buyouts. Two departments of the *Globe* will cease to exist by the end of the month. A few select employees will be asked to stay on in other capacities."

The ripple over the room is instantaneous. Carter raises a hand, forestalling the murmured outbursts. "It affects editorial and circulation."

I look around the room. While I don't know everyone's name yet, I've been introduced to a few in the affected departments. They're huge. Surely he's just restructuring? I see Mona sitting with her head in her hands, covering her eyes. She'd been so nice to me on my first day.

Something twists inside my chest.

He's destroying their careers.

"I understand this is difficult news," Carter says. My eyes zero in on him. There's no kindness or playfulness on his face now, set in serious lines. It makes him look older than he is.

At least he doesn't seem to be reveling in it.

"These decisions were a long time coming and were not made lightly. The relevant department heads will be your points of contact for severance and logistics. Thank you all, and if there are no further questions, I'll let you get on with your day."

He nods toward us and turns. Is he leaving?

If there are no further questions, he'd said. But he hadn't asked if we had any.

I raise my hand.

People around me turn to look, but I keep it up high, my heart pounding in my chest. If no one else is going to challenge him, then I will.

Wesley notices me. "Mr. Kingsley?" he says.

Carter turns back to the crowd, his eyes searching. They widen when they stop on me. It's tiny, but it's there, the acknowledgement. "Yes?"

"You said this decision didn't come lightly," I say, my voice carrying across the room. "Will you explain why it was made in the first place? And why these two departments?"

His eyes leave mine, traveling across the crowd of people, all turning toward him for answers. The air is thick. "As many of you know, the *Globe* has been struggling for years. The landscape for print media is changing, and we have to change with it. While the affected departments are important in their own right, cuts are necessary, and after doing the math... these departments don't add up."

His gaze returns to mine. There's finally a challenge in it. *Was that good enough?*

"Will there be more cuts?" I ask. Adrenaline is like a hypnotic beat beneath my skin, warning me about the danger here. But the words come out without shaking.

Carter shakes his head. "I can't tell you that, Miss...?"

He knows it, so he has to be pretending for my sake. "Ford," I say.

"Miss Ford," he echoes, eyes lighting up. Like he's enjoying this. "I understand the desire for more clarity, but I assure you, as soon as I have more information I will share it with you. That will be all for today."

Judging from his tone, he means it this time.

People disperse. There are hushed conversations, murmured laments. I watch one person race toward the

40

bathroom, their steps hurried and a hand pressed over their eyes.

It's carnage.

I wander into the main corridor in a daze. People's jobs, gone in a heartbeat. Just like that. People shuffle around me, heading off in different directions, but I just lean against the wall. I'd spent time with Carter. I'd laughed with him. The memories feel dirty, now. Tainted.

Maybe I'm overreacting, but all I can see is Mona with her head in her hands. I don't know how long I stand there.

"Hello."

It's Carter. I push off from the wall, looking around, but people aren't milling about. They've fled this room. Fled from him, more likely.

"I read the interview you put together for the newsletter. Good job," he says.

The smile in the corner of his mouth is back. Like he hadn't just ruined people's lives.

"Don't patronize me," I say. "It was a puff piece."

"Yes," he says. "But it was a well-written one."

I turn to him and hate that I have to tip my head back to meet his gaze. "All those people had jobs. Livelihoods. It's all gone, just like that."

His smile disappears. "I'm aware."

"Are you?"

"Yes. You think I'm not?"

I shake my head. "You're not even trying to turn this paper around, are you? You're just interested in cutting away the fat. Bleeding it dry, just like the other vulture hedge funds. We all know what's happened to newspapers all across the country."

Carter raises an eyebrow, but beneath the bemused expression, I see his clenched jaw. It gives me a small sense of victory that he's not as nonchalant as he pretends to be. "This isn't the first company I've turned around."

"Not the first departments you've slashed, either," I say.

"No, and they won't be the last," he says.

I glare at him. He glares at me.

"We shouldn't be talking like this," I say, looking behind me. But I don't see anyone.

"You interviewed me for the newsletter. It's perfectly all right for us to be friendly."

Friendly, I think. I can't be seen as friendly with this man in front of the *Globe* newsroom, not while he keeps cutting people's jobs. And he wants our bantering friendship, if that's what we have, to continue? It's impossible.

So I do the only thing I can think of. I turn and leave him there, leaning against the wall, and I don't look back.

Late that night, when I've just gotten cozy in bed with the latest monthly issue of *The Reporter*, my phone vibrates with a text.

It's from him.

Carter: I appreciated the way you stood up to me during the meeting. Good job, kid.

Audrey: We shouldn't be texting.

Carter: Nothing's changed.

I look at his text. Two tiny words that couldn't be more wrong, even if I wished they were different. I picture Carter's smile and Mona with her head in her hands.

Audrey: Everything's changed.

SIX

> Audrey

It's three days later, and people in my department still won't let my questions go. "Spitfire," Booker had commented afterwards, even going so far as to pat me on the back.

Declan had given me a short, approving nod from his desk. It must be the equivalent to *good job* in Declanese.

My gumption even went so far as to become a joke during the newsroom staff meeting for Booker's Investigative team. She handed out all the story beats, and in the brief pause after, a man named Raymond raised his voice.

"Doesn't Audrey have something to ask?"

People had laughed, and I'd stood and pretended to bow, accepting it. But it didn't feel earned. I'd taken a risk, sure, and Wesley had looked at me with death in his eyes when I passed him in the hallway earlier. But something told me Carter would hesitate to fire me because of it.

"Bored?" Declan asks me from behind his computer screen. "I know I am."

I sigh. "Yes. But I'm trying to see the positive side."

"Which is what?"

"We're perfecting our editing chops."

He doesn't respond, which shows just how poorly he thinks of my silver-lining skills.

Since all of our solo-initiative projects were put on hold, our only tasks are doing research and transcribing for the reporters who don't have *junior* in their job titles. It means very little original thinking, but a lot of precision work.

I'm finding that I don't mind, though. I'm at a cutting-edge newspaper that's been at the forefront of reporting for decades, regularly challenging authority across the world. I can do worse than handling research for some of the Pulitzer-winning journalists in my department.

It's just before midday when a text lights up my phone. I angle the screen away as soon as I see the name.

Carter: Want me to explain my plans for the paper? Have lunch with me at 23 Northbourne and I'll tell you. Off the record.

I read the message three times. Is he serious, or is he just messing with me? This sounds like something he'd send before I found out he was the new CEO. The *off the record* part makes me think he's joking about my job, investigative journalist and all.

But if he's serious…

This would be true investigative work. Talking to someone, learning their tells, pressing them for information. Luring someone with a hidden motive to share more than they'd anticipated.

Audrey: You're serious?

Carter: Dead serious. I swear it on your beloved coffee creamers.

Audrey: I'll be there. One o'clock?

Carter: Sounds good.

I look over at Declan in his tweed blazer, as if he might

somehow have seen. But he's focused on the monitor and not on me.

The lunch place Carter chose looks nothing like I'd imagined. It's hardly even a restaurant, and with a neon sign askew outside, it looks ready to be demolished. I step inside to the scent of stale beer and fries. It's a dive bar, with a counter occupying one half of the restaurant and old newspapers covering the walls. They look yellowed with age.

"Audrey," Carter calls. He's sitting at a booth in the back, a vinyl menu splayed out in front.

I take a seat opposite him. "This place is... interesting."

He looks down at his menu. "It is. New York journalists have frequented it for decades."

"Really?"

"Yes. It's got a fascinating history, you know. Secret meet-ups and off-the-record conversations." He looks around the place, jaw sharp beneath his five-o'clock shadow. "Scandals about congressmen and senators, a leaked sex tape, wire fraud. All of it has gone down here. There's a book about this place, actually."

"There is?"

"Yes," he says. "It came out about a decade ago. Never made it big—it's a niche subject. I'll send you a copy."

"Right... thanks. And thanks for showing me this place." I play with the edge of my notebook. "Why did you want to meet with me?"

"I told you," he says. "I want to tell you my real plans for the *Globe*."

"With no strings attached?" I open my notebook.

He reaches over and puts a large hand on the cover, shutting it firmly. "No strings, but this is off the record."

"Then why tell me?"

His heavy gaze tells me I should already know. It clicks into place a moment later. He still wants us to be friends, for some reason. "Audrey," he says, and his voice is low. "Hear me out before you judge me."

I push my notebook to the far end of the table and put my pen on top of it. They're out of reach. "Off the record," I agree. "I'll listen."

He leans back in the booth. "You asked me if I'd considered that all the people I fired the other day had jobs. Livelihoods. Entire careers, of which the *Globe* was the pinnacle."

"I did, yes."

"I had. Every single person I've laid off at the newspaper was a well-thought-out decision. I promise you that. But," he says, raising an eyebrow, "the *Globe* is dancing at a knife's edge. Some of the department heads know just how bad it is, but not all."

"A knife's edge," I repeat. "It's one of the biggest newspapers in the country. In the world, even. Good investigative reporting is the backbone of a country. A free and independent press is the fourth estate." I can tell my voice is getting passionate, and I shake my head. "It's worth so much more than just dollars and cents."

Carter looks amused. "Yes," he says. "*Free* press being the key word. But the *Globe* is currently beholden to advertisers every single issue to keep it afloat."

I frown. "I'd noticed a lot of ads. But most print media has that now."

"Yes, because all of print media is struggling. You haven't seen the numbers, Audrey, but if you had…" He shakes his head. "This place is a week, a month, from ruination. People don't read the news anymore. They certainly don't open their local newspaper to see which albums the music expert has reviewed when debating whether or not to buy a CD. Because they don't. We have to adapt."

"By firing some of our greatest people?"

"Not all have been fired," he corrects me. "Some will work as independent contractors. Phil, for example, who you seemed so concerned about in my office last week. He will continue to write monthly op-eds for the newspaper. He doesn't need to have a full-time office space and be on the payroll for that."

"That's job security," I say.

"Only if the job continues to exist," he says. There's a seriousness to his expression now, like he wants me to get this. To believe him. "The *Globe* is a great paper, Audrey. I know it and you know it. But it will be a hard few months before this place finds a way to right itself from the nosedive it's in."

I sigh. "I didn't know it was that bad."

"It is," he says. "What's worse, I don't like how much power the advertisers have. It compromises the kind of stories your department gets to tell."

I lean back in my seat. His words strike me like a thunderbolt. I'd never thought of that before, not deeply, even if it had come up now and again during my classes in J-school.

If we're really in such dire straits... "It's hard to take in, that's all. That these drastic changes are necessary."

"I'm not trying to butcher the newspaper," Carter says, and there's a quiet, passionate note in his voice I haven't heard before. "In time, I hope the others will realize that too."

"But more people will have to go?"

"It's either that," he says, "or the newspaper goes bankrupt."

I sigh, looking down at my menu without reading a single word. The letters might as well be in a different alphabet. "I want to believe you," I say.

He has no reason to lie to me, no reason to get me on his side... but he's every bit the moneyed, privileged, too-rich businessman I've read about a thousand times, in a thousand articles, slaughtering companies for parts and not caring about the employees.

"You should," he says. "Have I ever steered you wrong?"

"You have spectacularly bad judgement sometimes," I say, unable to stop myself. "Like when you suggested I go on a date at Cake."

"It's a nice place," he says. "I've been on plenty of dates

there. The guy you went out with last week, the insurance agent, he would've liked it, I'm sure."

"Yes, but Cake has a *two month waiting list.* You live in an ivory tower."

He frowns at me. "It does?"

"Yes. How do you usually book a table?"

"I call them, or my assistant does."

"And you say your name?"

"Of course," he says. "You have to, for them to hold a reservation, you know."

"Right. Well, *that's* why you can get a reservation at Cake."

He crosses his arms over his chest. "Doesn't mean I have bad judgement."

"No, you're just out of touch," I say.

"At least I don't need sweeteners and creamers to drink a normal cup of java."

"Low blow," I say. *"One-and-a-half pumps."*

He opens his menu, a smile on his lips. It transforms him into the man I'd met at the bar all those weeks ago. The one who'd teased me out of my nervous breakdown. "Order something, kid," he says. "You only have an hour-long lunch break."

"Are you pulling the boss card?"

"Boss's boss's boss, I believe it was," he says. "They have decent burgers here."

We order by the bar, and the food arrives a suspiciously short amount of time later. It should stop me in my tracks, but I'm too hungry to hold back, biting into the burger.

"Oh," I murmur. "This is decent. Delicious, even."

"Told you," he says, looking at me over his bun. His eyes glitter. "You moan when you eat, you know. When it's tasty."

"I do not."

"You do."

I reach for my glass of water, self-conscious. "You're being mean."

His eyebrows rise. "Not the response I was expecting."

"Why did you bring me here, really?" I ask. "Just to tell me why the paper is doing so bad? That doesn't feel like information a junior employee is entitled to."

Carter takes another bite of his burger, his sharp jaw working. He doesn't seem in a rush to give me an answer.

So I put my food down and wait.

He looks out at the empty dive bar. "Couple of reasons," he says finally. "You see a different side of the *Globe* than I do. You're right there, talking to others as a colleague. You're in the newsroom."

"I won't spy," I say.

His mouth quirks. "Wouldn't expect you to. But if you're so concerned about this paper, then… help me set it to rights, Audrey. You'll see what departments do the most work. You'll see what departments barely do anything at all."

I'm already shaking my head. "I can't be the reason people lose their jobs."

"But can you be the reason dozens, if not hundreds of others, maintain their jobs?" he says. There's enthusiasm in his tawny eyes. "You don't have to give me any information that makes you uncomfortable. But you clearly have opinions. I want to hear them."

"Is this just because…" I trail off, unable to find the words I'm looking for. Him and me, in a crowded bar, arguing over trivial things with dancing eyes.

"Because of what?" he asks.

I shake my head. "Never mind. I'll help you, if I… if my opinions really can help."

"They can," he says. "I need as many perspectives as possible into the *Globe*, the organization, the way it works."

"Not happy with just Wesley?" I say dryly.

"He's good, but he doesn't know everything," Carter says. Then he gets a gleam in his eyes. "You know, I'll help you in return."

"With what?"

"Men. Just like I did before."

I roll my eyes. "By suggesting *Cake* for one of my dates. You have to realize the men I go out with aren't like you."

"They're men," he says, "and I am one. How hard can it be?"

"Dating is nerve-wracking enough for me without having your bad advice in my head," I say, smiling now too. "You've seen just how worked up I get."

"You have no trouble telling me what you think," he says. "You're not nervous now."

"Well, no. But you're my boss, we're working. It's not like you're serious about… me, you know? It's not like *that.*"

"Right," he says. "Because you and I would never go on a date."

"Of course not," I say. Is he joking? A frisson of nerves bursts through my stomach, there and gone. He has to be. He's the CEO of the *Globe*, and he's also… *him*, handsome as sin and charming and someone who dates models.

Carter raises his glass to mine. It's ice water to ice water, nothing special, but the smile on his face says something else. "To friendship," he says.

I touch my glass to his. "To friendship," I say, and think that this must be the weirdest, most unexpected one I've ever had.

SEVEN

Carter

It's rare for more than two of us to be at Acture Capital's offices at a time, and considering which numbers released today, it's my damn luck that two of my three business partners are in.

"The *Globe* is doing abysmally," Victor says. "Worse than we anticipated."

I'm not surprised he takes the pessimistic view. "So it'll be a challenge," I say. "We knew that going in."

On the other side of the table, Tristan runs a hand over his jaw, skepticism in his voice. "I don't know, Carter. This might be more than we can handle."

"The *Globe* has had a tough six months. If they didn't, we wouldn't have gotten the company at such a steal."

"If they tank," Victor mutters, "we'll be the ones who get robbed."

I brace my hands against the table. "They won't tank. We've cut the personnel costs by significant amounts already, overheads are shrinking, and two donors who said they were ready to back out have stayed their hand."

"Because they can write it off on their taxes," Tristan says dryly. "Not because they believe in the *Globe*."

"Look, I'm not going to sugarcoat it. It's in a bad place.

Advertising prices are dropping at the same time as our subscribers are decreasing, but that's temporary," I repeat. "The newspaper is one of the most illustrious in the country."

"Reputations won't pay the bills," Victor says. But he's flipping through the paper with interest. "It has good bones, though. We could sell off the parts."

"Not yet. Let me try to build something on those bones first."

"Can't hurt to try," Tristan says. "We all knew the *Globe* would be amongst the hardest companies we ever tried to turn. It'll be a damn feather in a cap if we do, though."

"It's not like we bought a profitable consulting firm that we just expanded," I say. It's a low punch, perhaps, but for the past years both Tristan and Victor have served separate terms as CEO of Exciteur Consulting. It's now the world's third-largest consulting firm. But it had already been the seventh when they began.

Tristan snorts. "Noted."

"I'll attend the Reporters' Ball next weekend," I say. "We all know there will be plenty of traditional donors there. I'll schmooze, show them the new leadership. Might help us tide things over for a while."

"Sounds like a good place to start," Tristan says.

Victor crosses his arms across his chest. "Anthony would be on my side, were he here."

"Perhaps, but he's not," I say. Our fourth partner has finally taken an overseas vacation with his fiancée Summer, and the two of them had gone completely off the grid for three weeks. I know exactly which one of the two had been responsible for that decision.

But I also know they're visiting Winter Hotels for his brother, inspecting a few of the hotel chain's new luxury locations. What a sacrifice.

"I don't know," Tristan says. "Anthony's family has long supported the *Globe* as donors. He might be emotionally attached."

Victor shakes his head like we're all idiots.

"We stay the course," I say, "for at least three more months. I'll keep you informed. But there are still changes to be made, and possible profit in the future, and I'm not willing to give that up."

"Fine by me." Tristan pushes the papers with the *Globe*'s latest numbers away. Conversation finalized, he shoots Victor a smile. "Freddie and I got the save-the-date."

Victor nods, looking toward the windows. "Good. Well, if you've got the time, you're welcome."

"Of course we'll be there," Tristan says. "You two cheated us all out of a proper wedding ceremony, so this is the least you can give us."

I grin at Victor. He's so obviously uncomfortable talking to us about this, try as he does to hide it, and it's hilarious. The man has no ability to handle the public aspect of his marriage.

But I've seen him with his wife Cecilia. When he thinks nobody's looking, he's a different man entirely.

"I'll be there too," I say, having already blocked off time in my calendar for their vow renewal. "Have to make sure it's a real party."

Victor frowns. "It's not a big thing. Small, just family and a few friends."

"So much the better for my dance moves," I say.

He stares at me for a long moment before he sighs, realizing I'm joking. Tristan chuckles and pushes back from the table. He's in the process of purchasing a medical company, although one that will require a little oversight. "Gentlemen," he says. "Always a pleasure."

"Likewise," I say.

Victor doesn't comment, and I grin at him again. He rolls his eyes. I had no siblings growing up. It was me and my mother, living together in a one-bedroom in Queens, and the relationship I have with my co-partners is something I value.

Despite pretending not to care most of the time.

I head out of the office soon after. The *Globe* needs more

hands-on time than I'd like in these early stages. Truth be told, the numbers had been awful. Abyss-level awful. But I'd meant what I said. The paper has too much history for us to give up so soon.

A brunette with bouncing curls and blue eyes flashes through my mind, too. Her sharp mouth and eyes that seem to look straight through me. This job clearly means a lot to her.

I don't want to be the reason she loses it.

Just thinking about her makes me smile. She's a paradox. A spitfire with me, but nervous to the point of hyperventilating with others. I don't know why that makes me feel ten feet tall.

She'd agreed to being friends. Just friends, in fact, which is likely for the best. Not only is she an employee, but she's sweet, and ambitious, and passionate. Anything with her would be serious, and I don't know how to handle something that is. Never had it before.

And yet, absolutely none of that stops me from texting her on my way to the *Globe*'s offices.

Carter: Do you have your date with the piano teacher tonight?

She answers right away. She shouldn't, because it's during work hours, but I fully encourage this use of company time.

Audrey: No, it was postponed until Wednesday.

Carter: Who postponed?

But even as I wait for her answer, I'm pleased with her response. I shouldn't be, and I know that very well. But here I am regardless.

She takes a long time to answer. Long enough that I return to work, swatting away the incoming emails. They're always one missed swat away from overwhelming the inbox.

An email comes up with a reminder for the Reporters' Ball. It's this weekend. Man, Audrey would have a field day. An entire evening of press-themed mingling, with the guest list a mile long and so illustriously decadent. She should go. But the invites are closely guarded, and coveted, and I doubt I have the clout necessary to pull some strings.

To the best of my knowledge, only a few people from the *Globe* are attending, and they're all senior with a capital S.

My phone chimes again. It's a distracting way to work, texting with her, but I wouldn't change it.

Audrey: He did, he had to fill in for another teacher tonight. Huge sigh of relief for me.

Carter: Still gets your nerves going, huh. What will you do instead? Go home and watch back-to-back documentaries about political scandals?

Audrey: Lol. I know it doesn't seem like it but I have a few other interests outside of my job. Emphasis on "a few," though.

Yes, and that's just it. She'd love the Reporters' Ball.

Fuck, I wish I could take her as my date. My invite includes a plus-one, but I can't ask an employee. And even if I could, I'd mentioned the event to Becca weeks ago, a long-term friend with occasional benefits. She'd said yes before I met Audrey. But it was in a casual way, a mutually beneficial way. She loved fancy events and I liked having someone there to talk to who wasn't interested in my industry opinions. Now it seems like a waste of both our time.

Audrey would appreciate it more.

EIGHT

> Audrey

"Spitfire," Booker says. It's a week later, and the nickname shows no signs of fading. "Get the draft of the Decker story to me by lunch tomorrow?"

"On it!" I say.

"Declan, how's the research for Emery coming along? Give me an ETA."

"Just dotting some i's," he replies. "I'll forward it to Emery before I leave for the day."

"Dot them faster," she says, and then she's gone in a breeze of sensibly heeled shoes and determination. I watch her disappearing form, the queen of this office, the master of the story beats. She must keep the next day's edition of the newspaper in her head at all times. Moving stories around, editing, polishing, pushing and pulling to put together the best edition every single time.

Just being near her makes me a better journalist.

"Dot them faster," Declan mutters by my side, but there's reluctant admiration in his voice too. It's hard not to have any for Booker, even if she can be mean and harsh when needs be.

I've lived at the office for the past few days. With less staff than usual, but with the same printing requirements and story beats to fulfill, the newspaper is struggling.

And every single person knows who to blame.

Well, maybe not, I amend, watching as Tom Wesley walks through the investigative floor. There is little love lost between the staff and the *Globe*'s editor-in-chief.

He catches me looking and I quickly focus on my computer screen. The Decker story. It's an interesting one, and my fingers ache to write the article myself instead of just researching it for one of the senior journalists.

From the corner of my eye, I watch him come closer. Damn. Where Booker is stern but encouraging, Wesley's voice is syrupy with falseness.

"Audrey," he says.

I meet eyes that hold no humor, despite the smile on his face. "Mr. Wesley."

He leans against the edge of my desk and crosses his arms over his chest. "Quite a performance last week. In front of our new CEO and owner, no less."

The all-hands meeting. I wet my lips, keeping my hands clasped tight on my lap. "I felt we were owed answers, sir."

His smile widens and a shiver runs down my spine. "How fitting, for a junior investigative reporter."

"Uhm, yes."

Wesley's eyes shift to my screen, evidence of my research. "Well, good luck, Audrey. I hope the new owner looks as favorably on your... spirit, as I do."

My lips part in shock, but not a single word comes out. Wesley knocks twice on my desk and saunters off without another word.

Declan meets my eyes, and for the first time, there's no competition in them. No I-told-you-so, either. "If the CEO cares about investigative journalism," he says, "then he appreciated your questions."

"Thank you," I say.

He nods solemnly, like we've just brokered peace between two warring nations, and returns to his work with frenzied typing.

I spend the rest of the night working, fighting against the deadline. The story is good. But it's not great, and I want to impress Booker. I want her to turn me from someone junior into someone, well, not senior, but someone with a long-term permanent contract and preferably a little pay raise.

I want her to read the article and be impressed.

Perhaps that's not a reasonable goal to set for myself, but damn it, I was always the one who got As in J-school. I worked overtime at the school newspaper, I did every extra assignment, I aimed for valedictorian.

So I'm not about to stop a lifetime of overachieving when I'm finally in a place where it'll be rewarded.

"Spitfire," Booker says.

I startle in my seat. "God, sorry. Yes?"

She gives a half-crooked smile. "It's late. What are you still doing here?"

"Working on the Decker story."

"That piece is no more than seven-hundred-and-fifty words."

"I know, but that doesn't make it less important."

A snort. "You're so young."

I discreetly shut the screen to my laptop. "Thank you?"

Booker looks over her shoulder at the near-empty newsroom. Declan had left an hour ago, too. "You love this job, don't you?"

"It's all I've ever wanted to do," I say honestly.

"I can tell. Look, tonight is the Reporters' Ball. Have you heard about it?"

"Yes, absolutely," I say. "It's the biggest event of the year for journalists in the city. It's where—"

"I know what it is," Booker says with an uncharacteristic smile. "I've been a few times, and was planning to go tonight before my sitter cancelled."

"Oh, I'm sorry about that."

She shrugs. "After one ball you've been to them all. Want to go in my place, Spitfire?"

I stare at her. "To… the Reporters' Ball?"

"Yes." She looks at her watch. "The doors open in an hour and a half, so if you're interested, I suggest you head home right away."

"I'm interested," I say. "Definitely."

"I suspected you would be," Booker says. "I'll send you the e-vite. And Spitfire?"

"Yes?"

"You're a good enough writer, so learn when to stop polishing."

"Thank you. Will do."

Booker gives me another nod and strides off, leaving me spinning in my chair. Metaphorically, despite the fact that it does spin. The Reporters' Ball in an hour and a half. And she thinks I'm a *good enough writer!*

I make it back to my tiny room in Queens in time to have a shower in the bathroom I share with the student across the hall. My hair is a lost cause of curls, and I pin most of it up, only bothering to style the tendrils that fall around my face.

I have no idea how they dress at the Reporters' Ball. I know it's black tie, though, and there is decidedly *nothing* in my wardrobe that looks black-tie appropriate. It's also early fall and the evenings are chilly.

My office attire wardrobe I'd so painstakingly and expensively put together over the past year and a half had not included a beautiful floor length dress.

Hesitatingly, I pull out my old prom dress. It had been an impulse decision to bring it with me to New York. *As if I'll ever need a gown,* I'd thought, *but just in case I do…*

It's black and long, with see-through lining over my shoulders. I'd thought it was the coolest thing ever nearly a decade ago. It could work if I pair it with the sling-back heels I sometimes wear to the office. When I look in the mirror, I look just how I feel. Bewildered, excited, nervous, adrenaline pumping through my veins, with a flush to my cheeks.

I splurge on a taxi. It's an extravagant cost, taking me all the way to the city, but I spend the entire ride pretending this is normal for me. I'll arrive and talk to interesting journalists who are my peers and not my superiors.

War reporters. Political correspondents. Pulitzer-prize winners.

"This is where you're heading?" the driver asks me as he pulls up outside the venue. "Looks fancy."

"Yeah, that's me," I say. "I think."

I feel like an imposter, walking up the steps to the security guard. Any moment now they're going to stop me. Toss me out. Remind me where I live and what my salary is and how much student debt I have.

But the attendant only flashes me a wide smile when I show my e-vite.

"Welcome, Mrs. Booker. You'll find a coat check to your left and refreshments further inside."

My heels echo across the marble floor of the grand entrance. *You're not in Kansas anymore,* I think, and I've never even been to Kansas. Two men in tuxedos pass me, engrossed in conversation. In the center of the room is a string quartet and a harp player.

I've never seen an actual harp player.

A waiter stops by my side. He has an arm behind his back and extends a tray my way. "A drink, miss?"

"Yes, thank you."

I accept the glass of champagne and wonder how I got lucky enough to attend the Reporters' Ball as a newly hired junior reporter. All around me are people whose work I've read hundreds of times. I see Dean Allen, a journalist who once guest-lectured at my university. He's laughing with a colleague.

And I'm at the same party as him.

It's a pinch-me moment. An I-can't-believe-I'm-here moment. It's an—

Carter Kingsley is here too.

I spot him by the bar. He's taller than the men around him,

his dark auburn hair looking almost black in the dim lighting. All I can see is his profile, but I would make him out anywhere.

My friend-turned-asshole-boss-turned-tentative-friend-again.

He's in a tuxedo, the fabric clinging to him like a well-tailored second skin. It's impossible to see him like this and reconcile the man I'd texted with for weeks, that I'd shared dry jokes and commentary and nonsense with.

He doesn't fit into a neat box in my head.

"First Reporters'?"

I jump, and the woman to my left gives me a quick smile. "Sorry. Bad habit of mine. I'm Juliette."

"Audrey," I say.

We shake hands and I learn she's with the *Chronicler*. A few years older than me, perhaps, and chatty. Turns out she's also a killer at working a room. I lose sight of Carter somewhere amongst all the mingling, and soon forget about him, too. There are too many names to remember and people to meet.

By the time I make it over to the bar for another drink, I have a parched throat and a smile on my face. I'll need a month to digest the conversations I've had here tonight. A year. A *decade*.

"You look like you're enjoying yourself," a man says, amused flirtation in his voice. He has glasses and is holding on to a glass of red wine. He smiles at me.

And I'm instantly nervous.

It hits me right in the gut, the same way it does with first dates, and my breathing grows shallow. "I am," I say. "Absolutely."

He shifts closer. "Haven't seen you around before. Where do you work?"

"The *Globe*," I say. He's cute enough. Very smiley. About my height, and probably similar in age. Clearly an option, which is why my insides feel like they're on fire, and not in a comfortable way.

Exposure therapy, I repeat. Exposure therapy.

"Wow. Impressive," he says, shifting closer again. "Here alone?"

"Mhm, yes. Having a blast, though. There are incredible people here."

"They sure think so themselves, too," he says beneath his breath. Then he laughs and fits his arm next to mine on the bar top. "You look new. Not from New York?"

"I'm from upstate."

He laughs again, like I've told a joke. "Well, I know all the best spots in the city. Why don't I show you around one day? I think a connection at the *Globe* would be excellent. Doesn't hurt that you're easy on the eyes, either," he says with a wink.

I lean back. Everything about his charm is backwards. "Where do you work?"

"The *Quintessential*," he says, naming an online-only publication. It's renowned for posting articles without citations or facts and not caring at all. "Tell me something. Why is a girl like you here alone?"

I grip my glass tighter. "I think I'm going to do a sweep of the floor now."

"So soon? Why don't we—"

"There you are," a familiar voice says from behind me. It's smooth and cultured, but there's no mistaking the masculine edge beneath it. "I'm sorry I was late, baby."

Carter puts a hand on my shoulder and I catch the scent of him, cologne and aftershave and something that's clean like soap.

Creepy-guy's eyes drift between us. "You two are a couple?"

"Yes," I say, leaning into Carter's side. "Going on three years."

He puts his empty glass on the bar with a sharp twang. "Shoot," he says, all graceful subtlety, and stalks off.

Carter takes his hand away and turns to me. "You looked cornered."

"A bit, yeah. Thanks."

"Saving you from awkward situations with men seems to be my forte." He raises an eyebrow. "Didn't know you'd be here tonight, kid."

"Me neither, until about two hours ago. Booker had a ticket she couldn't use, so she very kindly gave it to me."

"Very kind indeed," he says. "Enjoying yourself?"

"Yes. I can't believe who's here. I spoke to Eugenia Lee earlier. You know, the woman who reported from—"

"The cartel wars," Carter says. "I know."

I smile up at him. "You know a lot about this industry."

"More than you expected me to?"

"Well, I didn't say that."

His voice is dry. "You didn't have to."

"I should have known better, after you showed me that dive bar."

He shrugs and looks out over the crowd. But he's angling toward me. "Maybe I just read about that place to impress you."

"Impress me? Oh, thank you," I tell the bartender, accepting another glass. I should take it slow with this one. "As if you'd work to impress me."

Carter's gaze returns to me, eyes teasing. "You're right. You're already suitably impressed. I'm surprised you've held off on asking for my autograph for so long."

I can't help but laugh. "Autograph? Who do you think you are?"

"The co-owner of a very successful venture capitalist firm," he says. "Some people would be impressed by that, you know."

"Oh, I know. How many people have tried to con you out of your money tonight?"

"A few," he admits with a crooked smile. "A nice woman spent a solid ten minutes trying to, subtly and very tastefully, get me to invest a couple of million in her arthouse newspaper before I told her it had absolutely no future."

"Carter!"

"Well, I said it more delicately than that. Are you going to tell me off for being rude again?"

"I shouldn't," I say. "You're my boss."

He shrugs with elegant ease. "Not here, I'm not. Besides, I let her know I'm in more than enough trouble with the *Globe*, but thank you very much. You'd have thought someone in the newspaper industry would do their research."

"Again with the snark," I say, but I'm chuckling despite myself. It's hard not to around him. Leaning against the bar, he looks just like he had the night we first met. A man from a different world, a god come down to play with mortals, and I'm somehow his chosen confidant. It's intoxicating.

"Admit it," he says. "You love it."

I take a sip of my drink to keep from answering, but he sees the answer in my eyes, because he smiles wider. "Of course you do."

"Do you know I called you peanut guy in my head the first night we met?"

"*Peanut guy?*"

"It's true."

"Like the little guy with a top hat? Mr. Peanut?"

I shrug. "You offered me peanuts the first time we met."

"It was a good ice-breaker," he says. "It wasn't intended to become a moniker. I hope you've never thought of me as that again afterwards. Peanut guy," he mutters. "The indignity."

"It's not bad, as nicknames go."

"It's awful."

"Somehow I've gained one in my department."

His eyes dance. "Have you, kid?"

"Ugh," I groan. "Not that one."

"I love that you hate it."

"I hate that you love it."

"Touché," he says. "Now tell me what your nickname is in

the newsroom."

I look down at my glass and trace the rim with my finger. My admission suddenly seems foolish. I'd gained it, after all, for standing up to him. "Spitfire," I say.

He chuckles. "Do you tell your colleagues off for their manners too, Audrey? Or is it only your bosses?"

A blush climbs up my cheeks. "I don't know what came over me that first night when we met. Or at that all-hands meeting, for that matter. I'm usually not as... forward."

"I think that's a lie," he says. "You probably get fired up all the time. I think you have to, to work as an investigative journalist."

"I do, but it's mostly in my head. I rarely act on it. Not like these greats," I say, sweeping my hand out at the mingling guests. "Did you see that Dean Allen is here? He spent a year living with militia to get the most accurate story. He was there, in the trenches and in the dirt, and he won the Pulitzer for it."

"Is that what you want to do? Get down and dirty for your stories?"

I nod. "Yes. I haven't yet, not properly... but one day."

"Well, there's no shortage of wars to report from," Carter says dryly. "Although the idea of you camping with militia in a jungle for a year doesn't exactly put my heart at ease."

I roll my eyes. "As if you have time to worry about a lowly employee."

"A single employee, no," he admits. "But a friend? Yes."

I smile at him. Maybe it's the champagne, and it's definitely the adrenaline from being in this beautiful place, but my words flow freer than they should. "I'm sorry I judged you so harshly before."

Carter's face turns inscrutable. "You're talking about the *Globe*?"

"Yes. I still don't like your methods, and I'm still... worried, but I shouldn't have assumed you wanted the worst for the paper."

"I don't," he says, eyes meeting mine. The gold in them seems liquid. "I've recently found myself more interested in the investigative side of things, too."

"Have you?"

"Yes. A friend told me investigative journalism was the fourth estate. A defender of democracy and crucial to civil society."

I smile at him. "A friend said that, did she? Sounds like a smart woman."

"She has her moments," Carter says. He leans against the bar on his elbows, turning toward the crowd. Standing elbow to elbow with me. "I've been meaning to ask your thoughts about the *Globe* and some of the changes I'm considering."

My palms immediately feel sweaty around the glass of champagne. "Oh?"

I don't want to be the reason anyone gets fired, and yet the chance to have an impact—to actually help change the face of the *Globe*—is more than any ambitious junior reporter can turn down.

And I hate it, but there is dead weight around. I've been there long enough to see it now. I open my mouth to admit that.

"But not right now," Carter says. "It wouldn't be fair of me to pry business secrets out of you when you're three glasses deep."

"Two," I say.

"Sure, kid."

I laugh this time, shifting so our elbows touch. "So, which of the beautiful women here did you bring as a date?"

"What makes you think I brought a date?"

"Come on, Carter," I say. "Like you're attending an event like this on your own."

He snorts. "You're right. I usually need a minder. A carer, perhaps. That's what happens when you reach my esteemed age."

"You're *six* years older than me."

"Don't worry," he says. "You'll reach my level of wisdom eventually."

"Doesn't wisdom come with humility?"

"That's a common myth," he says. "Happy to bust it for you."

My smile is on the verge of breaking into laughter, giddiness rising in my chest like the champagne bubbles in my glass. "You're the silliest man I've ever met."

"A superlative, and so early in our friendship?"

"I'm sorry," I say, nudging his elbow again. "It's all downhill from here."

"It's okay. We had a good run," he says. And then, spoken beneath his breath, "Peanut guy."

"So, no date?"

He's quiet for a beat, but his voice is as smooth as always when he speaks again. "I didn't say I came without a date. But she left a little while ago."

There's a brief pang of something in my chest. Disappointment, perhaps, even if it makes little sense. It's not like I'm his only confidant or friend, and I'm definitely not his date.

"You're good at cutting your dates short," I say instead, my voice playful. "You did it the night we met too, remember?"

This time, his smile warms his eyes to amber. "Only when you show up."

I laugh at the absurdity. "Right. You're too charming, you know. You're not allowed to exercise that on friends, not to mention employees."

"Sorry. I don't know how to turn it off."

"Don't," I say, bumping his elbow again. He's big and solid by my side, taller than most and more handsome than all. "It's good practice for me, you know. I don't lock up around you the way I do when I go on dates. If only I can get that way all the time."

Carter looks at me for a long moment. "Isn't your date with the piano teacher tomorrow? You postponed."

"Yes," I say, forcing down the nerves in my stomach. They're instinctual at this point, coming whenever I hear the word *date*. I wish they'd call it something else.

Something with less expectations.

"While I'm more than happy to be your guinea pig," he says, "you really don't get nervous around me?"

"No," I say with a grin. The idea of him, perpetually sarcastic and smiling, handsome and rich, ever dating me is ridiculous. He's so firmly outside of the box of romantic possibility.

He grins and flashes his dimple, proving my point. "I don't know if I should be flattered or hurt by that."

"Relieved, probably," I say. "Couldn't help you turn the *Globe* around if I was tongue-tied around you, now could I?"

"Valid point," he says. "You're all business, spitfire. I admire that about you."

I drain the last of my champagne. His eyes widen, and then he gives a quiet laugh. It's dark and sensual, just like his voice, and sends shivers down my spine.

"Liquid courage," I say. "Think I can introduce myself to Dean Allen?"

Carter takes my glass, our fingers brushing against one another, and sets it down on the counter. "Of course you can, although I can make the introductions, if you'd like."

"You know him?"

"Not well," he admits, "but we sat next to one another at an industry event last year. I was scoping the *Globe* and attended them all."

"A year of just speaking to people like this?! How do I live your life?"

He chuckles again and nods toward the crowd. "Come on. Dean Allen awaits. Do you have your notebook?"

"Very funny," I say. "I'm not going to write down his answers."

Carter bends to whisper in my ear. "But admit it. You want to."

I grin, feeling fierce and free and confident, a woman in charge of her destiny. "Yes."

It's late when I finally get my coat from the check. I don't know how late, exactly, because I haven't looked at my phone in hours. But judging by the rapidly thinning crowd, I'm amongst the stragglers.

Worth it.

Carter's voice has the same dry humor as before. "Had to pry you two away from one another," he says.

"Thank you," I tell him earnestly. "Thank you, thank you, thank you for making the introductions. I think that was the best conversation of my life."

He runs a hand over his jaw. "Well, I'm going to have to top that."

"What?"

"Never mind," he says, holding up my left sleeve and helping me into it. "Judging from the smile on your face, you two had a good time?"

"I did, at least. I think he enjoyed himself but he has that stoic face, you know? It's difficult to read him. Do you know what he said?"

"Tell me," Carter says.

"That he'd keep a lookout in the *Globe* for my articles." My heart feels like it's fluttering as I say it. Dean Allen is a legend, working far past his retirement age, with more accolades than one can count. This event is black tie and he'd worn a tweed jacket with a hole near the sleeve.

Declan would have died and gone to heaven, seeing that.

"I'm glad," Carter says, a small smile on his face.

"Okay, okay, I know I'm fangirling, but I think I just had the best night of my life. God, I have to thank Booker for this. But how? Is it too much to get her flowers?"

Carter laughs, his arm finding mine. "Come on, kid. You've had too much champagne."

"I've had exactly the right amount. If I'd had any less, I wouldn't have dared ask Dean Allen all those questions."

"Think you can call him just Dean now?"

I shake my head. "No. You don't end up on first-name basis with a person like that. He's a bit like you, you know. Not for us normal people."

Carter snorts. "Well, I'll address that comment in a bit. How are you getting home?"

I stop our descent down the steps. The New York air is cold, and a faint drizzle hangs in the air. We're well and truly in fall now. "I'll go… in that direction," I say, pointing to the nearby stop.

"You're taking the subway home," Carter says.

"Yes. How else would I get there?"

He takes a step back and gives me a once-over, from my black work pumps to my prom dress. It hadn't looked *too* out of place in there, but I doubted I'd fooled any fashionistas.

Maybe I should just start rocking tweed blazers too.

"In that?" Carter says. "You'll be accosted."

I look down at my chaste dress with a frown. "This was my prom dress."

He's quiet for a long moment. "Your prom dress," he repeats quietly. "Really?"

"Yes. I went with Sveinn, an Icelandic exchange student, and we spent most of the night behind the bleachers. I got food poisoning."

"Wow," he says, and then has absolutely no comeback.

"Are you speechless? This has to be a first."

He shakes his head. "There's just so much to process. So many questions to ask. But first, you're not taking the subway. Come on, I'll drive you home."

"You've had champagne too," I point out. "And no one drives in New York."

"Well, my driver for the night does."

That shuts me right up. A driver. I've never met anyone who has a driver on standby. We walk down the steps in silence, him on his phone, me with my mind spinning. Every time I settle into the idea of being friends with him, despite our differences, they whop up to hit me over the head.

"It's not a big deal," Carter says. "Think of it as a taxi driver on retainer. My own Uber, essentially."

He'd read my silence correctly. He does that a lot, I've realized. "That doesn't make it less weird, you know. You don't have a butler as well?"

"I don't even know where you'd get a butler in modern-day New York."

"You can find anything on the internet."

"Yes, well, I don't want to hire a middle-aged man who's watched too much *Downton Abbey*." He slides his phone into his pocket and guides us to a spot on the sidewalk. "We'll be on our way in no time. Now, something you said earlier."

The wind whips at the loose tendrils of hair I'd artfully framed around my face hours earlier. No doubt they're out of place, the lipstick smudged, my mascara runny. And I couldn't care less.

Tonight was everything I've ever wanted career-wise.

"Oh no," I say. "Being quoted is scary. What did I say?"

"That I'm like Dean Allen. Not someone normal people get close to."

"Oh, that. Well, I stand by it. Great statement. You could put it on a T-shirt."

His mouth twitches, but it's not with his usual charming smile. It looks like he's trying to stop a genuine grin. "You really are drunk."

"No, and even if I were, it would be very unladylike of you to point it out."

"Do you mean ungentlemanly?"

"Yes. What did I say?"

He rolls his eyes. "You're a normal person, and you're getting to know me."

"Am I?" I ask. "We've texted about all kinds of things, but they're not *real* things. All we do is laugh and joke. I like it. I mean, you're funny, Carter. Some of your texts make me laugh so much my stomach hurts."

His smile flashes briefly. "Right."

"But I don't know who you're dating, where you grew up, where you live… I don't know. You're up here," I say, raising my hand to the level of his collarbones, before lowering it down to mine. "I'm here. You're not really for the likes of us normies. Tomorrow you'll fire an entire department of people again before buying Zanzibar over lunch."

"Buying Zanzibar," he repeats. "Well, I usually do my nation-shopping at night."

"Right. Are there infomercials for that?"

"Too many. I couldn't sleep one night and accidentally bought the entire Scandinavian peninsula, and I don't even have the space for it."

My laughter is cut short by a black town car pulling up beside us. Carter unbuttons his dinner jacket and opens the door to the back seat for me. "Come on."

I take a deep breath, and then I step into the luxe interior and leather scent. He closes the door behind us and we're instantly in a world apart. Gone is the drizzle and wind. We're alone, side by side in a dark car.

"Your address," Carter says. I give him the details and he relays them to the man in the driver's seat. Absurdly, I thought he'd wear a hat, and then feel stupid when I think it.

And all of a sudden my heart speeds up. Carter's nearby and he's a man and what if he has expectations, too? What if I've misunderstood and despite the fact that he could never, ever date someone like me, he might—

"Tell me something honestly," he says.

"Uh-huh?"

"Think you can be friends with your boss, despite his… business practices?"

I smile. Friends, of course. That's what he wants. I have

nothing to worry about. "I'm considering it, yes. Even if it makes no sense and is definitely not advisable."

"Wondering if I should be offended," he says. "Deciding not to be."

I bump his knee with mine. His legs are long, stretched out in the ample space of the town car. "Then tell me something honestly in return."

"Yes, I was born this handsome. My mother has been contacted repeatedly by the press, but there's no real explanation. I'm just a beautiful accident of nature."

"Are you ever serious?"

"Life forces me to be sometimes," he admits, "but I avoid it at all costs."

I chuckle. "Tell me something, then. Someone like you—I don't mean someone as handsome as you, although you are, and you know it. But I mean someone as successful and social... why did you and I end up texting so much? What did you gain from it, you know?"

He arranges the cuff of his jacket and I can't see his eyes. But his voice is the same confident drawl as always. "Is it so crazy to imagine I wanted a friend?"

"You must have a hundred people in this city that are better friends than me."

"No," he says. "I don't. People are intimidated by me, you know. It's the face."

I laugh again. It's hard not to, around him, and even harder when you're drunk off champagne and the best night of your life. "The clothes, perhaps, the expensive watch, the town car, the easy wit..."

Heated gold eyes meet mine. "Compliments?"

"You were fishing for them," I say, but I lean back in my seat.

He smiles slowly, and his eyes drop down to my dress again. "Well, kid, for being a grown woman in her prom dress... you look fucking gorgeous."

My eyebrows climb all the way up to the sunroof of the

car. "What?"

"We're exchanging compliments, are we not?"

"Yes, but they have to be believable."

"You don't think you're beautiful," he says skeptically. "Don't play that card. How many damn dates have you been on in the past month?"

I shake my head. "No, no, I'm not trying to be falsely modest. I like how I look. It's not like a supermodel or anything, but I'm happy with it. But I've seen the women you date."

Just not the one you brought tonight. The thought immediately sours my thinking. Was he like this with them too? Like he wants nothing more than to make them laugh?

"That's a comment we'll dissect another day," he says. "You live in Queens."

I nod. Outside the windows, the streets are becoming familiar. We're getting closer. "Yes."

"Rent your own apartment?"

"I rent a room in a house. The owner lives on the first floor."

Carter nods. "Right. I grew up in Queens."

"You did?"

He runs a hand over the back of his neck. "Yeah. So now you know where I grew up."

I recognize a tentative gesture when I see it, and through my drunken haze, I wonder if he'd meant exactly what he'd said earlier. If some of his jokes aren't jokes at all, the self-deprecation hiding things beneath the surface.

"I grew up in Alrich," I say. "It's a town upstate."

His smile is small and crooked. "Nice to meet you, Audrey."

I extend my hand. "You too, Carter."

He takes it in his. It's so much warmer than I expected. His fingers curl a moment longer around mine, long and firm, before he lets it go.

"We're here," he says. "Thanks for tonight."

NINE

Carter

I rub a hand over my eyes. Despite the sleep I'd gotten last night, better than I had in weeks, I'm bone tired. The *Globe*'s poor financials are an antidote to any kind of rest.

A man would have to be mad or inspired to take this project on. I'd been inspired when I bought it, but increasingly I'm wondering if I fall in the other category instead. All I need is a hat and I could host myself some tea parties.

Wesley's quiet opposite my desk. He probably knows what's coming, and I know it too, but I have to say it.

"Are you seriously telling me," I say, "that the Deckson ads account for *eight* percent of our profit margin on the paper?"

"Unfortunately so," he says. "One of the previous board members was close with the Deckson family. Things escalated from there, I suppose."

"I'm sure that was well and good thirty years ago, but the company is a PR nightmare today. We can't have their name plastered across our pages."

Wesley takes off his glasses and rubs them clean on his shirt with meticulous swipes. "It would undermine confidence in our reporting."

"The Investigative team is working on a deep exposé on

their industry and the production methods. Undermine? We'd lose any credibility we have left, running that piece on the front cover and having a Deckson ad on the next page."

"You're right," Wesley says.

I stare at the man. He's been nothing but helpful once I got here, quick to engage with my suggestions and even quicker to implement them. But this exposé had been in the works for over a year. He'd been editor-in-chief all that time.

Had he never seen the clash?

"We can sell the ad space to other retailers," he says. "I'll have our sales department draft a list of possible candidates during the day."

I run a hand through my hair. The *Globe* shouldn't be this reliant on ads. It's stifling the company's originality, credibility, and most of all, it's losing trust with the very people we want to reach.

"Do that," I agree, even if I hate the necessity. "Investigative will have a part to play in this whole thing, you know. If we're to draw new subscribers to the *Globe*, we want to keep our reporting relevant. Break new stories."

"I'm with you on that, sir," Wesley says.

He leaves my office soon after, and I relish the closed door. No one to impress or charm, just me and my thoughts. This fucking media company is like a minefield. I make one department redundant only to discover some of the employees in it were actually pulling a load on the side for another. The man I thought was competent enough to head a new department is poached by another newspaper with higher pay, and the bastard doesn't even confront me about it —or HR—to ask for a commensurate raise in pay first.

The internal structure of this newspaper is a disaster.

But I can't blame my mood entirely on the *Globe*, try as I may. There's a single, tiny little reason why I can't.

It's the text I got last night. I haven't responded to it yet, and it's lying on my phone, innocent and unanswered.

Audrey: I survived the date!! It went so well. I think I've nailed the art of small talk now. We're going on another one tonight. I'm supposed to pick the place. I want to suggest the movies, but does that have other implications for a man?

Her date went well. As a friend, I should be happy about that. Hadn't I been the one to make the damn suggestion about helping her with dates if she helped me with the company? So far we'd done neither of those things. It would be cool by me if we kept it like that.

Of course this guy wants a second date. Any man who wasn't an idiot could see the catch she is. Honest to a fault, beautifully optimistic without being naive, and true in a way I've rarely met. There's no artifice to her.

She's quick to laugh and quick to stand up for her beliefs.

Audrey might give me flack for being a charmer, but mine is all bluff. Her kind of appeal runs deeper.

The idea of her having trouble dating is ridiculous. I'd understood that the second I met her. It's in her head, the nerves, the expectations, the build-up.

I want her to realize that... just not with some random guy from a dating app.

I tuck my phone into my pocket and go searching for Wesley again. He looks up when I enter his office. "Yes?"

"You said you'd introduce me to the investigative team. I want to do it now."

"Right, okay. Let's go." To his credit, Wesley never seems off balance with my suggestions. Not even when I'd slashed half of the circulation department.

We reach the newsroom and walk through the busy corridor. People fall quiet as we pass, the sound of animated voices quieting down to a hesitant murmur. They still don't trust me around here. I wonder if I have a giant sign over my head that says *your job is in danger* whenever they see me. One person I don't recognize actually ducks back into his cubicle, as if he's safe as long as he can't see me.

Wesley stops in the center of the office. "Anyone seen Booker?" he calls.

A gangly man in a tweed jacket answers. He's sitting next to a wide-eyed Audrey, her eyes moving from me to Wesley. "She's finishing up a phone meeting," he says.

Wesley clears his throat, but I step in. This is the team Audrey waxed poetically about. It's the kind of reporting that, I have to admit, she has a point about. It could put us back on the map.

"Sorry to disrupt your work," I say, projecting my voice to the entire room. There has to be at least forty people working here. "We've met before, but not on a personal basis. I'd like to get to know this department better and familiarize myself with the work you all do. I'll do a lap of the room with Wesley here, and speak to each one of you."

Quiet murmurs break out as soon as I've finished. The journalists are hesitant. A quarter of them aren't even in the office. But some tell me in open, excited terms about the stories they're working on. One man, older than most, informs me that he's working toward a deadline and doesn't have time to hold my hand. Wesley pales by my side, but I grin at him.

"Someone who understands the value of time. I appreciate it. I'll talk to you at a better time, then."

"Looking forward to it," he says with the enthusiasm of someone talking to their dentist.

So this team doesn't like me very much. That's all right. As long as they produce great content for me, they can think me the devil and I'll be happy.

Audrey's table is the very last I visit. I speak to her deskmate first. "Declan, is it?"

He nods. "Yes. Nice to meet you, sir."

"No sir here," I say. "Tell me what you're working on."

"I'm fact-checking some things for Emery's Sunday article."

"Right. Junior investigative reporter, right?"

"Yes. Together with Audrey here, we mostly support the other journalists." He reaches up and rearranges his glasses. Despite the stern expression, there's a bead of sweat on his forehead.

Audrey clears her throat. She's been following the conversation, and I've been watching her from the corner of my eye. Her hair is pulled into a low ponytail and she's wearing a blazer, no lipstick, a world away from the woman I'd spent time with at the Reporters' Ball. She'd been almost giddy then, filled with so much excitement for her job and life that it excited my own.

"Well, we used to work on our own stories," she says. "Before the freeze on our articles. Declan's idea was fascinating."

He shoots her a glare.

"Oh?" I ask. "Tell me about it."

He does, reluctantly at first, but his eyes soon glow with enthusiasm. Audrey had been right. These people are self-starters, and assuming they can write, they're one of the paper's greatest assets.

"Don't forget to look into the other perspective," I tell him. "I want you covering both sides."

"Will do," Declan says. "Thank you."

"Anytime." I turn toward Audrey. She meets my eye with a careful one of her own, her face composed like she's sitting for an old-time portrait. The obvious attempt at casualness makes me want to smile.

"Audrey Ford," I say. "You interviewed me for the newsletter."

"Yes, that's right," she says. Even her voice sounds stiff.

I crack a smile. "It was a good interview. Well, what are you working on now?"

She tells me about the three research projects she's helping with in short, professional tones. Even goes so far as to open the file on her computer, her voice heating up with excitement.

"Excellent," Wesley says by my side. "Mr. Kingsley, let me show you—"

"I'd like to hear about what story you're working on," I ask Audrey.

She meets my gaze with a strong one of her own. "The focus is on a bodega in Queens. The owners are being evicted by a construction company on false grounds. It's all an excuse to level the place and build expensive condos."

"You care about the area?" I ask.

She nods. "We're a big-picture paper, but I think we've lost sight of the customers at home over the last couple of years. The New Yorkers who are our true supporters. They care about their city and the things that happen in it."

A quiet apprehension lands in the air. She's criticized the leadership of the newspaper to the current and former heads, and she'd done it with an enthusiastic smile.

And *that*, I think, is why she deserves to be called spitfire.

"It's a good story," I say. "The freeze on solo reporting will be lifted. I want you to find time to work on it."

She nods, and I can tell she's biting the inside of her cheek to stop a smile. "Yes, sir. Excellent. I'll… do that."

"No sir," I repeat.

I leave her at her desk, the terrible actress with her glittering eyes. Wesley walks beside me on our way back to the executive floor. There's agitation in his silence.

"Just say it," I tell him.

"Several of them overstepped," he says. "I'll speak to Booker tomorrow. Saying they didn't have time, sharing their unsolicited thoughts on the direction of the newspaper…"

I frown at him. Is this how he usually runs the paper? "I don't want sycophants, I want a functioning newspaper," I say. "You won't tell Booker a thing."

A brief flare-up of irritation in Wesley's eyes, but then it's gone, and he's once more the helpful second-in-command. "Noted."

As soon as I'm back in my office, I reply to Audrey's text.

Carter: You're a terrible actress.

Well, *reply* is a loose term. I'd promised her help with her dates. But I never promised to be prompt.

Audrey: You terrified everyone in this room, you know. Announcing you wanted to get to know the department. I swear two people in the back fainted.

I frown down at my phone.

Carter: You're exaggerating.

Audrey: Only slightly. What made you want to get to know Investigative better?

She has to know it's her. Audrey's words and her burning enthusiasm for the topic. I still have plans for the other departments, not to mention the *Globe*'s app. But her passion is contagious.

Can great journalism really be the savior of this newspaper?

Carter: Someone told me it's the backbone of this paper.

Audrey: Someone very smart, right?

Carter: Moderately, I'd say.

Audrey: I'll take it. Thank you for allowing solo initiatives again. You know, we all work on it on our spare time. It's what keeps a lot of these journalists' flames burning.

I'd never considered that. Booker handles the story beats, but all of them want to pursue their own stories. Like Audrey's bodega. *Flames burning.* Christ, she has a way with words.

I take another hour to answer her first text. It's a dick move, because it's already past five and she's likely left the paper already, but I couldn't bring myself to give her advice before. Half my text is a lie.

Carter: Glad to hear about your date. The movies is a good suggestion. If you're wondering if he'll think about handsiness in the cinema, the answer is yeah, he might hope for it. But he's an asshole if he expects it.

It's only half-an-hour before she texts me back.

Audrey: Thank you, you're right. But he just cancelled :(No movies for me!

And with that single text, I see an opportunity.

TEN

Audrey

It should have bummed me out. On all accounts, Ben was great. A musician with a steady gig as a piano teacher, well-mannered, didn't seem like a closet psychopath. He was cute in that teacher kind of way, and I'd always been a teacher's pet. His text to cancel had consisted of no less than three different ways of apologizing. *I'm sorry, forgive me,* and *I feel terrible.*

But me? All I feel is relief.

I don't have to go through with another nerve-wracking date, where half my brain spends the entire evening nervous about what he's thinking. I wish I didn't care. I wish I could be like Nina, my best friend, who throws herself off metaphorical dating cliffs with reckless abandon.

I'd texted her right after I texted Carter, and she's written me an essay in response.

Nina: You can't let this one setback turn you off. He might have a legitimate excuse. But I want you to know I'm so proud of you. How many first dates have you been on now? Who are you, and what have you done with Audrey??

She means well, and I smile at the double question marks.

But these dates aren't leading anywhere. I'm overcoming my nerves of first dates, yes, but nothing more.

The fifteen minutes I'd spent re-doing my makeup feels like a waste now. I lift up my long hair and arrange it into a bun. Should I go out anyway? Eat at a restaurant alone, a woman empowered?

But Lord knows I'm not made of money.

So I let my hair down and sit at my kitchen table instead. I have three separate notebooks open, filled with my sprawling handwriting. With the heavy pressure at work, I spend most of my evenings on the story about the evicted bodega owners and violated zoning regulations.

I hit play on my recorder and listen to my interview with the owner. My voice is steady, if a bit nervous. His grows agitated as he describes how predatory gentrification is pushing them out of the area.

I start transcribing.

The owner has just finished describing the construction company in very colorful terms when my phone rings.

Carter Kingsley, my phone screen informs me.

We've never spoken on the phone before.

"Hello?" I say.

"Your date remains cancelled?"

"Uh, yes. Nothing's changed since I texted you."

"Come on then, I'm downstairs."

I walk to my window. "What?"

"I heard you were in need of a white knight."

I push back the curtain and peer out. To my amazement, he's telling the truth. Carter's standing outside Pierce's brownstone, leaning against the stoop.

"Why," I say, "are you wearing a tux?"

Down on the street, Carter runs a hand over the snugly fitted suit. It makes him look sharper, his edges clean and his form tall. "White knights need their armor," he says. "I was at an event before. Come on, kid. Let me buy you dinner."

I can't stop myself from grinning down at him, so out of

place amongst the regularly dressed passersby. "All right. I'll be downstairs in a minute!"

I pull on my thick puffer coat and stick my feet in a pair of sneakers. We'll look like the world's most mismatched couple... which we are. At least it's a truthful representation.

I close the front door behind me. "Hey."

"Hello," he says. His mouth pulls into a smile as he looks me over. "Cold?"

"I don't know how you aren't. Are you wearing thermals beneath that suit?"

He puts a hand over his chest. "A gentleman never reveals his secrets."

I make a show of looking around. "There's a gentleman here?"

"Ouch," he says. "Hungry?"

"Starving."

"Good. I know a place." He nods up the street and I fall into step next to him, shoving my hands into my pockets. I can't stop smiling. He'd shown up, just to hang out, had he?

For all the reasons why we shouldn't be friends, I can't help wanting to spend time with him. Somehow everything he says is intriguing. He could be talking about laundry detergent or the national debt, and he'd make it interesting.

Maybe it's his voice or his turns of phrase.

Maybe it's just him.

"Didn't you say you just came from a dinner?" I ask. "Now you want to eat again?"

"I did, but calling it dinner is an insult to the institution itself. The only thing they served was tiny quiches."

"Ouch." I look over at him, the strong line of his jaw, the crisp suit. "But you went anyway? What was it?"

He lifts a shoulder in an elegant shrug. "Something I'd accepted a long time ago and couldn't get out of. It was a networking thing at the British Chamber of Commerce."

"Must be tough being so popular. How do you sort through all the invitations?"

"It's a problem," he says solemnly. "My apartment regularly floods with them."

"Poor rich businessman."

"We're a struggling minority."

I roll my eyes, but I'm grinning. "You never answered my text about sending the newsroom into a panic today."

"Honestly?"

"Yes. Coming down unannounced and declaring you want to get to know the department better? Every single person there was thinking they'd be fired."

He's quiet for a moment. "Well, not you."

"Not me," I say. "Well, I couldn't be quite sure, but I suspected you weren't there to lay us all off. You didn't have your serious face on."

"My serious face?"

"Well, now it seems a bit silly, saying it out loud." I pull the sleeves of my jacket down to cover my hands. "But I saw what you looked like when you gave the speech during the all-hands meeting. You didn't wear that expression today, you know. The one where you're bracing yourself against blowback."

We walk the length from one lamppost to another in silence.

"You're observant," he says.

"It's a good trait in a reporter."

"I'm sure. So you weren't scared today, at any rate, seeing as you can apparently read my intentions from my face. How did people react after I left?"

I shrug. "People didn't know what to make of it. Most people assumed, and I think correctly, although let me know if I'm wrong, that it was a good sign. Was it? Does this mean you're considering giving Investigative more resources?"

"You don't give up, do you?"

"Never."

Carter doesn't reply. He stops outside a restaurant instead. "Have you ever eaten here?"

I peer through the windows. The place is Italian and kitschy, with a painted mural of the Colosseum on one of the walls. The tables have red plastic tablecloths.

"Nope," I say.

He pushes the door open. "Come on. They have the best pizza in Queens."

I don't move right away. I stare at him instead, tall and with a pressed tuxedo on, holding the door open for me. "Volare" plays softly from the speakers.

Carter's eyes are steady. "Audrey?"

I step past him into the warm restaurant. We're greeted by a smiling hostess in her mid-fifties and ushered into a booth in the back. Her gaze lingers on Carter.

Probably wondering what a man dressed like him is doing in a place like this.

"You've been here before?" I ask.

"Might've been, yes." He pushes the menu across the table at me. "Their calzone is delicious."

I open the menu without reading any of the items. Just when I think I have him figured out, he changes. But nothing about our friendship is normal. Why should I expect him to be?

"They have passable house wine as well," he says. "But I think the beer is a safer bet."

"Oh, I'm not drinking around you anymore. I get too... talkative when I do."

"It's entertaining when you do, though."

I roll my eyes. "Christ, I'm sure. But I can't stand by the things I say."

Carter's mouth stretches into a wicked smile. "You remember what you told me at the ball?"

"I remember all of it," I say, heat flooding my cheeks. "And there was so much of it that I'm not even sure *which* embarrassing thing you're referring to."

"You didn't embarrass yourself."

I look down at the pizzas on display. Far too many for any

mortal person to sort through. "You're nice, but I definitely did."

"Hmm. Would one of them be getting food poisoning at your senior prom?"

"Oh God. I really did admit to that, didn't I?" It had been one of the most embarrassing moments of my life, throwing up on the dance floor. The teachers threatened to call my parents about my underage drinking.

It was *mildly* humiliating to have to explain to them, my hand clasped to my stomach, that I'd never tasted a drop in my life, because I'd never been invited to the frequent house parties the cool kids threw.

Carter's voice drops. It's soothing again, the deep register washing over me like a balm. "Was the Icelandic boy nice to you?"

"Yes. I think he was secretly a bit put out that I ruined his American prom experience, though." I chuckle at the memory. "But I told him to go inside and have fun, and he informed me sternly that he would never leave a sick friend."

"What about your parents?" He reaches out to grab hold of the salt canister, twisting it around in large hands. I'd never really looked at them before, but I watch them now, long fingers moving with dexterity. There's a light dusting of hair across the back of his hands. "Tell me about your family."

I smile at him, but he's looking down at the salt. Is this because of my stupid comment about not really knowing him? Are we getting deeper?

"Well, my dad's a dentist and my mom's a chiropractor. Kevin is three years younger than me. He lives in Brooklyn now, in an art collective with six of his friends."

"You have a brother?"

"Yeah. We were best friends growing up. I'm a bit worried about him right now, though, but I think he's just finding his way." I shrug, closing my menu. "It's tough to be young and idealistic."

Carter raises an eyebrow. "Speaking from experience, are you?"

"Well, I don't know if you've noticed, but I *might* be a bit idealistic too."

"You? Never."

I grin at him, and he smiles right back at me. Something flips over in my chest. It feels like the beating of a pair of wings, light and airy and launching into flight.

"Ready to order?" the hostess asks. I look away from Carter's golden eyes, breaking the magic, and we order. The food arrives quickly, almost suspiciously so, but Carter accepts his giant pizza with a solemn thank-you.

"Better than a miniature quiche?" I ask him.

He cuts into his pizza with strong, energetic moves. "Kid, never get rich. It's all events and *sir, would you please look at this?* and tiny fucking food. People never stop trying to con you out of your money, either."

The words prick at my memories. I see my father's crestfallen face, the bone-deep disappointment in himself after the man in a suit had swept through his life with honey-sweet promises. My entire college fund, gone. My brother's, gone. A life's worth of savings gone. "You don't have to be rich to have people con you," I say.

"No, you're right about that," Carter says, and there's a trace of bitterness in his own voice. "Poor choice of words."

I shake my head. "No, I'm sure you're more likely a target. People always have investment schemes for you, don't they?"

"Yes. Ninety-nine percent of them are pure bullshit."

"That's what you do as a venture capitalist, right? Find the one percent that's worth your time? Like the *Globe*?"

He takes a bite of his pizza and chews slowly, eyes on mine. "Are you interviewing me?"

"Part two of the company newsletter," I say. "Got a lot of requests for a follow-up."

He snorts, reaching for his beer. It's all deceptively normal, but I can't look at him without seeing the well-fitted suit, the thick hair swept over a face that is, admittedly, unusually handsome. It's no less so while he's eating pizza and drinking beer.

I shrug. "Well, you're fascinating. You don't make sense to me, you know. I'm still half-convinced you'll pull the rug out from under me one day and say 'what, you actually thought we were friends? I own the company you work for!'"

Carter nods, like this is a distinct possibility. "Would I laugh maniacally as well?"

"Yes. Twirl your moustache."

He smooths a hand over his jawline, across the five-o'clock shadow. It makes him look deliciously masculine. "I could grow one for you."

"That'll be the sign, then," I say. "If I show up to work one day and see you with a moustache, that means you've decided I'm beneath you. No more socializing."

His lips twitch. "I'll bear it in mind. Don't hold your breath, though."

"I won't. I rather like texting you," I say, taking a bite of my pizza to avoid his gaze. It feels like a vulnerable thing to admit. To put into words the weird connection we have, this... non-thing that's a thing all of its own.

It feels safer to keep it in the gray zone.

"I like talking to you too," he says. His voice sounds gruffer than usual. Not the smooth, cultured suaveness.

I prefer this version.

We eat in silence for few minutes, the weight of our mutual revelation settling between us. Like sand sinking to the bottom of a lake, shoring up the bed.

He takes another deep sip of beer and meets my gaze. "Will you finally tell me why dating is so scary for you? It wasn't the Icelandic boy, then, but it was someone, right? Tell me who and I'll have him killed."

I burst out laughing and have to put my pizza slice down. Carter's mouth quirks into a half-smile, eyes glittering. He likes to make me laugh. The knowledge makes my chest warm.

"It wasn't anyone in particular," I say.

He raises an eyebrow. "Audrey."

"It really wasn't." I run a hand through my curls. A flush creeps up my neck. "I wasn't exactly... popular in high school. And in college I spent all my time studying or at the school paper. I was the editor for one term, you know."

"The newspaper was best that term, too?"

I shrug, but I'd loved being at the helm. Judging from the look in his eyes, he knows it too. Funny how I never have to hide my ambition around him. "It ran like clockwork," I say. "But I also worked extra at the school's pretzel shop."

"The pretzel shop?"

I clear my throat. "Would you like your pretzel bites with a dipping sauce? We have cheddar cheese, curry and barbecue, or for a sweet touch, caramel, maple or chocolate."

Carter chuckles. "You still remember it?"

"I'll remember it until the day I die," I say. "God, I've eaten enough of them to last me a lifetime."

"Did you put yourself through college?"

I look back down at my pizza. "Partly, yeah."

And if it wasn't my father's greatest shame. I'd only mentioned my student loans a few times at home, before the pained look in his eyes became too much. I hated seeing him beat himself up.

"That's impressive," Carter says. "But all that left little time for dating?"

I chew the inside of my cheek. "I've never had a boyfriend."

His hands slowly lower to the plate, pizza slice forgotten. "Never?"

"No. Nothing... confirmed. I haven't really been on dates, either. Before this past year."

Carter looks at me for a long, silent moment. Is he judging? I know the conclusions people draw. The ones that aren't true, not really, but sting nonetheless.

"That's a fucking disgrace, Audrey."

"You called me Audrey," I whisper.

"I'm embarrassed on behalf of my sex," he says. "How the hell did none of the college boys scoop you up? Someone on the paper?"

I rub a hand over the back of my neck. "Well, my one college fling was with someone from the paper."

"Ah. Here it is, the big scandal. Come on. How awful was he, and what was his social security number? I can have a SEAL team give you justice in four hours. Ten, if he's abroad."

I laugh, shaking my head. "No, no, it was nothing like that. It was good. It was just not traditional. We never went out together. I never had to do that awkward first date dance where you're both pretending to be someone else."

"There's an easy solution for that," he says. "Stop pretending."

I roll my eyes. "What, just be myself right off the bat?"

"Yes. You were yourself with me, from the first moment we met, and I'm still here."

"Well, I wasn't trying to impress you."

He raises an eyebrow. "And yet you have. Perhaps you don't have to pretend, kid."

I give him a teasing smile. "If I stop pretending, you have to, too."

"I don't pretend anything," he says.

"I'm not convinced. You're the biggest charmer I've ever met. Were you yourself at that Reporters' Ball, with the date you brought? Or with the blonde I saw you with the night we met?"

Carter leans back in his seat and gives me a calculating look. "You've been paying attention."

"Of course I have. I don't know many venture capitalist billionaire CEOs."

"I know too many," he replies.

"Wouldn't you agree, though? That you wear a mask?"

He's quiet for another beat. "Maybe I do," he says, reaching for his beer.

"I get that it's probably safer for you in some cases," I admit. "With all the people trying to con you. If only they could see you now, eating twelve-dollar pizza in a worn-down restaurant in Queens."

"They'd never stop calling," he says.

"So, we've psychoanalyzed me. I want to know the same things about you. What do your parents do?"

His lips quirk in a half-smile. "My mother's a teacher. She works at an elementary school right around here."

"So that's why you grew up in Queens?"

"Yes. We lived just a few blocks over."

"Normal childhood?"

"Normal enough," he says. "No mini quiches, if that's what you mean."

"No one really needs mini quiches," I say. "So, do you also have a sibling who answers your texts sporadically?"

"Not really," he says.

"Not really? Isn't that a yes or no question?"

His mouth twists into another one of his smiles, but this one feels more rehearsed. "Not really," he repeats, voice smooth.

I laugh. "Mysterious. I respect that."

"It was mostly my mother and me," he says. "She still lives in the area, actually."

I put two and two together. "You've been to this restaurant a lot, haven't you?"

"Every other Friday, like clockwork," he says with a grin.

"That's why the hostess recognized you!"

He looks over at the woman, busy with showing a new party to their table. "Fiona. She recognizes me, but isn't quite sure who I am, I think."

"Wow."

He gives me a level look. "I'm a normal person, you know. Even if I am your boss's boss's boss."

"I'm starting to realize that, yeah."

"I have a question for you," he says. "Did you always know you wanted to be a journalist? All that work, college, the paper... what put you on this path?"

I chew slowly, drawing out the pause. The real answer is complicated, but I don't have to give the long one. "I've always loved to write," I say. "But I've always been interested in the world around me too. My father, he reads the *Globe* every day. On Sundays he stretches it out into a half-day event. I'd sit next to him and ask about articles. It seemed like a magical thing. Stories, information, hot takes. It felt like the whole world was contained inside those thin pages."

I shake my head, smiling. "I know that sounds fanciful. But I grew older, and I learned that stories have power. They can mobilize. They can galvanize, polarize. They can change a person's life, a person's business. Some are huge, like the whistleblower stories. Others are smaller. A construction halted because of a petition."

"Idealistic," Carter says softly. "And young."

I smile at him, a bit sheepish. "Yes. There's more to it, I know. Politics. Advertising. Propaganda. But the best of journalism is about people and change. It'll always be magic to me."

"I'm amazed you're sitting here with me," he says, "when I'm the one rolling a bowling ball through the newspaper you love."

I look down at my pizza again. "True, I love it. But it's struggling. Has been for years, same as all print media. Your changes are hard to swallow sometimes. But I know you're doing it because you genuinely want to save this paper."

"I do," he says levelly. "I have no doubt that you'll help me do it, too."

"Right. You said you had some changes planned, right?"

For the rest of the meal we talk about the *Globe*. Still teasing, because I can't seem to stop around him, and he makes me laugh more often than I should. But we talk about the future of the newspaper and numbers and a tentative plan to ramp up resources available for the Investigative team.

And the birdwings in my chest beat on.

He insists on paying the bill, and I insist on splitting, until he finally sighs and puts a large hand on mine. He pins my card to the table and extends his own to the machine.

"Next time, then," I say.

He pretends like he doesn't hear me.

"Thank you," Carter says to Fiona when we leave. "Just as good as always."

Her face shines up in a smile. "Oh, I'm so glad," she says. "Say hi to your mom for me, will you?"

"Will do."

We walk in a slow amble toward my apartment. I'm full and warm and happy. I'm nervous, too. Not a lot. Not like a proper date. But it tickles my insides with anticipation.

"You know," Carter says, voice smooth. "I wish I would have gone to the Reporters' Ball with you."

Those little tickles increase. "We ended it together, at least," I say. "Did you really send your date away?"

"Will you berate me if I say yes?"

I focus on the sidewalk. "I should, perhaps, but... What did you tell her?"

"It was booked weeks in advance," he says. "I didn't want to cancel last minute, so we went."

"Right. That's nice of you. But what did you tell her, at the ball?"

"She seemed relieved, at any rate. I think she'd expected an event where the median age wasn't forty-five. Told me thanks."

We stop outside the stoop to my house. I face him, forced as always to look up and up to meet his eyes. There's hesitation in them, and something else, a look that sets my stomach ablaze. "What did you tell her?" I ask again.

His mouth quirks into a half-smile. He reaches up and pinches a lock of my hair between his fingers.

I can't breathe.

"I told her," he says, "that someone very special had arrived."

"Oh."

We're silent on the sidewalk, staring at one another.

"Thank you for keeping me company tonight," I murmur. "It was very nice of you to come all the way out here from your dinner."

"You're welcome," he says. "Were you nervous tonight?"

"No." *Just now*, I think. *I'm nervous right now.* "Why would I have been?

He smiles again. It's smaller this time, and something about it makes my heart hurt. "You and I were on a date, spitfire."

Air feels stuck in my throat. "We were?"

"Yes," he says. "Had a good time?"

I nod. "Excellent food. Excellent... company."

Carter's hand smooths from my hair to my cheek. Long fingers flit across my skin, fitting themselves to my jaw. Tilting my head up.

I didn't think he liked me like this. I didn't think...

And then I can't think at all, because his golden eyes are burning on mine. "Glad you had fun," he says. "But I'm not going to ask you out again."

Oh.

"Good?" I whisper.

He smiles. "I know how you feel about dates, so I want you to think about this. Consider if you'll let me ask you out. Can you do that for me?"

"Yes. Yeah, I mean. I can do that."

"Great." Then he bends his head, and I close my eyes, heart pounding. But he only presses his lips to my cheek. The rough feel of his stubble against my skin sends a shiver down my body, all the way to my toes. "And Audrey?" he says. "The guy who cancelled on you is an idiot."

"Right. Sure."

Carter straightens to his full height. His smile is cocky, full of himself. Every inch the man I'd met in that bar weeks ago. "I'll be out of town for a few days. Think about it until I get back," he repeats. "If you'll let me take you out for real."

I nod, not finding words, and watch him disappear down the street. Hard to imagine I'll be thinking about anything else.

ELEVEN

Carter

I spin the pen around in my hand, the solid weight of the metal cool against my skin.

"With our budget constraints," the speaker drones on, "a gradual increase is the better option. But that would mean…"

My mind wanders again. It's done that a lot this conference, and at damn inconvenient times, too. During meetings and panel discussions. Thank God I'd managed to hold it together long enough to give the short speech I was required to.

Tristan has asked me twice what's on my mind, and both times I'd answered the *Globe*. Strictly speaking, it's only a half of a lie. Audrey is a *Globe* employee, after all.

We haven't texted much since I said goodbye to her outside her apartment. She'd looked shocked and flushed and wide-eyed, like I'd taken her completely by surprise, drowning in that oversize coat. It had hurt to kiss her cheek instead of her lips. It had hurt to turn and walk away from her. To put the power in her hands.

Tell me, I'd wanted to ask, *what you need from me.* I'd wanted to make her comfortable, to banish the nerves, to coax her into telling me the real reason dating scares her.

But I'd swallowed every single one of those traitorous words.

Audrey wants it all. A boyfriend who cooks her dinner and reads the paper with her on the weekend. And she deserves it all.

And I can feel myself standing at the ledge—wanting to give her that. Wanting to be the man she turns to for all of it, and doubting I'll ever be able to live up to it.

It would kill me to be less than she needs, I think.

I spin the pen faster.

What do I know, anyway? About loyalty and family and being a man who keeps his word?

Tristan leans in closer. "You bored?"

I force the pen down. Leave it abandoned on the table. "To death," I lie. Truth is I could be anywhere and thinking about her right now.

Whether or not I blew the whole fucking thing by crossing the line between us.

He chuckles. We're far enough from the speakers, sitting opposite the long conference table. Both of us don't have to be here, strictly speaking, but it was clear the organizers very much wanted two-fourths of Acture Capital here.

No doubt there'd be a photo op with the speaker after this.

"The *Globe* could benefit from his budget theory," Tristan says. "If you can convince Anthony and Victor it's still worth keeping intact."

I nod, jaw working. A few more months to turn the ship around in the eyes of my partners, or they'll want to sell it for parts. If the roles were reversed I'd probably advocate for the same exact thing.

But they're not. And I've promised to save the paper.

I run a hand through my hair and re-focus on the speaker. Whatever happens with Audrey, I know one thing. I can't be the reason her dream job falls through.

When the talk's over, Tristan and I are carefully asked if

we'll consider taking a picture with the speaker. "For posterity's sake," the organizer says with an artful chuckle.

For your PR team, I think. But I give him the charming smile I've perfected over the years, the one that never fails me. The one that Audrey seems to see right through.

"Definitely a moment to preserve," I say.

His smile falters a tiny bit. My cynicism had bled through, and damn it, I'm turned all the way inside out.

Tristan and I make our way down to the social afterwards. The hotel is filled with people already, a sea of suits and blazers. We're escorted straight past the line for the open bar to the section where the other keynote speakers and investors are waiting.

"Here we go," Tristan mutters at my side. He'd always been good at this too. It had been him and me playing good cop with investors, and Anthony and Victor playing bad cop.

We'd been a team.

But it seems like neither of us are feeling the charm tonight. Tristan has bigger things to concern him now. He'd married his longtime girlfriend earlier in the year, and together with his young son, his interest in networking has dwindled.

It takes time from the people who matter to him.

I accept a glass of bourbon and have a seat. It burns going down. What would it feel like? To know you have a wife and child at home. A family waiting for you, a puzzle where you're one of several pieces fitting perfectly together?

I imagine going home to a wife after this. The image in my mind is of a woman curled up on my couch, a blanket around her knees. She's reading a book. Maybe she'd even look up at me with warm eyes, eyes that are happy I'm home, eyes that don't expect me to perform.

I take another deep sip of my bourbon. My mind has given her Audrey's looks, and I like the image a little too much.

"Mr. Kingsley," the man to my left says. He's giving me a courteous smile. "Of Acture Capital, is that right?"

"Just so," I say, extending my free hand. "A pleasure."

"Likewise. Jacob Finch of Rosen Investing. We've heard about your purchase of the *Globe* and have been following the development closely."

I push all thoughts of Audrey down. Of a life outside of this.

This is what I know, this is what I do. I network and I perform and I talk.

"That's right," I say. "Care to hear more?"

I'm three bourbons deep when I step away from the VIP area. It's guarded off by a pathetic little rope, more to signal to the other minglers to stay out than for any security reasons. When did I start living my life in roped-off areas?

I click her name on my phone. We haven't texted at all in three days. Not a word, my phone quiet in my pocket.

Carter: Having a fun night?

Tell me about it, I think. Tell me about anything that's not here and anything that's about you, so I can pretend I'm there too.

When Tristan calls the night to an end, I do the same. We shake hands with the people who haven't gotten to us yet. Our joint Acture assistant gives us a tired thumbs up.

"Only one more day," she says.

Tristan rolls his neck. "I'm heading out after lunch tomorrow. Carter, you'll handle the dinner tomorrow?"

"If by handle," I say, "you mean I'll gain Acture thirty new potential investors, then yes."

He smiles. "That's the spirit."

"Good night."

"You too, man." He holds up his phone and gives it a little shake. "Gotta call Freddie. We... well."

I raise an eyebrow, my hand stilling on the door handle to my hotel room. "You what?"

Tristan looks sheepish, at odds with his usual competence and calm. "We're not telling anyone yet."

"Oh," I say. And then I understand what he's saying. "Jesus. Is she…?"

He nods, and the sheepishness dissolves into a grin. "Six weeks."

I reach for his hand and he lets me pull him in for a half-hug. "Christ, man. You'll be a father of two."

"Yes." He shakes his head, still grinning. "Don't know how I'll manage."

"You have a decade of experience as a father," I say. "You'll be fantastic."

He lifts a shoulder in a shrug. "It was never like this with Joshua, you know. It was never my wife pregnant, I wasn't in the delivery room… and I never had him as an infant. There are so many things that could go wrong."

"But so many things that could go right," I say. "Congrats, man. To both you and Freddie. Don't worry, I'll still act surprised when you tell us all."

Tristan's smile widens even further. He looks like he's lit up from within with joy. "Thanks. I'd better call. I'm driving her insane, probably, asking her to report how she's feeling several times a day."

I chuckle and nod toward his hotel room across the hall. "Go, then."

"Thanks. Night, man."

"Goodnight."

I close the hotel door behind me and lean my head against it for a long moment. He's having a second kid. The first with his wife, and the two of them—the three of them—will go through that together.

I look around the hotel room. It's bland and beige and about as personal as a franchise chain can be. The bed is huge and doesn't look slept in. I haven't felt lonely in years, but here it is, elegantly decorated and acidic.

My phone vibrates in my pocket. It's Audrey.

Audrey: It was all right. I was actually out on a date. The guy who cancelled last week, you remember?

Fuck.

My mouth tastes like ash, the pleasant aftertaste of bourbon long gone. Is this her answer to my question, then? If she'd consider letting me ask her out.

Defeat feels like a poison in my blood.

She'd gotten ready for him. Done her makeup and hair. Sat across from someone who didn't know her, didn't understand her, and made pleasant small talk.

Three little dots appear on the screen as she types another message. I stare down at them. Waiting for the verdict to fall.

They disappear. One second. Two seconds. Then they appear again. She's writing for so long that I'm half-expecting an essay, and if it's a polite no-thank-you, I don't know what I'll do.

The dots disappear.

Oh, for fuck's sake. My finger hovers over the call button. The one we've rarely used. I hit call. Audrey takes four long signals to answer. Maybe she's looking at her phone, just like me, wondering why I'm calling.

"Carter?" she says.

I close my eyes at her voice. "Yeah, it's me."

"Is everything all right?"

"As good as I can be," I say, "after a day of back-to-back meetings." There's an edge to my voice. I can hear it, and I can't stop it, not when I think of her and her date. Still looking for the man she'd told me about, the one who would cook her dinner and share the newspaper with her.

On the other end, Audrey's voice softens and turns teasing, all at the same time. "Poor little CEO."

"Someone pulled out my chair for me at dinner."

"How dare they?"

"Nearly had them fired on the spot," I say. For a few seconds neither of us speaks. The tension in my shoulders drops, just a tad.

"Did you just get back to your hotel room?"

"Yes," I say, and reach up to undo my tie. "And you just got home."

She's quiet for a beat, and I hear rustling on the other line. Is she lying in bed? I wish I'd have seen her apartment, to imagine where she's sitting now. "I did," she says quietly. "It was with the guy from last week. When you and I went for dinner instead."

I push away from the hotel door and walk through my suite. Toss my tie in the direction of my suitcase. "Right. The one who cancelled last minute."

It takes her a moment to answer. "Yes. I didn't... know how to respond when he asked for a rain check that night, so I said yes."

Her voice sounds apologetic. Fuck, I can handle being turned down, but I can't handle her walking on eggshells. "And how was it?" I brace my hands on the desk, wondering how I'll sleep after this call. "The date?"

"It was okay. Not bad or good, really," she says. "At least I'm not getting so nervous anymore, beforehand. It's getting... easier."

"Good," I say. "That's good."

"Yeah. I think that means I'll be less nervous when I go out with someone I'm genuinely interested in."

I reach for the buttons of my shirt. I feel too hot, my skin scorching to the touch. Maybe it's my pride burning up inside of me, because I'm seconds away from asking if she's given any more thought to my question.

"Great," I say.

Another quiet beat. We're never quiet this much, but if there's a joke to crack here, I can't find it. Can't make my way to the banter that will make it feel okay. "Did he kiss you?"

"No, God no," she says. Instant relief floods through me. "We're not going on another one either."

"And why not?"

"Well, I..." She sounds embarrassed, voice soft.

"Audrey," I say. "You can tell me."

"I don't want to go on any more dates while I'm considering, you know. The thing you told me to think about? I only went out with him because I'd already agreed to the rain check."

Something speeds up in my chest. I can't remember feeling nervous, not for years, but around her it's like an ever-present thing. She's in my ear and so close and yet wildly out of reach.

"Sounds like you'll need more time to think about it, then," I say. My voice comes out smooth. A miracle.

"A bit," she admits. Another rustle and yes, she has to be lying down. I stretch out on the hotel bed and imagine her doing the same on hers.

"Want to talk me through your thought process?" I ask, sounding like I'm asking about the weather, and not if she'll let me ask her out. "No worries if not."

"Okay," she says. "Well... you and I are friends. Weird ones, maybe, and definitely new, but friends. I like that, and we might lose it."

I close my eyes. She sounds like she's made a pros and cons list, and the idea of Audrey sitting down and attacking this like a story she wants to write makes me smile. "We might, yes. But we might have more fun."

"Right. Well, that's another issue. Fun. At some point we'd stop having it, and you'd still be my boss."

"I'd never interfere in your career. I should have made that clearer, spitfire. Would never happen. You could do anything to me and I wouldn't."

"I believe you," she says, yet there's a *but* in her voice. Of course there is. Because it's her livelihood and her dream, and what am I put up against that? There are too many cases of men who abuse their power over women in the workforce.

"You can say no," I say, "or you can say yes, and there will be no repercussions."

"I know. Carter, I don't... I know. But the idea is still scary. What if someone at work found out?"

I'd researched it. It's not an HR violation, isn't mentioned anywhere in the company's policies. But telling her that feels like admitting to how much I'd thought about this, so I don't.

"All good thoughts. Great ones, even. You keep thinking them. But I want you to remember that I won't be in charge of the *Globe* forever." I reach down and rest my hand on the belt of my slacks. "You can consider it for a long time."

"Hopefully I won't need a long time," she says.

The silence stretches out between us. It's not heavy. I hear her breathing faintly on the other line and wonder what it would feel like to have her resting on my chest instead.

Audrey speaks again. "Carter. Would it be like it was last week?"

"You and me, you mean? Yes. I think so."

"We had fun."

"We always have fun."

This time, I can hear the smile in her voice. "You make me laugh so much. It's ridiculous, actually."

"And you accuse me of being charming," I say.

"You are that, too. Nothing like how I expected a CEO to be, and especially not when I saw all the changes you brought."

The mass layoffs. They're still uncomfortable to think about, even if they'd been necessary. Upending so many lives. "I live to surprise," I say.

"Well, you surprise me," she replies. "Regularly."

Maybe her words give me the inspiration, or it's still the lingering image of Audrey out for dinner with her date, her cheeks flushed with life and eyes glittering as she laughed at *his* fucking jokes. But I ask the question anyway.

"Did you want him to kiss you tonight?"

"No," comes the soft answer. "I didn't."

"We never spoke about that."

"About what?"

"Intimacy," I say. "Where it fits into the equation for you, in relationships and dating. With your nerves."

The silence between us feels heady this time. I could take back my words. But I don't, letting them hang there, my stress like prickles beneath my skin.

I hear a soft click on the other end and I know, without knowing how I know, that Audrey has turned off her bedroom light. Cast her room into darkness. "It's complicated," she says. "I do want someone to be intimate with. Just not him. None of the men I've been on dates with, really."

"That's terrible luck," I say.

"Maybe, or maybe it's me," Audrey says. "I think I need more than just some polite small talk to know if I want to be... close to someone."

I smile at my ceiling lamp. *You and every woman*, I think. "That's not odd."

"It's not? Feels like it is." There's a shuffle on the other end and I imagine her turning over. Tucking her arm under her head.

"Say you met someone you connected with. You went out with them, had a great time. You found out he read the newspaper, and not just digitally."

"You remember?"

"Of course," I say. Her criteria for men. "What would you want him to do?"

Her voice is low. "Kiss me."

"You like being kissed," I say. The words feel hot on my tongue, and I know what I'm doing, and I know I should stop. I'm also more likely to be hit by a meteorite or be nominated as a presidential candidate.

But then Audrey takes it one step further. "I love being kissed," she says. "I like having sex, you know. I don't want you to think I don't, just because I'm not... experienced with relationships."

She said sex, she brought it up, and my mind floods with images. It's not like I haven't imagined it before. How she'd look beneath me, my arms on either side of her face. How the soft insides of her thighs would feel clutched around my head. If she'd whimper when I pushed inside.

"You like having sex," I repeat. The words send an instant ache up my thighs.

"I do," she whispers. "Don't you?"

Banal conversation. Banal, and absurd, and my hand glides down to stroke the hardening outline of my cock through my pants. "It's one of my favorite activities," I say.

With you, though, it would be worship.

"Think we'd have good sex?" Audrey asks. Her voice is small, but also determined, and I go rock hard in a second. It happens so fast I get a brief flash of lightheadedness.

I can't believe she'd brought up us and fucking.

"Carter?" she says. "Ignore me."

As if I could. "I think we'd have *great* fucking sex."

Her breathing catches on the other line and I close my eyes. Imagine her sitting across from me, watching the flush creep up on her cheeks. "We would, wouldn't we," she murmurs. "Even if it might be awkward at first."

I chuckle darkly. "It won't be awkward."

"It often is, the first time," she says, and I experience a brief and violent impulse to kill every man she's referring to in that statement. It passes, and what I'm left with is a burning desire to prove her wrong.

"It can be. Won't be for us, though."

"Oh?" Her voice is a caress in my ear. "What do you think we'd do?"

"If you want me to go there, I will. But fair warning."

"Wait," she says. "Just give me a minute, okay?"

I can't believe she didn't stop me. Adrenaline and something else, something darker, pulses through my veins.

Her voice is a whisper in my ear, along with the rustling of fabric. "I'm back."

"Did you just get into bed?"

"Yes," she says. "Is that... okay?"

I run a hand through my hair. "Fuck yes, that's okay."

"Well, I'm ready, Carter. Tell me what it would be like."

"I know what I'd like to do," I say. "If you were here with me at this conference. We'd go out to eat, like we did last week. Just the two of us."

"Would you be in a suit?"

"You like me in one?"

A brief pause. "Yes. You look handsome."

I haven't started touching myself properly yet, and I'm already edging closer to the finish line. Her words are too sweet. Sweeter still, knowing that she's in bed, that she's considering this. Considering us.

Actually *asking* me to tell her what we'd do. I could tell her I've fantasized about this, but I don't want her to run.

"Well, then. I'll be in a suit. You'll have your curls out, the way you did last week. We'd talk. I'd tell you how beautiful you look, and I'd mean it, too. I'd kiss you right there at the table."

"In the restaurant?"

"Where anyone could see," I say. "I wouldn't be able to stop myself."

Had a damn hard enough time last week, when I'd dropped her off.

"Oh," she breathes. "We'd kiss for a long time."

I grin. "Would we?"

"Yes. I love kissing. Slow, teasing... not too much tongue."

"Are you giving me tips here, Audrey?"

"Maybe." Her voice sounds flustered. "Is that okay?"

"I thrive on critique," I say. "So I'd kiss you a long time. Draw it out. Make you beg for more."

"Beg," she repeats. "Beg for you to take me back to the hotel, you mean?"

"Yes. Would you?"

"If you kiss me good enough, I just might."

It instantly becomes a goal. "Then I will. We'd get back to my hotel room. It would be slow at first. I'd get you a drink. Kiss your neck."

Even though I'd want to go very, very fast. But from her comments, it's been a while for her. She needs trust and friendship and I can't think of anything worse than wasting the chance to fuck Audrey properly because I get too eager.

"This is going very slowly," she says.

I make my voice mock stern. "Didn't you say that's what you liked? Are you critiquing my phone sex skills too?"

"So that is what we're having," she says. "It feels different to hear you say it."

"We're heading in that direction, at any rate," I say. My voice feels hoarse. "It's a poor substitute, but…"

"Good preparation," she says, and I bite my tongue to stop from groaning. So she's saying we'll have it one day. "I think I'd take off your shirt. Before you take off mine, I mean."

"That's allowed," I say.

"I'd want you to unzip my dress slowly. Run your hands over me. Make me feel…"

"Make you feel what, Audrey?"

"Wanted," she whispers.

I close my eyes. "I could do that. Wouldn't be difficult at all."

"Oh."

"I'd show you just how much I wanted you, too. Tell you how fucking hard you make me."

"I'd make you hard?"

"You already do," I say, and tuck my phone against my chin to undo my belt buckle. My pants feel uncomfortably tight, stretched over my cock.

"Did you…" Audrey says, then clears her throat. "Did you just undo a zipper?"

"Yes. Wanted to make it clear just how hard you make me."

"Right now? You're hard right now?"

"I'm thinking about fucking you, aren't I? In this hotel room, if you were here."

There's a breathy sigh on the other end. "I've never done this before."

"It's not hard," I say. "Well, one thing is. But it's just you and me talking. We've done it plenty of times before."

Her voice is low. "I'd want to take you in my mouth. Right there, in the hotel room, after you undo your zipper."

"Jesus Christ." I wrap my hand around my liberated cock, imagining my familiar fingers are her warm mouth, and start to stroke slowly.

"You'd groan just like that, too."

"I'd have to stop you eventually, too. Or I'd come from that alone."

"That would be okay," she says.

I stop my stroking, biting the inside of my cheek to hinder the dizzying sensation at the base of my spine. She can't talk about me finishing in her mouth. Not when I haven't even undressed her in this fantasy yet.

"Spitfire," I say, "if you think I'm not worshipping your body the first time we fuck, you have another thing coming."

"Oh. Wow."

"I'd undress you slowly. Kiss my way down your body. Suck on your nipples. Fuck, I'd do that for a very long time too. Slide a hand inside your panties. Would you be wet?"

"Yes. I… yes."

"Are you wet now?"

The line goes quiet on the other end, nothing save for her breathing. It's heavier than before. The single-word answer I receive makes my hardness twitch.

"Yes."

"Fuck."

"Carter?"

"Yes, Audrey?"

"You're touching yourself right now. Aren't you?"

I chuckle. "Yes. I want you to do the same, if you'd like."

"All right, I'm... okay."

"Tell me what you're doing."

Her voice is like velvet, smooth over my skin and sending goose bumps down my arms. I pump myself harder. "You go first," she says.

"I'm stroking myself, thinking about you," I say. "What I'd do if you were here in this bed with me. How incredible you'd look, after I'd slide your panties down your legs. How good it would feel when you'd let me fuck you for the first time."

"For the first time," she repeats. "There'd be many?"

"Do you doubt that?"

Her breathing speeds up. "No. I can see it."

"You can, can't you?"

"Well... I'm touching myself too."

"Where?" I demand. Something hovers at the edge of my vision, threatening to turn it dark, I'm so turned on. Images of her flicker in my head. In that dress at the ball. Teasing me in the back of my car. Eyes burning with passion as she tells me off for laying off her colleagues.

The shape of her in that dress. What she'll look like underneath it.

And most of all, how it'll feel to have her beneath me. To be inside her.

"I'm touching my clit," she says, and there's just a tiny hint of embarrassment. It heightens everything. She hasn't done this with anyone. Doesn't do it often. And here she is trusting me with it.

I groan, my fingers gripping my cock so hard it's almost painful. "That's it. Do you have your legs spread?"

"Yes. Knees bent, too."

"Did you take your panties off or just slide them to the side?"

"To the side," she murmurs. "God, Carter, I can't believe we're doing this."

"Don't think at all," I tell her. "Just close your eyes. Can you do that for me?"

"Mhm."

"Imagine it's me between your legs. My tongue against your clit. I'd push you down on this hotel bed and I wouldn't let you up again until you're screaming my name."

"Oh my god."

"Slide your finger down. Fuck yourself for me."

We're quiet for a few long beats, if quiet is the right term. My breathing is labored and hers comes in small pants. The sound is right there, in my ear. I imagine she's panting against my cheek as I drive into her. She'd have her legs around me. Fuck, and she'd be sweet, and mine, and I'd—

"Carter," she whispers. "I can come."

She says *can*, not will, and something tightens in my chest. "Then come."

"Will you stay on the line?"

"I'd rather die than hang up."

"Talk to me," she says.

I'm more than happy to. "You have no idea how much I want you. How badly I want to taste you. You'd be sweet against my tongue, I know you would. I want to see you so fucking bad. Want you here right now. My cock's about to burst, I'm so hard, and the only place I want to come is inside of you. To feel your sweet pu—"

"Oh my God." Her breathing catches on the other end, and then catches again, before she moans softly in my ear. It's long and drawn out and I can't bear it for a second longer. Pleasure explodes from my spine, down my thighs and through my cock. I spill onto my stomach, pumping myself in hard strokes.

Behind my closed eyes is only starlight and Audrey.

"Fucking hell," I curse.

She gives a breathless laugh. "Wow."

My tired right hand falls to the bed bedside me. I stare up at the ceiling, trying and failing to catch my breath. "I haven't come that hard in ages."

"You came?"

I laugh. "Only with the force of a thousand suns, yeah."

"I like that," she says, and she sounds pleased. Almost proud. "I did too, actually."

"I noticed. I liked that, too."

I smile at the ceiling. I feel ten feet tall. A hundred. I wonder if I could ask her now if she'd go out with me and if she'd say yes. If she'd ask me the same, I'd give her anything.

"When do you get back? To New York?"

"Saturday evening," I say.

"Oh. That's good to know," she says. "Carter, I don't know… what happens now? Will this make it awkward?"

"You and awkwardness," I say. "No. It won't. You and I are the same as we were before."

"Friends. And potentially daters," she says, and then she giggles. It's a very un-Audrey sound and it makes me smile. "God, I can't believe I just did this with you. The wine definitely helped."

"You'd been drinking before this?"

"Yes. Just a bit. We went to a wine bar."

I close my eyes, and it's not in pleasure this time. She's been drinking. Did I pressure her into this somehow? And that fucking date. "Right."

"Thank you, Carter. I don't… wow. I think I'll sleep like a baby after this."

"Good. I'll see you when I come back."

"I look forward to it," she says, and the shyness in her voice cuts straight through my chest. I don't know what to think. Don't know what to do. "Good night, Carter."

"Night, kid."

TWELVE

Audrey

"Heading out already?" Declan asks dryly. He's looking at my jacket with a frown. The blazer he's wearing today isn't tweed, but it has elbow patches. His hair looks like it's been in a wind turbine and I bet it's a hundred percent intentional.

"Yes," I say, tying the waistband of my coat. "I have a dentist's appointment, and I've already run it by Booker."

His frown turns into a sympathetic smile. "Oh. I'm sorry. Good luck."

"Thanks. Two wisdom teeth, and then an evening spent working at home. It'll be fantastic."

"Think you'll be able to work on that anaesthesia? Send me a copy of the article you write, will you? I need a laugh."

"Very funny," I tell him, but I'm smiling, and he gives me a little wave. He's warmed up to me, it seems.

I leave the frenzy of the office behind. The newsroom has two new staff members, which raised more than a few eyebrows company-wide considering the general hire freeze. Both are former private investigators.

"Snakes," Booker had called them, but her tone had been admiring.

Carter is beefing up this department. There was an email

just last week to the entire department that encouraged all personal projects. Pitches welcome, it had said.

Carter.

Just thinking about him sends a shiver down my spine, and it's not uncomfortable. I can't believe what had happened on Friday evening. It's Monday today, and we haven't spoken since. Not a single text.

I've written three different ones and then deleted every single one. Nothing feels normal. Nothing feels the same.

There had been something so freeing about our conversation… and about what had happened. He gave me the feeling that I could say anything, do anything, and he would be on board. He'd never laugh or reject me.

But he's also my boss's boss's boss, the man who quite literally *owns* the newspaper I work at, and a relationship is so beyond inappropriate that it's practically a crime. My colleagues would never respect me. Booker would… I don't want to think about what Booker would say. Wesley would look at me like a bug.

None of that matters, though, when it's just him and me.

When he's sitting across from me in a diner in Queens or on the other end of the phone, his deep voice hoarse with the sound of his pleasure.

The elevator is empty as I ride it down. It's only a little after lunch, and people are still hard at work. The lobby is mostly empty. I tug my bag up higher on my shoulder and look at my watch. I should make my appointment if the C-train isn't late.

A group of suit-clad men enter the lobby. I pause to the side, waiting for them to pass through the revolving doors.

"Thanks," one of them tells me.

"Of course," I say.

At that, a tall man looks up. Auburn hair. Tawny eyes. Carter is among them, and he turns his head to meet my eyes as they pass.

My cheeks heat up with memory. He raises an eyebrow,

and I give a tiny, teeny shake of my head. Not here. Not now. Not in front of other members of the executive team. He turns his head forward and keeps walking.

Disappears with the others into the elevators.

I breathe a sigh of relief. He'd looked just like he always did. Larger than life, impossible to understand, an enigma in a suit. Handsome and powerful and very clearly *not* for me.

I've almost convinced myself Friday was a fever dream when my phone chimes.

Carter: Leaving your post? It's the middle of a work day.

My fingers shake just a little as I answer. Wasn't he heading into a meeting?

Audrey: Keeping track of your employees, are you?

Carter: Someone has to. Are you following a lead?

Audrey: Yes. It's leading me all the way to the dentist's office. I have the honor of losing two wisdom teeth.

There's a two-minute break before he replies, and I imagine him listening to someone pitching ideas, to Wesley talking in his ear, fingers tapping against a desk.

Carter: I'd make a joke about that, except nothing about it is funny. Sorry, spitfire. Taking tomorrow off too?

Audrey: Working from home. Or I'll at least attempt to.

Carter: The paper will survive without you.

Carter: I realize how that just sounded. You're crucial for the *Globe*'s success, but not so crucial that you can't rest after surgery.

Audrey: Not offended. Just determined to cut your negativity out of my life. Don't text me again.

I'm grinning as I write that, standing on the subway platform. This, I know how to do. Talk about nothingness with him until I can forget the sound of his hoarse breathing in my ear.

Even if it feels burned into my memory and stamped on my bones.

Carter: Fair. This is the final text before I leave you alone forever. Is someone picking you up afterwards? You get pretty out of it from the drugs they give you.

Audrey: My brother was supposed to, but he just cancelled.

Carter: Damn. Tell me the name of the clinic, at least? Just in case. Someone should know.

I consider it for one whole subway stop. Is it a good idea? But he's right. I'd wanted my brother there, but he couldn't make it now. Nina, my best friend, is still painfully far away after her job transfer to DC. My other friends in the city are all at work.

So I text him the address. Just in case.

———

Much later, a kindly nurse leads me into the waiting room. "Have a seat for a while," she tells me. Her voice comes from far away. "I'll get you a glass of water. It says on your sheet that your brother is coming to pick you up?"

"Oh, he's not," I say. My voice sounds bouncy. I say the words again, just to hear them soar.

"I'm sorry? He's not?"

I shake my head, and the sensation feels weird. Even

bouncier than my voice. "He had a gig in Hoboken. It was only a lunch gig, but his entire band is counting on him. Even though I counted on him first." I laugh, because that almost rhymed. "Why? I don't know."

"Miss," the nurse says, and now her voice sounds sharp. "We wouldn't have proceeded with the anaesthesia and surgery if we knew you didn't have anyone to escort you home."

It's difficult to parse her words. Too many of them. "You speak very sharply," I tell her. "You sound like... a squid. Every direction. They're pointy, too, their tentacles. God, I want ice cream."

"You can't eat any solids for another twenty-four to forty-eight hours. Honey, please let me call someone for you. A friend or a colleague? Maybe a neighbor?"

I close my eyes at the waiting room's bright lights. It's hard to focus on them *and* her voice at the same time. How do other people do both?

"I'm here to pick her up," a voice says.

The nurse releases my arm. "Oh, thank goodness. Honey, your boyfriend is here."

That makes me giggle, and then I can't stop, even though my mouth feels round and cottony and like I've swallowed a hippo. Carter is standing in front of me, with an oddly concerned look on his face. I've never seen him look concerned before.

"Audrey," he says. "It's me."

I giggle harder, until it wheezes out of me. As if I wouldn't recognize him. But he seems to be waiting for something, and the nurse peeks around his shoulder too.

I form words. "Hello. You're skipping work too."

His mouth softens at the corners. "Yes. Don't tell my boss."

It takes a few seconds to make sense of the words, but when they penetrate I dissolve into laughter again. He means himself. "You're funny. Why are you always so funny?"

Carter's arm slides around me, and then we're walking. "And you thought you'd be able to get home by yourself," he mutters.

But I'm still on his last joke. "Stand-up," I tell him.

"Stand up?"

"Yes."

"I'm already standing. So are you."

"No, you and stand-up! People would love it. I'd be... I'd sit... front row."

Carter snorts. It makes him sound like a horse, and my mind races to the memory of a family vacation. We'd been in Arizona and Kevin had begged, so we'd all gone on a horse tour along the canyon.

Wide-open spaces. It had been so beautiful.

"I prefer to perform my comedy in private," Carter says. "Don't worry. I'll always save you a front-row seat."

I shake my head. "We need to go to the canyon."

"The... canyon?"

We're moving. An elevator, I think, and then a lobby. His arm is strong around me. "This way," he says. "Now what's this about a canyon?"

"I don't have one," I say, and the thought makes me sad. They are so far away. "It's been forever since I saw the red earth. The desert wind."

"Okay, you hippy. If you really want to visit a canyon we can go to one."

I shake my head. "They're all disappearing."

"They are? Where are they going? Come on, this is my car. Let's get in."

I duck my head and settle in the leather backseat of his car. The smell feels sharp in my nostrils. I lean back against the seat and close my eyes.

Wow, I'm tired. Exhausted. Can't feel my mouth either.

"Miss Ford's apartment," Carter says. Then he says my address.

"Got it," a voice says from the front seat.

I crack my eyes open. "How do you know that place?" I ask him.

Carter chuckles. "That's where you live."

"I know that. How do you?"

"I've dropped you off there before. I've also picked you up from there, last week. Remember? When we went out and ate pizza?"

Pizza… pizza… delicious cheese. "I want pizza."

"You'll have to wait for a bit, kid. Can't eat for a while."

I lean back against the seat. "Why? And why does my mouth feel weird? Does it look weird? I feel like I've lost it." But when I reach up to touch the cottony area, something closes around my wrist. A warm hand.

"Don't," Carter says. "You shouldn't touch it."

"But I've lost my mouth."

"No, you haven't. It's still there. I can see it."

"You might be lying."

"Would I lie to you?" he asks. "I've been more honest with you than I have with anyone for years."

It takes me a few seconds to process the words. Honesty. Okay. If he says I still have a mouth, I probably do. So I twist my hand over and grab a hold of his instead. "Fine," I say.

"Great," he murmurs, and our intertwined fingers drift to my lap. I lean my head back and close my eyes. Nothing feels real, nothing feels tangible, except the seat beneath me and the tight grip around my hand. For a long moment I just let myself drift.

But maybe it's more than just a long moment.

"Spitfire, we're here. Can you get out of the car for me?"

I blink my eyes open. It's bright again. Why is it so bright? "Yes."

"Come here, then. Let's get you home."

I emerge on shaky legs on the sidewalk. It's cracked beneath my feet, and I stare at the crack for a long time, daring it to move. It feels scary. What if the asphalt breaks apart?

Carter's hand squeezes around mine. "Ready to go inside?"

"Yes," I say, and give the crack in the sidewalk a last look. "Don't move," I warn it.

"Well, we have to," he says. "Do you have your keys?"

I reach inside my jacket, searching for the inner pocket. My arms feel heavy. They weigh tons and tons, but I finally find it.

Carter takes it from me. "Great. Come on, up these stairs."

I catch sight of a curtain on the first floor shifting. Old Man Pierce watching me come home, no doubt. He keeps his eagle eyes trained on the stoop most days from the comfortable perch of his century-old armchair.

"He's watching," I tell Carter.

Carter's focused on unlocking the front door. "Interesting," he says. "Are you referring to God? But come inside."

"Not God. Landlord."

The front door clicks closed behind us and I'm just about to point toward the stairs, up to my room, when the door to Pierce's apartment swings open. He's standing there, dressing gown on and glasses perched on his nose. He looks like a turtle. Or a vulture. A giggle escapes me and I press my entire hand against my mouth to stop it.

It hurts.

"Audrey?" he says. "What's the matter?"

"She's had her wisdom teeth removed," Carter replies. He sounds like he does at work. Cool and slippery, like rocks beneath a stream. Distant somehow. "I'm helping her home from the dentist's."

"Oh. I've seen you around before," Pierce says. "Good, good. Always told you to get a boyfriend, Audrey."

I giggle harder. *As if.* Pierce gives me a final nod and closes the door again, retreating back into his apartment. The door closes and only the smell of mothballs remains.

"Boyfriend," I whisper. "Everyone thinks that."

"Yes, well, it's a logical conclusion. You live up here?"

Carter asks. There's a hint of disapproval in his voice. He doesn't sound smooth anymore. He sounds raspy, like sandpaper.

I walk after him up the stairs. "You don't want people to think that. Of course you don't. I get it. I geeeeeet it," I say, drawing out the word.

"Kid, I have no problem with people thinking we're in a relationship. But I don't like you living in a place that smells like mold."

"Oh." I look down at the carpeted stairs. "There was a leak... a few years ago. Ergo, mold. People don't use 'ergo' enough. I should start adding it to my articles."

"No, it sounds pompous," Carter says, "and why hasn't the mold been fixed? You breathe this on a daily basis."

I grip his arm to get him to look at me, to tell him off about complaining. But his arm feels huge in my grip, and I'm distracted by the width of his bicep. *Bicep.* Also a weird word. Bi-cep.

"Audrey?"

"You never call me Audrey."

He looks down at my hand on his arm. "Sometimes I do. When I need you to take me seriously."

"I always take you seriously. When you're not being silly."

"I'm never silly," he says solemnly, and I break into laughter again. I've never met anyone who's sillier.

"Is your room on the right or the left?"

"Left," I say. "The right one belongs to Jonah. He smokes pot all the time."

Carter mutters something under his breath and reaches for the knob to my room. Then he pauses. "Where's the lock?"

"I don't have one."

"Fucking hell, you *live* in this place?"

I push past him and open the door to my little palace. My home. It smells softly of lavender from the essential oil dispenser I'd splurged on last week, and that's about the only great thing about it. But it's mine.

In all of its tiny glory.

"This is me," I say, and head straight for my bed. The world is swimming and I sit down heavily. Close my eyes again.

Right. I had two wisdom teeth removed. Two. That's why my mouth is starting to ache.

"You don't have a proper kitchen," he says. He sounds vaguely offended by the notion, and I smile. I instantly regret it when a sharp stab of pain ricochets through my jaw. "Just a microwave and a sink," he says.

"A mini-fridge, too," I correct him.

"Your landlord has clearly just put this in as a way to make money. And you... where's your bathroom?"

"In the hall."

"You share it with your pot-smoking neighbor."

"Mmhm." I lean back against the bed and watch him move around my space. It feels much smaller with him in it. Like he's too much human for a poorly decorated mini-apartment. I wish I'd gotten around to cleaning last weekend.

Carter stops at my table-turned-desk. He reaches for some papers and leafs through them. "You're writing articles in your spare time."

"Mhm." Concentrating on this conversation is difficult and I lie down on my bed. If the world would only stop spinning softly on its axis, I'd be all right.

"Hold on," Carter says, and then he's there. Untying my shoelaces. "Want your jacket on?"

I run my fingers over the slick material of my coat. It had been an investment piece. Nina had been with me when I'd bought it, and we'd said it back and forth to one another until the word was meaningless. *You're investing, Audrey,* she'd said. I'd twirled around in it. *Look at my* investment *piece!*

"Keep it on," I say. "It was expensive."

"Great logic. Lie down for a while, will you?"

"But your clothes look expensive. You look so handsome in your suits."

He laughs. "You're making me want to ask you for more honesty here than I should. Did you stock up beforehand with food?"

"I have food," I say and close my eyes. My bed seems to rise and fall beneath me.

Carter opens my mini-fridge and curses. He's done that a lot today, it seems. "You have apples, carrots and half-a-box of takeout."

"Exactly," I say, pleased. Should get me though the next twenty-four hours.

"You can only eat soup or ice cream. What were you thinking?" He sighs, and then I hear the sound of a keychain. "I'll be right back. Don't go anywhere, okay?"

I have no intention of ever moving.

"And I can't even lock the door to keep you safe," he mutters. Then it closes behind him and I drift away on a magical carpet of anaesthesia.

When I finally wake up again, my head is pounding. My mouth tastes bad and I feel like I've had my first ever drunken night. Still a little bit inebriated and a lot hungover. It's awful.

Carter is sitting by my table, on the single chair in my apartment. He puts down the newspaper he's reading when he sees me. "Hey."

"Hi," I say. "Where'd you go?"

"Stocked your fridge. You have four different kinds of soup now and five ice cream flavors. Lots of juice too."

I blink at him. "Oh."

"Wasn't sure which one you liked." He leans forward, golden eyes on me. "How are you feeling?"

"I've been better," I say and cautiously move my jaw. "Oh my goodness."

"I can't believe you would have gone home alone. I'd be mad at you, if you didn't look so battered right now."

"Oh." Then I remember what we'd done, what we'd

spoken about the last time, on the phone, and I squeeze my eyes closed.

"There it is," Carter murmurs. "You just remembered, didn't you?"

"Yes. I can't believe we... that I actually..."

"It was great," he says. "I won't let you feel awkward about it."

I press my hands against my eyes. "God."

"Do you regret it?"

It takes me a few deep breaths to answer. "No. Maybe I should, but I don't."

The faint sigh from his direction sounds like it holds relief. "Well, then. We're both adults. We can do whatever we'd like, or not do."

"I can't believe I came," I say, and then immediately regret it. My head still feels loose. "God. Ignore that, will you? Please. *Please.*"

Carter chuckles. "I didn't hear anything. And even if I did, the thing I didn't hear wouldn't displease me, you know."

"What?"

"Never mind."

I lower my hands and look at him. Folded onto the chair, long legs stretched out in front. Still in the same suave suit I'd seen him in earlier. His dark auburn hair looks almost brown, and it's ruffled from where he's run his hands through it.

"You came from work," I say. "You... left your meetings? What time is it?"

He shakes his head. "Didn't want to be there anyway."

"But you have things to do. I didn't mean to force you to be here."

"I don't feel forced," he says.

"Carter, I'm sorry."

He rises from the chair, stretching to his full height. "One of the perks of being the boss," he says. "Don't think about it."

I grip the edge of my comforter. Why am I still in my

jacket? The thought comes and goes, slippery, my mind unable to hold on to too many things at once. But one thing is important.

The most important.

"Thank you," I tell him. "I don't know what I would have done without you today."

His lips twist into a half-smile, and I lose myself in his steady eyes, looking down at me. "My pleasure, kid."

I reach for his hand. He realizes what I want and captures mine with his. Warm fingers twine with my own. My pulse thunders through the simple contact and up through my head.

It's not the first time we've touched, but it feels like it. "I've thought about it," I say.

Carter goes still. "Ah. About what I asked you?"

"Yes," I say. "I'd very, very much like it if you asked me out, I mean."

His thumb moves in a slow arc over mine. "I'd be happier about this if you weren't drugged. When we spoke on the phone you were drunk, too."

I don't smile—I've learned my lesson—but I want to. "This isn't the anaesthesia speaking."

He looks down at my hand in his, but there's no hiding the brilliant smile spreading across his face. "I'll ask you tomorrow, then. When I'm sure you're not under the influence."

My heart stutters in my chest. "I'll say yes."

THIRTEEN

Audrey

It wasn't a dream. That's the first thing I realize the next day, when I wake up clear-headed. The second thing is that my mouth really, *really*, hurts. I take care of the second thing right away by way of aspirin and orange juice. He'd bought the fancy, organic kind.

Carter had been here. In my apartment.

I look at my jacket, thrown on the floor. My shoes spilling out from the too-small closet. There's a grim-looking avocado that's, inexplicably, resting on an old copy of the *Globe* like a sad paperweight.

He'd been here. I smile down at my orange juice, ignoring the tug in my cheeks. He'd showed up to my dentist appointment. He'd called me when he was out of town. And somehow, some way, I'm not nervous about going on a date with him.

Correction—I'm nervous as hell. But it's the excited kind, the one that makes me feel so alive it's like my soul is abuzz. I spend most of the day working lazily from bed and watching old re-runs at the same time. Try as I may, concentrating is difficult, and the double dose of painkillers knocks me out every so often.

He texts me after lunch to ask how I'm feeling. The

conversation is quick as usual, texts that make me smile down at my phone.

Until it includes the thing we'd spoken about.

Carter: Is your head clear today?

Audrey: Yes. Clear enough to know that I meant what I said yesterday. Before you left.

He calls me a few seconds after I send my answering text.

"Hi," I say.

"Hey. Sleep well?"

"Surprisingly, yes. I guess being knocked out does that to you."

"Hurting today?"

"A bit. Feeling significantly less wise, too," I say.

Carter's voice warms. "Listen to you, joking. You're in a good mood."

"I am, yeah."

"A definitely clear-headed one?"

"Exceedingly so. I've never been more in my right mind than I am right now, this very second."

"That's good," he says. "Exactly what I want to hear."

"Oh?"

"Mhm. So. Will you let me take you out this weekend?"

Hearing the words makes it real, and that reality is terrifyingly exciting. "Yes, I will."

"Well," Carter says. And then nothing else.

I smile. "No quip about that? No joke?"

"I'm searching for one," he says. "Give me a few minutes."

"Speechless. That's a first."

"Are you free this Friday?"

"I am, yeah. Hopefully the swelling will have gone down by then," I say, biting my lower lip. A date. I have a date, and for the first time in months, it's one I'm truly excited about.

"If anyone would look good with swelling, it's you," he says. "I'll have to figure out a way to impress you. What about—"

There are muffled voices on the other end, and then I hear the distinct words of *Mr. Kingsley*. He's working. Of course he is, I'm the one taking a day off.

When his voice is back, it's professional in tone. "I'm afraid I have to go. Sorry to cut this short."

"Were you in a meeting when you called me?" I ask.

"Yes," he says. "Just stepped out. I'll talk to you later."

"Okay. Well… good luck at work today, honey," I say, my voice teasing.

He gives a surprised laugh. "Spitfire," he says fondly, before hanging up.

I rock back on my heels, bag in hand. He'd said wait outside my house and dress nice, whatever that means—is it nice enough for a ball? Or we're going to a bar? The lack of specificity feels like a very masculine oversight.

He's also late. Well, two minutes, but it's given the nerves in my stomach ample time to go crazy. They multiply at the speed of light, and if the graph is exponential, I'll be in trouble in ten minutes.

But I don't have to wait long. A familiar black car pulls to a stop in front of the curb. My heart explodes with nerves, and I bite the inside of my cheek. Carter steps out, and the moment I see him, something inside me stills. It's him. I can do this. I have done it many times before with him.

"Hello," he says. He's wearing a suit, no tie, topped with a crooked smile. "How do you feel?"

"Much better than when you saw me last. My teeth feel all better now."

He bends to kiss my cheek. "Glad to hear it. Ready to go?"

"Where?"

"I think I'll keep that a surprise."

"Sneaky." We get into the car and it takes off, weaving through traffic and back toward the city. Neither of us speaks.

Carter shifts closer. "I'd tell you that you look beautiful, and I'd mean it, but I don't want to set off those nerves of yours."

I chuckle. Acknowledging them feels better. "They're already set off," I say. "But strangely enough, it's not that bad."

"A resounding success. Does that mean I can say it?"

"You can." I glance toward the driver, but he has his eyes on the road. Is he listening?

Carter doesn't seem to care. "You look stunning," he says. "Far better than nice."

"Nice is hard to shoot for," I say. "It's a moving target."

His eyes dip to my lips. "Well, you overshot it. But I'm not complaining."

"Aren't you nervous at all? About us and… dating?"

"I'm terrified inside. Shaking like a leaf, kid." It's so obviously an exaggeration, with him sitting there his usual composed self, that it makes me laugh.

The car pulls to stop outside a bar. It takes me a moment to recognize the place. "Wait. Is this…?"

"Where we met, yeah," Carter says. "I thought it would be poetic to have our first date here."

Something warms in my chest. "Our first?"

"Yes. Is that okay?"

"It's more than okay."

He leads me inside, his hand light on my lower back. I lean into his side and breathe in the familiar scent of his cologne and soap and something else, something that's just him.

We have a seat in the back. It's far away from where I sat with my obnoxious blind date, and even further from where Carter had lounged at the bar.

"Did you really watch my date?" I ask him. "Last time we were here?"

"Of course. Someone had to make sure you weren't meeting a serial killer on that blind date of yours."

"I saw who you were meeting, you know. The blonde."

He gives a half-shrug. "It wasn't serious."

"No, that much was clear," I say, and throw caution to the wind. "Do you ever date seriously?"

"Not if I can help it," he says with a wink.

I laugh. It's what I expected, anyway, and having it confirmed feels good. Safer, somehow. Whatever happens, I know we can bow out with a laugh and a smile. "Right. So how long will I keep your interest on this date?" I say. "Until dessert, at least?"

Carter tilts his head, considering. "Yes, but give or take a decade, probably."

We talk about everything, drifting from one topic to the other with a fluidity that feels preordained. The *Globe*, journalism, movies we've seen, his business trip, his hotel room, and then inevitably, the call.

I ignore the heat in my cheeks. "I didn't expect it," I admit.

"No," he says. "Neither did I. It wasn't what I called you for, you know."

"Why did you call? Not that I minded."

He leans back in his chair and gives me a studying glance.

"Come on," I say. "Tell me. I can take it. Had you been drinking?"

"I didn't call you because I was drunk," he says. "I called you because I was jealous."

"Oh. Really?"

He runs a hand over the back of his neck. "Yeah. Not very chivalrous, perhaps, but that's the truth. I'd promised to talk to you about dating, to give you a male perspective, but truth be told I stopped enjoying that a while back."

The world tilts on its axis. Had I misread things from the beginning? Had he always… was this… "Oh," I say again.

"You look shocked," he says. "Can't be the first time a man admits to wanting you?"

No, I think, *but it's the first time in forever I've wanted him back.*

"I didn't mean to talk your ear off about my dates. I had no idea you minded," I say. The memories feel awful now, somehow. Forcing him to listen to things he didn't want to hear. "I didn't think you…"

"Don't worry about it," Carter says, his half-smile back. "I know you had your reservations about me. Slashing jobs and all that."

I shake my head. "No, I just didn't know it was an option. Didn't really consider it, even. You seemed so far above me. And you always wear a suit."

His eyebrows rise. "You told me I looked handsome in suits."

"I did? Oh. The anaesthesia."

"Yes. You were lovely, by the way. You mentioned canyons for some reason, and never told me why."

"Canyons. Like… the Grand Canyon?"

"I assumed, but who knows what went on inside your brain."

I laugh and reach for my glass. "You do look handsome in suits," I say. "I don't need to be drugged to think that."

He gives me a wide smile. "What a compliment. But why did that make you hesitate in the beginning?"

"Well, it's… I suppose it's a long story." I say. "But the world of businessmen and briefcases and suits has always struck me as kind of fake."

"Fake," he repeats.

"Yeah. Like, snake-oil charmers and Wall Street bankers. People who can't work with their hands, who don't know a trade, you know. I realize this is all pretty insulting, and I really don't mean it that way. I know you're not like that."

He shrugs. "Well, others might disagree. I help build

companies and occasionally dismantle them. It's a trade but it's not a very visible one. I don't get calluses from it."

I shake my head. "It's definitely a job, and an important one. It was really my own prejudice that got in the way. And combined with all the layoffs in the beginning, well…"

"You didn't have a high opinion of me," he says softly.

"Not in the beginning, no." I hesitate for a moment, meeting his eyes. The oddly golden eyes, so often dancing with humor. They're serious now. "You asked me why I wanted to be a journalist a while back. Didn't you?"

He nods. "You spoke about reading the newspaper with your dad."

"Yes, and that's definitely part of it. But something else happened to my family when I was fifteen." I twist my glass around, looking at the red liquid. "My dad's a dentist, right? And he was approached by a businessman with a great investment opportunity."

Carter's voice is hesitant. "Ah."

"Yes. It was a textbook con, but the man knew so much about Dad's industry. Had statistics and books and could show why this dental company would revolutionize the industry. Several dentists in the area had already signed on."

"I'm sorry," Carter says. He's already caught on.

I nod. "Well, Dad invested way too much. College funds, retirements. Thank God he didn't take out a second mortgage on the house, at any rate. And the businessman—a con man, really—took everything."

"Did you try to press charges?"

"Yes, but there was nothing to tie him to. The name was an alias. The addresses were PO boxes. The accounts were cleaned."

"Let me guess," he says. "He wore suits?"

"Impeccably tailored ones, yes. He had dinner with us all a few times too. Really wined and dined my parents." I'll never forget him, for the rest of my life. Nearly as tall as Carter and with dark hair. Lines around his eyes that crinkled when he smiled. A man who radiated warmth and trustworthiness. A shiver of unease runs through me, as it always does when I think about him.

To have laughed with someone who, all the while, was planning on stealing every last cent my parents had worked so hard for.

"Audrey, I'm sorry," Carter says.

I shake my head. "It was a decade ago. My family's recovered. Dad still... smarts from it, but no one got physically hurt at least. That's what matters."

"And you never trusted a man in a suit after that," he says, fingering the lapel of his jacket. "I'll burn every single one I own."

I laugh and reach across the table, finding his hand. It's warm beneath mine. "Absolutely not. You're not the same as him, I know that. I knew that from the first time we met!"

"What was his name?" Carter asks. "Did you ever manage to find him? Get justice?"

I shake my head. "Will C. Jenner was the alias he used. We didn't find anyone who matched his description with that name."

"Fuck. What a scoundrel," he says.

"Yeah. We tried talking about it to the papers, too. Dad didn't have a picture of him, but he could describe him very well. But no one was interested in running the story," I say. It still feels like an insult. A good investigative journalist could have followed a trail. Found other families devastated by this man. Made it into a bigger story of con artists in the country. But no one was interested. "I guess only the Bernie Madoffs attract national attention."

Carter's voice is low. "That's why you want to be a journalist. Why you're working on the story of that construction company evicting tenants in Queens."

"Yes, I think so. A problem can't get fixed if people don't know about it, you know? That's my job as a journalist. Our job as a newspaper. Equip people with knowledge."

His mouth curls into a small smile. "Do I sound naive?" I ask. "I know the *Globe*'s numbers aren't the best."

"No," he agrees, "they aren't. But you keep making compelling argument after argument to keep it running."

"Am I convincing you?"

"Kid, you convinced me a long time ago," he says. "I just have to get the numbers to add up."

It's late when we leave the bar. Late enough that the bartender is cleaning off the counter, and only a few stragglers are left. The drinks have left me happy and lightheaded and a little brave.

A lot brave.

"I'll drive you home," Carter says. His hand brushes against mine as we walk along the curb. "Say goodnight outside your deathtrap of a house."

"It's not so bad. It has… charm."

"You don't have a lock on your door," he says, like that's the end of the conversation.

I shrug. "I guess I'm just more of a trusting person than you are."

"Probably, but I wouldn't say that's a good thing."

We pause on the sidewalk and wait for his black town car to arrive. I rock back on my heels, butterflies dancing inside my throat. "Well… it's got one redeeming feature."

"Yes," Carter says. "Its tenant."

I laugh. "Thank you. But I was referring to something else. The fire escape."

"A way to leave your apartment in case of a fire isn't a redeeming feature. It's a legal requirement."

I nudge his shoulder with mine. It's solid, a brick wall. "But it's so *New York*. For a girl from out of town, I feel like a character in a sitcom."

"You sit out there?"

"Sometimes. It has a pretty good view. And well… I have a bottle of wine at home."

Tawny eyes look down on me. There's a light in them. "Are you inviting me in for a glass?"

"Yes," I say.

"Well then," Carter says. "I've never been more excited to see a fire escape."

FOURTEEN

Audrey

Carter's legs are almost too long for the cramped space outside my window. He extends them, the tips of his lacquered suit shoes emerging through a slab of bars.

"Isn't this a great balcony?" I say. I climb out after him with a bottle of wine and a blanket tucked under my arm. Despite the unusual warmth, it's still night in New York, and we'll need to keep our jackets on.

"Yes," he says. "Fantastic. It's definitely a reason to overlook the fourteen other health hazards."

"No ragging on my place while you're a guest," I inform him sternly.

He holds up his hands, a half-smile on his face. "Sorry. I'll keep my thoughts to myself."

"Don't even think them." I hand him the bottle and sit down opposite him, struggling to fit my legs into the space. He reaches down and, as if it's nothing, as if we've been intimate before, lifts them across his lap.

"Better?"

"Yes, thanks." The railing is lit with tiny fairy lights, the one decoration I'd added to the fire escape. It's most definitely not up to code and I don't care.

Carter unscrews the wine and doesn't comment on the

poor quality. I'm treating the owner of one of America's oldest newspapers to a bottle of six-dollar wine. I lean back against the bars and watch him fill up two wineglasses.

The impossibility of him, here, makes me smile.

He notices. "Why are you looking so happy?" he asks, handing me one of the glasses. But his eyes dance in the dim light.

"I don't know. You being here, drinking this awful wine with me."

"It's awful?"

"My best friend bought it for me when I moved in and we never ended up drinking it. It's cheap."

He takes a deep swig, and then raises an eyebrow. "It's drinkable."

"Wow. I was aiming for oaky undertones or full-bodied, but I'll take it."

"Smart-ass," he says, He rests his right hand on my calf, still draped across his lap. Connecting us even further. "Was it okay that I took us to the same bar where we met tonight?"

I nod. "We kinda came full circle, didn't we? Returning to the place where it all started."

"That was the idea," he admits. "I also thought that..."

"That what?" I nudge him with my leg, and his hand shifts. Moves to my knee. "Tell me."

"It wouldn't be intimidating. You know, I didn't want you hyperventilating at a bar and needing some handsome stranger to save you."

I grin. "That happens, does it?"

"It happened to a friend of mine quite recently, actually," he says. "Tonight was just you and me and alcohol, and I figured there was no way either of us wouldn't enjoy it."

"It was a good date. Great, even." I feel brave, filled with liquid courage. "I invited you up for a nightcap, didn't I?"

His eyes flash with heat. "You did. I'm grateful."

"Grateful?"

"Maybe the wrong choice of words. Intrigued, perhaps.

Definitely encouraged." He looks down at my legs over his, thumb moving slowly over the edge of my knee. I feel it, even through my stockings. "So you thought I was awful when we met, then. My suit gave me away as a man who couldn't be trusted."

I roll my eyes. "I wasn't thinking clearly at all. I was just trying not to throw up from nerves."

"Right. Peanuts, water," here he points to himself, "savior. I should be grateful to your panic attack, I guess. It meant you gave me a shot."

"But you weren't aiming for a shot," I say. "Were you? I mean, what did you think of me when we first met? Be honest."

I'd been a wreck at that bar, and not particularly kind to him either. I remember berating him for the way he spoke to the bartender when ordering another drink.

Carter's smile is intimate. "You don't see yourself particularly clearly. I've noticed that before."

"What do you mean?"

"You're fucking gorgeous."

I scoff. "Right."

"I mean it. You were that night, too, you know. All big eyes and smart mouth and this long, curly hair. You didn't know me, but you spoke to me like you did. I liked that."

I've never been one to suffer from false modesty. My looks are good if I put some effort in, but I know my limitations. I'm pretty average.

Carter seems to read my thoughts. He takes another deep sip of his wine, eyes still on mine. "You don't believe me."

"It just seems... excessive. You're you. Handsome, tall, rich, capable. I was panicking at a bar."

"You saw me," he says. "Even back then."

The words fill up the space in my chest, warm me from the inside out. It could be snowing right now and I'd still be hot, on this fire escape with him. "Oh."

He reaches for my glass of wine and puts both of them to

the side. "You still do, you know. I'm myself with you in a way I haven't been in over a decade."

"I'm glad," I say. "Don't ever be anyone else around me."

His lips curve. "I don't think I could be, even if I tried."

My fingertips feel cold, curving around the steely roundness of a bar. "What are we doing, Carter? Really?"

He captures a curl of my hair and watches it slip through his fingers. "We're spending time together," he says. "We're getting to know one another."

"But what about work," I breathe.

He smiles. "I'm trying my damndest to seduce you, and you think of the *Globe.* I love how your brain works."

"Not the paper," I say. "But us... and my job. Our colleagues."

"No one will know," he says. "Your job won't be affected."

"We won't tell anyone?"

His breath ghosts over mine. "What happens between us is nobody's business." Carter slips a hand under my chin and tilts my head up. Forces me to meet his eyes, and there's a question in them. I give the tiniest nod and lean closer. My heart is racing like it's trying to run away.

He closes the distance between us. The kiss is a soft brush of his lips against mine, once, twice, controlled and steady. I blink my eyes open to find him watching me with a half-smile. "What I should have done," he says, "before I called you from that hotel room."

I shake my head. My hands find the lapels of his suit, curling around the stiff fabric. "I don't regret it."

"Christ, me neither."

I kiss him this time. Press my lips to his, my fingers sliding back to find the soft hair at the nape of his neck. Carter groans into my mouth and deepens the kiss, the hot tip of his tongue meeting mine. The brief touch feels like a shot of electricity through my body.

His hands slide down my sides, smoothing over my body through the fabric of my coat. He kisses me like he's thought long and hard about it. Like it's an extension of our banter, another match of wits. Deep and soft, quick and slow, he varies the pace.

I grip him tight and melt against the onslaught.

Just when I think I can't take any more, he shifts his lips to my cheek and kisses a line down to my neck. "Audrey," he says, voice so thick as to be almost unrecognizable. "This is a great fire escape."

I laugh. It turns breathless when he finds *that* spot, right beneath my ear, and my hands tighten on his shoulders.

It's a long few seconds before I can form words. "Mhm," I say. "Redeeming feature."

His mouth returns to mine. "No," he says against my lips. "I told you, it's the tenant."

"You're biased," I tell him.

"And proud of it."

We kiss for a long time, and with every delicious touch I feel myself sinking deeper into lust with him. My mind feels heady, almost drugged, joy flooding through me.

Skilled fingers find the waist tie to my coat and tug. He slides a hand inside, touching my waist through the thin fabric of my dress. A frisson of nerves run through me, just faint enough to heighten the anticipation. But the hand stays there.

"You know," I murmur. "The fire escape is nice and all, but we can also go inside."

He closes his eyes. Dark lashes fan out against his cheeks, flushed with color. "Dangerous idea," he says. "I'm trying to behave."

"You can't behave inside?"

"It would be harder to. I'm not domesticated."

I press my lips to his cheekbone. "Maybe that's a good thing."

"It's our first date," he says, "and I'm angling for a second."

I climb onto his lap. He lets me, hands steadying my hips

inside my coat. I settle a thigh on either side of him and grip the railing behind him. "What if I told you that a second date is already guaranteed?"

"Then I'm a lucky man indeed," he says and draws me up for a kiss. I press my chest against his and when he groans, I feel it reverberating through his chest. We spend another eternity kissing.

Eventually he breaks away from my lips and leans his head back against the cold railing, closing his eyes. "Fuck," he mutters.

I run my fingers inside the collar of his shirt, touching hot skin. "Did I break you?"

"Yes. I'll reboot in a second."

I shift in his lap and notice the long, hard length beneath my thighs. Once I've felt it, it's all I can focus on. Red-hot nerves race through my body and leave me breathless.

I circle my hips once, tentatively.

His hands tighten on my hips. "Spitfire," he warns.

"Let's go inside."

"I could kiss you forever," he says. "Would be happy to."

I lean back in his arms. "Don't you want to?"

He chuckles darkly and looks down at me straddling him. "Clearly. But I remember what you told me the other day. About you and relationships."

And my lack of them. I tighten my hands around his neck. "I've had sex before. Been intimate with men."

"I know," he says. "But not very often, I'm guessing."

I shake my head. "Why are we talking about this?"

He smiles and kisses me, three urgent brushes of his lips. "Because I don't want to rush you. At all. Ever. And because you have me wound so tightly that I'm not sure I can go as slow as I'd want to for our first time."

"I don't feel rushed."

He grips my thighs and pulls me up against him, melding our bodies together. His erection is a rough, intractable object beneath me, making it hard to think. "When was the last time?" he asks me.

I bend my face to the warm skin of his neck. He smells like soap and man and the leather seats of his town car.

"Audrey?" he says.

The truth is embarrassing. "A little over a year and a half." Even then, it had been a weekend thing with a guy I'd known in college. He'd been back in town and we'd met up. Before that... seven months, I think. At least.

Carter's eyes are serious on mine. "A year and a half," he repeats.

"Yes."

He doesn't mock me for it, he doesn't smile, he doesn't laugh. He just kisses me again, and it's softer this time. It sends butterflies careening through my stomach, colliding and multiplying. "Spitfire," he murmurs, a hand sliding over my hair, "we're not rushing this, then."

I don't know what comes over me. If it's the clear need in his voice, the way his fingers grip me, but everything about him makes me feel wanted. Powerful. So I slide my hand down to where he's hard and run my fingers over the length.

He groans and leans forward, forehead against my shoulder. "Audrey," he mutters.

I move my hand away and smile into his hair. Whatever this is, whatever we're doing, isn't just a one-time thing, then. It's a bad idea for all sorts of reasons, but none of them come close to how happy I feel in this moment.

"Until next time," I say.

Carter nods, but his hand slides up to graze the underside of my breast. It's brief, and he groans, and then he locks his hands safely around my waist. "Next time," he says, and his voice is a promise.

FIFTEEN

Carter

"Are you sure you don't need anything else?" I ask.

Mom shakes her head. She's leaning against the kitchen counter, vivid against the yellow cabinets. I remember her painting them over a decade ago, singing to the radio, during one of my father's many absences.

"No, no, I'm perfectly all right," she says.

I cross my arms. "The new construction down the street will go on for years," I say. "But you're absolutely sure?"

She laughs, the wrinkles by her eyes fanning out. She's always been quick to smile. "I can handle a bit of construction noise."

"Sure. But at least look at the brochure I sent you. Please."

They're opening a state-of-the-art apartment building right next to mine in the Village, and she'd have access to a pool and a gym.

"I looked at it," Mom says. "It looks like a lovely place, although they need more greenery."

"You could add that," I say. "Be in charge of the condo plants."

She gives me an appeasing smile. "That would be nice, sweetie."

"You just won't leave this place, will you?"

"It's my home," she says. "It's where I raised you. Do you really want me to sell your childhood home?"

"You know I do. I can't believe you don't." The apartment is hers, yes, but it had been bought by my father. The man we both washed our hands of years ago.

"It's filled with good memories, too, Carter," she says. "You grew up inside these walls. Besides, it's close to work. I can walk to the school and I can make sure the students behave when I see them in the grocery store."

I sigh. "Fine. I'll drop the subject."

"Thank you. Although you won't like the subject I have to bring up," she says. She reaches up and rearranges her auburn hair. It's pinned up in a braid, silver hinting at the temples.

I sink down onto the kitchen chair. "You're moving to an apartment in a worse neighborhood."

She smiles at my bad joke. "I'd never. No, sweetie, I got a call from your father yesterday."

The world goes still. "He called you out of the blue?"

"Yes."

Anger rises through me like a tidal wave. How *dare* he, after everything. To open old wounds and force himself—

"He apologized," Mom says. "Profusely, actually."

"You can't believe him."

She shrugs. "I'm not ready to believe him. But I'm not ready to not believe him, either. He has nothing to gain from asking for our forgiveness."

"He always has something to gain," I say. "He hasn't done a selfless thing in his life."

"He gave this apartment to me with no strings attached."

"Yes, when he knew he was going to *prison,* and they were seizing all his assets," I say through gritted teeth. The past couple of years I've spent considerable amounts in lawyer fees to make sure Mom was completely and thoroughly protected from any of his illegal dealings.

And oddly enough, because their marriage was never

actually legal, she's off the hook. Another one of his lies that worked out in the end.

"I'm not making excuses for him," she says and sinks down on the chair opposite me. Her eyes are imploring. "I'm thinking of you."

"Of me? Mom, he—"

"I know what he did," she says. "He hurt both of us. I know you like to focus on me. But he lied to you too."

I look at the mustard-yellow cupboards and the seashell knobs. Another feature she'd installed, right after we got back from our trip to Florida. It was the one proper vacation we ever went on with him. "I'm aware," I say.

"He's out of prison and mentioned that he wants to see you, but doesn't know if you'd want to."

"I absolutely don't want to," I say. "He has no space in my life."

Her hand lands on mine. "That's your right, sweetheart. You never have to see him again for as long as he lives. But, and don't get angry, I wonder if maybe you have things you want to say too. Things you want to ask. Everything happened so fast there at the end, when all his... lies unravelled. If you met him, it would be on your terms. You could tell him anything you wanted."

"You mean I could yell at him for a solid hour and then leave."

She chuckles. "Yes. You're very forceful when you yell, you know. You were always the most intimidating soccer player."

"In little league," I say, but her idea sinks in. "I get what you're saying, but nothing good can come of it. I'm not going to meet him."

Mom lifts her hand from mine. "Okay. That's your right, sweetie. I just wanted to relay the offer to you."

"I don't want him calling you all the time either."

She folds a kitchen towel, hiding her face from view, but I can hear the smile in her voice. It's infuriating that she's so calm about this. "Calling once in ten years isn't exactly harassment. I have no love lost for your father, except for the fact that he gave me you."

I rub a hand over my neck. Mom is too good at this, too kind. I can't see it the way she does. She has an easier time forgiving the slights he committed against her than I do. Having a *real* wife, other children, a white-picket fence and house in suburbia… living a double life.

I'd driven past his other house once.

I've never told her about it, and I never will.

But I'd been twenty-three, and furious, and sitting in a rented car outside a house that looked like it belonged in a commercial for house insurance. A dog had barked from somewhere inside the house and a teenage girl had appeared in the window. Younger than me. A half-sister?

I'd floored the gas so fast I left tire marks on the street.

"There's no way I could trust him or anything he says," I finally say. "Especially not now, when I'm…"

"So wildly successful?" Mom says teasingly.

I roll my eyes. "Yes. Why is he reaching out now?"

She shrugs. "I have no idea. I'm not on his side, sweetheart, I'm on yours."

"I know," I say. Because if there's one thing I've never doubted, it's that. Every time he disappeared we'd become a single-parent household, with a single-parent income. And she'd picked up extra shifts without ever complaining. And now that I've made sure she never has to work again, she infuriates me by refusing to stop.

Mom's voice changes in pitch, and she crosses her arms over her chest. "You've looked at your watch three times while you've been here. Where are you running off to after this?"

"I'm in no rush."

"Pah, I know when my son has ants in his pants. Is she anyone special?"

I shake my head. A grown man, and she can still treat me like I'm eight years old. "She might be."

"Anyone you can tell me about?"

"It's early days still," I say. "But she lives around here actually. In the area."

"I like her already," Mom says. "You need someone serious. Someone with a proper job."

I raise an eyebrow. "Is this a comment on other women I've dated?"

"Yes. You're a smart man, and with just as much charm as your dad. I know you could have any woman you wanted, but the real question is, which woman do you want? You deserve the best, sweetheart."

I sigh. Of course she thinks that. But I see Audrey's eyes in front of me, her hopes for the future, her idealistic dreams about the world, and I know it would kill me if I broke that innocence.

And I'm not sure I'm capable of *not* breaking it.

"You think too highly of me," I say.

"That's my job. Go on, then. Go woo her and bring her home for me to meet."

I laugh. "You're that eager for a daughter-in-law?"

"Yes. You work too much. Balance, Carter. It's all about balance."

I'm still shaking my head at her words when I walk the surprisingly short distance to Audrey's crumbling deathtrap of a house. Dad had called. Out of the blue.

I don't know how I'd react if he did the same thing to me. Christ, will I have to start screening my calls? I can't be responsible for what I say or do if I answer the phone only to hear his voice on the other end.

For the past decade, I've pushed his existence to the bottom of my mind. But I should have known he'd refused to stay buried.

I wait outside Audrey's house, texting both her and my driver to coordinate the pickup. Tonight's date will be different. Anticipation and desire mingle inside of me. It's been a year and a half, for her. *A year and a half.*

I have to make it fucking spectacular.

Audrey opens the front door and stops when she sees me. A giant smile lights up her face, setting her eyes ablaze. Something falters in my chest.

It's criminal, to stare at a man like that. Like he's your favorite person in the world.

"Hello," she says.

"Hi, kid."

"Thanks for picking me up. What are we doing tonight?"

"Something you once told me was necessary in a relationship. I figured you should be given a chance to take me for a test run."

Her mouth falls open. "Oh. I mean… yes. Good. I'd like that."

I chuckle and reach out to clip her softly under the chin. "Not that, spitfire. Though it can be arranged."

Definitely, absolutely, *willingly* arranged.

She blushes. "Right."

The car takes us through the city, back into Manhattan and toward the Village. She seemed like the type to want lowkey dates. Ones where we could get to know one another, ones where we didn't risk anyone seeing us.

She catches on as soon as Tom stops outside my building. The doorman, recognizing the car, opens her door.

"Carter…?" she asks.

I put a hand on her lower back. "Remember how you wanted a man to cook dinner with?"

"Vaguely, yes. I said that, right?"

"You definitely did. Well, tonight's your night."

"We're going to your apartment," she says in a half-whisper.

"Either that, or I've rented an impressive hotel room to impress you. You'll have to guess when you see it."

She slaps me softly on the chest. I almost reach up to grab her slim hand and press it there for good. "Fool," she says.

"Always. Come on. The elevator is this way."

She's quiet on the ride up and the silence turns expectant. I haven't invited someone into my apartment in a long time. There was a time when afterparties were common. Even a time when I'd give women I was seeing access recklessly, relentlessly, asking them to be there waiting for me after I came back from work. I think we'd both enjoyed the ridiculousness of the notion. The fake sophistication and the play at a relationship both of us knew wasn't real.

Those days are long gone. It was superficiality and recklessness, and Audrey deserves neither of those things. This, in contrast, feels so real it threatens to break me.

"Oh," she breathes, stepping into the hallway. She looks small beneath the high ceiling. "You have a loft apartment."

"It's a bit industrial, perhaps, but it has great lighting."

Her voice is filled with awe. "There's no way to undersell this place, you know."

"So I shouldn't bother trying?"

"No." She stops in the center of the grand space and spins around slowly, taking in the giant windows, the curved couch, the open-planned kitchen. It would probably fit ten of her apartments.

"Like it?" I ask.

Her smile is teasing. "It's okay. But there's no scent of mold, and Carter, you don't have a fire escape."

I shake my head at her and cross the space. Her smile turns into a grin and she backs up, trying to escape, but my couch expertly blocks the way. It's a two-player effort. She's still laughing when I kiss her, like wildfire in my arms.

I'm dazed when I finally raise my head and there's a pit of heated need burning in my stomach. Every luscious curve of her in my arms is like holding a live ember... One about to ignite.

Audrey's hand slides down to curve around mine and she pulls me toward the kitchen. "Can I get a full tour?"

"Uh, yeah. Yes. Let me show you around."

"So this is the living room."

"Yes. This here is a kitchen. *I think*, but I'm rarely here."

She snorts. "Of course not."

"Home office is in there," I say, pointing to one of the rooms off the corridor. "Guest bedroom, guest bath, and here…"

"Your bedroom." She stands on the threshold, peering inside the large room. Seeing my bed sends another jolt of heat through me. It looks like it always does, large and made, but her presence changes everything.

The air feels electric. "Yes," I say.

"Your bed is so big."

Several inappropriate replies flit through my mind. One even hovers on my tongue, but I don't want her to feel pressured. Not ever.

"Mhm."

Audrey looks up at me with a grin. "That was a very tame response?"

"I fought against my impulses, believe me."

She laughs, her hand finding mine again. We head back to the living room and leave my bed, with all of its tantalizing promises, to itself.

She jumps onto one of the stools by the kitchen counter. "So?" she says. "What is this thing that I apparently said a relationship has to contain?"

I start rolling up the sleeves of my shirt. "Cooking dinner."

The smile that spreads across her face makes it all worth it. "We're cooking?"

"Yeah."

"I mean… *you're* cooking?"

I roll my eyes. "How hard can it be?"

"That depends entirely on what you want to make." She makes to slide off the chair, and I raise a hand to stop her.

"I remember you specifically mentioning having a man cook *for* you."

"But I want to participate."

I rummage through one of the cabinets for a cutting board. "You can chop the potatoes."

"Potatoes," she repeats. "What are we making?"

It's been years since I was nervous around a woman. Since I fretted about dates, or doubted my ability to charm. But here with her, I don't know if what I'm offering is enough. "Steak and potatoes."

"Very homey," she says, accepting the knife and cutting board I give her. "I wasn't expecting this."

"Bad surprise?"

She shakes her head. "Not at all. It just goes to show that more and more of my assumptions about you are flawed."

"Maybe not all that flawed. This will be the first time in... a while, that I've cooked in this kitchen."

"I'm glad I'm a part of this momentous occasion, then."

I grin. "Yes, you should feel honored."

She sits at the kitchen island and occasionally chops, occasionally gives helpful pointers, as I prepare our food. Her chin rests in her hand, her smart mouth teasing and encouraging, and quick to laughter. A deep sense of contentment spreads through me. It's heady, stronger even than the lust. She's here in my space with me.

We eat at my kitchen table. The lit candles send flickers of flame across her skin and her curls fall softly around her face.

"This," she says, "is really good."

I look down at our food. Potatoes and meat. It looks bare, somehow... I hadn't made a salad. No vegetables. And—oh Lord. "I think I forgot sauce."

She chuckles. "It is a little bit dry, perhaps. But not bad."

I curse and push my chair back. Open the door to my

fridge. "You can have... ketchup? Or BBQ sauce. No, it's expired. It's ketchup or ketchup."

Audrey's voice is soft. "I don't need anything, Carter."

"No sauce," I mutter, taking a seat opposite her again. "Should have thought about that."

"You don't do this often, then? Cook for the women you date?"

I reach for my wineglass. "God, no."

A tiny smile spreads across her lips. "Oh."

"Very few have been here, too," I say, extending my hand to encompass the entire room. "It usually feels a bit... I don't know. It's rare, anyway."

"But you do date a lot," she hedges.

"I have in the past," I admit. "Less and less, now. Some, like my date to the Reporters' Ball, aren't really dates. We've been friends for a few years and meet now and then."

Audrey's lips quirk, like she's heard the subtext. That I haven't had relationships as much as friends with benefits for years. There's a question in her eyes, but none emerges.

I take another sip of wine and wait. But there's only silence. "You can ask it," I say.

"It feels presumptuous," she says. "Asking where you and I fall on the spectrum. I mean, we work together. Or not really *together*, together, but... you know."

I bite my lip to keep from smiling. "I know."

"We went out on a date last weekend. We text all the time. We can't tell anyone about us, of course, and yet here we are. In your apartment."

Ignoring the half-eaten food on the plates in front of us, I reach out to tip her head back. "I'm not looking for another friends with benefit situation," I say. "Although I would call us friends."

"And hopefully there will be benefits?"

"There have been plenty already. I would have burned the steak if you didn't intervene."

She gives a breathless chuckle. "You make it very hard to keep my guard up."

"Do you need it up?" I ask. Her eyes are bottomless on mine, like two pools of water where I can't see the bottom. I think I might die if I can't have her in my arms soon.

Audrey shakes her head. "Maybe. But even if I did, it's come down."

It should scare me, perhaps. The honest confession. And the feelings inside of me do. It's been a long, long time since I felt out of control. Since words failed me and I couldn't just laugh something off. But her confession makes something inside me ache.

"Christ, I want you," I murmur.

She laughs, two spots of color appearing on her cheeks. "Already told you. Guard is down."

"Doesn't mean I'll stop complimenting you," I warn.

We clear the table and I watch her move through my space, the tight curve of her shirt around her chest, her body's sinuous movements. The temperature rises inside by degrees.

Audrey notices. She puts her plate in the sink and turns slowly, catching me. "Well," she says.

I swallow. "What do you want to do now?"

She smooths a hand over her skirt, curving down her hip. "Um, your TV looks gigantic. We could watch a movie?"

"Yes. Sure."

When I sit down on the couch, she takes a seat a solid few feet away from me. Tension is strong in the air and it's strung me tight. But I fight to keep my voice casual. "I have all the streaming services. Choose whatever."

"Oh," she says. "It's almost harder when there are so many choices."

"Then I'll give you none. Put on *Gladiator*."

It works—Audrey smiles. "That was fast. Also, it's too gory for a date. What about... this one?" She uses the remote to hover over a romantic comedy. I vaguely remember seeing it on a flight, years ago.

"Sure. I'll mostly be watching you."

She laughs and hits play. "Honest to a fault."

"Sometimes, at least."

Audrey grabs a pillow and tries to get comfortable. Slides a leg up underneath herself on the couch, curling up, eyes on the opening credits.

"How did you get a TV so big?" she asks.

"It arrived in a box."

She snorts. "Do they even make TVs this big?"

I rub a hand over my neck. Truthfully, it's a bit too large. Ostentatious. "It was a gift."

"From an engineer who made it themselves?"

"An investor, actually. After we made a deal. He also owns a Korean electronics firm."

Audrey looks over at me. Her lips look soft, and warm, and too far away. "So it's a bribe."

"Consider it more of a gift-in-the-hope-of-future-good-relations."

"Which is the definition of a bribe," she says.

"Can't fool you, can I, reporter?"

She scoots closer. "Never."

"Are you recording this whole conversation?" I reach out and drape my arm over the back of the couch. Letting my hand brush over her shoulder. "Will I be exposed on the front page of the *Globe*?"

"Watch out." She leans into my arm, her voice a bit breathless. "I might be wearing a wire."

I raise an eyebrow. "That sounds like something I should investigate."

Her hand comes to rest on my chest, fingers curling around the collar of my shirt. "I think you should," she murmurs.

I kiss her. My intention is to go lightly, to tease, but those thoughts derail when she parts her lips. Something short-circuits in my brain and I slip my tongue inside her mouth.

My hands find her hips and twist her toward me. Away from the stupid TV and the joyous tones of a pop song.

Audrey's hands slide into my hair again, the way they had just a few days ago, and I groan against her neck. The gentle tugging sends shivers down my body.

"There's something different," she whispers, breathless, "when we're not doing this on steel bars two stories up."

I grip her thighs, fitting her more snugly against me. "Yes. It's even better."

She chuckles, but the sound dies when I find the spot beneath her ear. It had made her tremble last time. I close my lips around it and lick softly, and as if on cue, she trembles.

I'm rock hard, near bursting in my slacks, and neither of us is undressed yet. I'm such a fucking goner for her.

She moans into my ear. It's a quiet, wanton sound, and my hands tighten around her thighs. "Fuck," I say. "I can't believe the first time I heard you make that sound was on the phone."

Audrey's hand grips my shoulder. "I can't believe I came with you listening."

"Best goddamn phone call of my life." I slide my hand up, brushing past the soft curve of her breast. Needing to see it bared. "I'm looking forward to listening to it again."

She rests her head against my shoulder. "Carter," she whispers. But I don't know if it's in approval or admonition, a plea or a question. She's breathing fast, and my fingers ache to reach for the hem of her shirt.

I reach for the buttons of mine instead. Audrey leans back and watches as I undo one after the other.

"Oh," she breathes. She reaches out and runs a hand over my chest, through the faint hair there. Down to my stomach, and the muscles tighten instinctively. Pleasure so intense it's almost pain makes my cock twitch.

Her hand is so close.

"You work out," she says.

It's the last thing I expected her to say, and I look down to see her fingers trace the outline of my abs. "Yeah."

Her hands move, and it's divine, feeling their warmth over my skin. She tugs at my shirt and I shrug out of the sleeves, tossing it away. Her eyes are wide and a bit glazed and I cup her face, making her look at me.

"You're so beautiful," I say. "We could do anything, or nothing at all, and I'd be happy with tonight."

Her lips curve into a smile. "You're good."

"Just being honest."

But she surprises me, then. Leaning back on the couch and reaching for the hem of her shirt, she drags it up and off. Her skin is so pale it's almost luminescent in the light. The curve of her waist begs for my hands.

She's wearing a lacy bra, and Christ, her tits are the perfect size. A pulse of desire sweeps through my body so strong it makes me lightheaded.

Audrey shakes her hair out and gives me a smile.

I'm on her the next second, and she laughs, falling onto the couch beneath me. I kiss her forever. Time stops, and the movie fades into nothingness in the background.

The scent of her skin is warm woman and faint perfume and something else, something all her, and I drown in it.

I tease the cups of her bra down, revealing sliver after sliver of soft skin. Her nipples are rosy and taut, and for a second I can't breathe. She's too beautiful. I close my lips around a pink peak and she sighs in soft contentment. I'm in heaven.

And God, I hope I never have to leave.

I remove her bra entirely and dedicate myself to worship. Her hair tickles my forehead, and her hands move through mine, clutching me close.

Then she does something that short-circuits my brain. Again.

She shifts her hips and opens her thighs to cradle me.

And now the only thing between us, between me being

inside of her, is a few layers of fabric. My cock is so hard it's begging to be released from my tight zipper, though that's not the only kind of release I need.

I rest my head against her stomach and breathe deeply.

But Audrey isn't hampered by raging erections, not even mine, and lifts her hips up. Like she's egging me on.

My fingers dig into her skirt. It's tight, and it's in the way, and I meet her eyes. They're dark blue on mine.

I tug it down to reveal light purple, lace-edged panties with a tiny bow at the front. Fucking hell. She's trying to kill me before we've even started.

She reaches down and puts her hand on my shoulder. "Carter," she says, and there's a thread of uncertainty through her voice. I force my heart to still.

"Yes?"

"I have an idea," she says.

SIXTEEN

> Audrey

His tawny eyes are deeply golden, his hair falling over his forehead from where I've run my hands through it. Half lying above me, he seems enormous. All wide shoulders and muscled torso.

"Yes," he murmurs. "Anything."

My sudden nerve in asking falls flat. It's a crazy suggestion. Only, something in me is frightened of going first. Of having it be all about me, of taking off my panties, of lying here naked when he's not.

"Audrey?" he prompts. He so rarely says my name, and there's soft seriousness in the tone. It reminds me that it's him, the same man who'd made it a sport to make me laugh, who texted me about how he drank his coffee, who'd picked me up from my dentist's appointment.

I push myself into sitting. He follows suit, not trying to hide the erection that's clear through his pants.

"I want to see what you did when we spoke on the phone."

Carter's mouth falls open. Then he grins, and it's filled with so much heat that it sends an aching pang through my stomach. "Not what I expected you to say."

"Only if you want to, of course."

"If I want to?" He palms himself through his pants. "Yes. I do."

I reach for the belt buckle and he lets me, strong hands resting beside mine on his lap. I undo the button of his pants and slide the zipper down. There's something reassuring about focusing on him and the inescapable evidence of his arousal.

Carter tugs his pants down and pulls himself out. He's long and hard and thick and dear God I can't look away. Especially not when his hand closes around the shaft and starts to stroke in slow movements.

I'm mesmerized.

"This is what I was doing," he says. "When we spoke on the phone." His voice is hoarse, head leaning back against the couch. His eyes move across my collarbones, my face, my bare breasts. Down to my panties. "Imagining you just like this. How beautiful you'd look beneath your clothes."

"You've thought about that?"

He raises an eyebrow. "About thirty seconds after we met."

"No. In the bar?"

"Yes," he says hotly.

My words form and die on my tongue, over and over again, and I can't look away from his hand gripping himself. The long fingers wrapped around rock-hard flesh.

"Well," I finally murmur. "I'd better not disappoint."

Carter's hand strokes lazily. "That would be impossible."

But the real impossibility is for me to remain a spectator. I reach out, and his own hand falls to the side, letting me take over. His skin is hot against my hand and moves like silk over the hardness. I echo his previous movements, stroking slowly from base to tip.

Carter rests his head against the couch and swallows thickly. The muscles of his throat work with the movement. "Christ," he mutters.

"You feel good," I say.

"Oh yes, I do," he says with a flash of his grin. It disappears when I trail my fingers around the sensitive head. A groan escapes him.

I don't know how long I touch him. Teasing, exploring, getting to know the man who is so comfortable sitting naked on his couch and letting me do what I want. It's tantalizing. He looks big, and thick, and I ache inside with the knowledge that I'll soon feel every inch.

"Spitfire," he finally says, voice hoarse. "As much as I'm enjoying this, I wasn't the only one touching myself during our phone call."

I meet his eyes, heavy-lidded and heated, and the last shred of my inhibition slips away. "You're right," I say. I give his erection a last, lingering stroke before I reach for my underwear.

It's now or never.

I lift my hips and slide them down.

Carter doesn't seem to be breathing. A large hand comes to rest on my knee, and I let him spread my legs. One hooks over his, my bare foot resting against his knee.

"I was lying like this," I whisper. "But under the covers."

"How modest." His warm hand rests on my inner thigh, his voice hoarse. "But what were you doing?"

I touch myself tentatively. Fingers moving in a familiar pattern. I'm already wet, and it's embarrassing, but then I hear the soft murmurs in my ear.

"Fucking hell, do you know how hot you are? Doing this?" His left arm curves around my waist, tugging me firmly against his body. Long fingers brush over my nipple. "Do you usually tease yourself for a long time or make yourself come fast and hard?"

"It depends," I whisper. "If I'm in a rush, or if I'm... very turned on."

He bends over my shoulder to see what I'm doing and strands of his hair tickle my bare skin. His hardness is a heavy, warm weight against my leg.

"Look at that," he mutters, watching my fingers circle. "That's it."

I lean my head against him and focus on the feelings. On the pleasure radiating from my own touch and from the erotic pinch of his fingers on my nipple. I'm breathing hard, but I'm keeping it together.

Until he kisses my neck.

I moan and a full-body shiver rushes over me. I have to pause my fingers or risk falling over the edge too soon.

Carter's large hand slides up my inner thigh until his fingers brush my own. Asking to take over, just like I'd done with him.

I let him.

Oh, it's so different when it's not your own hand, and by God, had I forgotten that? It's been too long, far too long, and I can't wait—

He slides a finger inside. We're both breathing hard, and when he adds his thumb, circling, I surrender entirely. Close my eyes and focus on breathing.

"You're not watching the movie," he murmurs against my cheek. "Pay attention."

I turn my face toward his. "Asshole," I say.

He laughs darkly and presses a kiss to my lips. With his fingers moving, pressed against him, it doesn't take long until my pleasure turns into a coil ready to spring.

"Carter," I breathe. "I can't—I'm not—"

"Let me hear it," he says. "Let me *feel* it."

Pleasure rushes through my body and makes my back arch. My legs close on instinct, his hand trapped between them, still moving. Drawing out the last of my orgasm.

I feel weak when I finally collapse back against him. My thighs are weak, and I'm sensitive, which he seems to know, because his hand just gently cups me.

"Fuck, you're sexy," he says in my ear. "Watching you come nearly made me explode."

"I can't believe that just happened."

He kisses my neck again. "I can. You felt so good around my finger. Clenching, and unclenching, like you were squeezing my cock."

"Oh God."

"Too much?" His hands move reverently over my body. "I've wanted you for weeks. When we've argued, when we've joked. I thought of this. The phone sex the other night nearly drove me mad."

I twist in his arms and reach for his neck, kissing him. My enthusiasm seems to take him by surprise, but he reciprocates, hands bracing my waist.

"To bed," I tell him. "Now."

In one swift movement he stands with me still in his arms. He walks and I kiss his neck and shoulders. It's a great division of labor.

Carter lays me down on the bed and stretches out above me. He's breathing hard, an arm on either side of my head, and the color of his eyes looks near-black in the dark room. "Can I fuck you?"

I'm nodding, my hands finding the silky strands of his hair again. He's a heavy weight between my thighs. "Yes, yes, God yes."

He reaches down, stops, and curses. "Condom," he says and reaches for the bedside table. I close my eyes and breathe in and out, arousal like adrenaline through my veins.

Carter rolls it on, still kneeling between my legs. No fumbling and no hesitation. We both watch as he grips himself and pushes inside, inch by inch. I gasp when he's halfway in. There's a faint burning right at the entrance. He's thicker than I'm used to.

His hand comes to rest on my hip. "Relax, Audrey," he murmurs. "You okay?"

I take a deep breath. "Yes. Keep going."

Carter eases inside with his hand still on my hip. His hoarse voice showers me with murmured compliments, words of encouragement, the sexiest kind of dirty talk. "You feel so good, that's it... Jesus fuck, Audrey, you're sweet. So beautiful too, the way you're spread around me..."

My body accommodates, and then he's fully in, a weight in my stomach. It's deep and it feels earth-shattering, earth-changing, and I'd forgotten how intimate this is.

"Holy shit," he mutters.

I lock my legs around him. Forcing him even closer, until his chest hair tickles my nipples and his mouth brushes across mine. "Told you it had been a while," I say.

He seems at a loss for words, and when he starts to move, the low groans in my ear sound like music. Just like they had on the other end of the phone. I run my hands over his back, fingers tracing smooth skin and rippling muscles.

His hips roll into me in a steady motion, deep and slow, and my entire body becomes languid with it. Carter bends to his elbows, mouth at my ear. He's covering me completely and I never want him to stop doing it. "Stay the night," he murmurs.

"As if I'd leave after this."

He chuckles. The sound stops abruptly as I flex my muscles around him, experimenting.

"I'm trying to perform here," he tells me. "Not come before I've hardly begun."

I run my hand down to his hip, fingers curving over his strong muscles. They flex with each thrust. "I thought I was staying the night?"

He makes a low groan and speeds up. There's no more talking after that, only our bodies moving, and I'm so attuned to his pleasure and the rapid beating of his heart that I'm right there with him when he falters. His body becomes taut, a bow strung tight, and I lock my arms and legs around him.

After a few deep breaths, he rises on to his arms as if to move away. I pull him down again.

He chuckles weakly. "That's the way it is, huh?"

"Yes." I close my eyes against his shoulder. He's warm, and big, and the weight is comfortable. "You know, I've been reading about those weighted blankets people use to sleep better? I think I understand the hype now."

Carter breaks my hold and lifts himself up, golden eyes meeting mine. He grins. "That's what you're thinking about right now?"

"The thought just hit me."

He kisses me for a long while, and when he leaves, I don't stop him. He walks into the ensuite with the condom and I turn over on my side, watching him.

"Your mind is a mysterious thing," he says.

"That's why you like me, isn't it? Because I'm mysterious."

"Tall, dark and handsome," he says with a wink and settles back on the bed. "Come here and let me weigh you down a bit more."

SEVENTEEN

Audrey

My first thought when I wake up is that I've overslept. I'm late for work, and I'm going to have to run for the subway. The second is a prayer that Jonah isn't hogging the shower.

But then I register the softness of the sheets, and my sprawl on a much-too-big bed. The room I'm in is beautiful and only faintly familiar. Dark gray colors with a large wooden dresser in a corner. An art piece hangs above it that vaguely resembles steel bars.

I'm in Carter's bedroom.

He's not in bed, either, but the sheets smell like him. I pull them up to my nose and take a deep breath. Linen, soap, and cologne. Beneath the fluffy down comforter, I wiggle my toes.

We've slept together. Twice, too. And it had been some of the best sex of my life. I smile beneath the comforter, feeling giddy and shy and well-rested.

I hear a sound from the ensuite. A tap turns on, and then off. The door opens and Carter comes into view.

He's running a towel over his hair. He's only in a pair of slacks, his wide chest and abs on fully display. He looks even better in daylight.

He catches me watching him. "You're awake?"

I nod.

"Slept well?"

I nod again.

"Lost your voice there too, kid?"

I pull down the comforter and shake my head. "No. Just overwhelmed."

"Overwhelmed," he says with a smile. "By my handsomeness?"

That makes me chuckle. "Yes."

"Well, when you feel like you've come to your senses, I'll be in the kitchen with breakfast." His smile turns crooked and he nods to the bathroom. "There are fresh towels in there. Help yourself to anything you find."

After my shower, I steal one of his shirts. My clothes are in his living room and while I don't think he'd mind, I'm not about to parade through his apartment stark naked.

Carter is sitting at the kitchen table. He's reading the newspaper, spread out in front of him, a large hand gripping either side. His hair is half-dried and his eyes focused on the article in front of him.

My heart squeezes painfully at the sight. *Mine,* I think.

He lowers the paper. A slow smile spreads across his face when he sees what I'm wearing.

"You said I could help myself to anything," I say.

"So I did... I approve wholeheartedly."

I catch sight of the spread on the kitchen table. Croissants, fresh orange juice, a fruit platter, fried eggs, bagels. Something that looks like... an açai bowl?

"What's all this?"

"Breakfast," he says.

"You didn't... did you *make* this?"

He chuckles. "What, you doubt my skills? After the gourmet meal I served you yesterday?"

I sit down on the chair opposite him. "I doubt."

"You're right to. This is from a brunch place down on Seventh Avenue. I ordered in."

"It looks delicious."

He folds the newspaper into a neat square and sets it down. He has two of them, I see now. The *Globe* and its sister publication in DC. "Dig in," he says and reaches for his cup of coffee.

I pour myself a glass of orange juice and pull my knees up beneath me. Rest my head in my hand and just look at him. An odd shyness creeps over me. Seeing each other like this, the day after, feels intimate in a different way than last night had.

I watch him, the casual T-shirt, the strong arms. He's cutting a bagel in two and it's so ordinary, yet so extraordinary, that I laugh.

Carter looks up. "What?" he says, but he's smiling too.

"I can't believe we had sex last night."

"As in, I'd never do it again?" he asks, raising an eyebrow. "Or as in—"

"You know exactly the kind of way I mean it in."

He chuckles. "Yes. I do. I'm pleased with it."

"You look it, too," I say.

"Says the woman wearing my shirt and a newly-fucked smile."

I laugh, covering my face with the wide sleeve. "Guilty."

"Come on. Eat. There's good stuff here."

"Did you buy the entire menu?"

"Pretty much," he says. "Oh, and there's ketchup in the fridge if you need sauce."

I laugh and grab one of the grapes from the fruit plate, tossing it at him. He deflects with a butter knife and shakes his head.

"An animal," he says. "The younger generations are so uncivilized."

"I'm still only *six* years younger than you, *kiddo.*"

He nods sadly. "And boy does it show."

I roll my eyes and dig into my food. Happiness is bubbly inside my chest. I've become a bottle of champagne. "But you are getting older soon. I did some research on you, after the interview for the company newsletter. Isn't your birthday next week?"

"You," he says, "have too good of a memory."

"So it's true?"

"Yeah."

"What are the big birthday plans? Private plane for your hedge fund friends? Hookers and cocaine? Strippers?"

He raises an eyebrow. "Good morning, Miss Stereotype."

That makes me laugh. "Sorry."

"I'll be working, mostly. Might have dinner with my mother in the evening." He pauses, like he's considering something. His voice is measured when he speaks again. "Actually, I'm having some friends over this weekend. There won't be any hookers or cocaine, I'm afraid, but you're welcome to come if you'd like."

My butter knife pauses over the bagel. "To meet your friends?"

His smile turns crooked. "If you want to, yes."

I nod slowly. "I do. Actually, it would be… I don't know. But I would, yeah. Except I'm going back to Alrich this weekend."

"Oh," he says. "No worries."

"It's for my dad's retirement party. It was booked a long time ago. But I can—"

"Absolutely not," Carter says. "You're going."

"But I'll miss the strippers emerging from cakes."

"I'll pop one in the fridge for you."

I pretend to wipe sweat from my forehead. "Whew."

He snorts and reaches across the table for a croissant, like he hasn't just asked me to meet his friends. Maybe it's a huge party and I'd barely get two seconds alone with him… but it means a lot, regardless. I wish I wasn't double-booked.

"We'll celebrate before," I say. "On the day."

He smiles. "We don't have to do anything special."

"Of course we do. I'll think of something," I say brightly. "What do you usually do on Sundays?"

"Catch up on work," he says. "It's a good day to clear the decks before the week."

I shake my head at him. "That's a terrible view of the best day of the week."

"Using it productively?"

"Yes. You should lounge on the couch or go to a museum. Eat a breakfast like this for a few hours."

"That's what you usually do?"

"Well, you've seen my kitchen. I rarely have this kind of spread."

"Kitchen," he says with a snort.

"Hey," I warn him. "Be kind."

Carter rolls his eyes, but he's amused. "Fine, fine. Your apartment is a palace."

"That's right." I wrap my arms around my raised knee, watching him. My hair is wet down my back and I can feel it leaving damp circles on his fine shirt. "What are we going to do at work?"

His lips twist into a half-smile. "Work, I imagine."

"It'll be weird to see you," I say, "walking down a corridor with Wesley and your other retainers, and not be able to say hi. To know you're just a few floors above me."

"My retainers? I'm not a king."

"You wield about as much power at the *Globe*, you know. You can make oceans rise and fall with your buyouts, layoffs and re-organizations."

Carter meets my gaze, and he doesn't look troubled by my words. But faint color rises on his cheeks. "I suppose, yeah."

"Does it bother you? Having to make decisions that affect so many people?" I'm genuinely curious about this one. I sometimes spend thirty minutes agonizing over the opening sentence of an article I'm writing. I can't imagine having to consider firing someone.

He takes a moment to answer. "Yes," he says finally. "It shouldn't, perhaps. I know it doesn't bother my business partners. Two of them, anyway. But it's still an awful day when you have to look someone in the eye and tell them they're out of a job."

I dig my nails into my palm, thinking of the line of people who had been let go during the first few weeks. I'd been so angry, then. Everyone had been angry.

"People understand, of course," he says. "That you have to cut costs. Sacrifice a limb to save the body. But that doesn't mean people enjoy being the limb in question."

I shake my head. "Not to mention there are plenty of hedge funds who don't have the same ambitions you do."

He raises an eyebrow. "That I do?"

"Yes. To save the paper, I mean. You genuinely believe in the importance of newspapers, of local reporting. But there are others—you've heard of them, haven't you? They buy newspapers and bleed them dry, emptying the newsroom journalist by journalist, and rack up prices for subscribers."

"I'm aware," Carter says. "I've met some of them."

My fork drops. "Really?"

"Yes."

"They *never* grant interviews."

"Not surprising," he scoffs. "They don't want to be pushed on what they're doing. As far as business models go, theirs is profitable. They live off the goodwill the newspaper has garnered over the years, until dwindling subscriber numbers force it into bankruptcy."

"Vulture funds," I say. "Everyone feared the worst when your company took over, you know. That the *Globe* would go down the same route."

Carter's eyes meet mine. "I figured. It looked similar in the beginning."

"I was so angry at you," I say, looking down at my bagel. "When I went up to interview you for the newsletter. To tell you the truth, I'd even prepared a bunch of questions to press you on the issue. I knew I'd be fired, but... I figured you'd probably gut the newsroom anyway."

He grins. "You were going to grill me?"

"Yes. But then I opened the door and you were, well, *you*. Peanut guy."

"That fucking name," he groans.

It makes me smile. "Yeah. Threw me off my game."

"Even thrown, you were a formidable opponent," he says. "I had to hold my own during our lunch."

I shake my head. "I wanted to believe you, even then. Have since the first time we met."

"Oh?" Carter grins, all charm and confidence. "You wanted me from the first time you saw me. Admit it."

I laugh and take a bite of my bagel to keep from answering. His smile deepens, eyes dancing on mine. "Yeah. That's what I thought."

"I plead the fifth," I say. There's no reason to admit that I'd thought he was so wildly out of my league that I'd never entertained the thought.

Carter sorts through the newspapers and hands me one. The paper crinkles in my hands as I unfold it, watching over the edge as he returns to his article. Sunday morning, in a beautiful New York apartment, eating brunch over the newspaper. My chest feels tight with a sudden burst of joy.

"So we'll see each other outside of work," I say. "Weekends… evenings?"

He flips a page and looks across the table at me. There's a promise in his eyes. "As many as you can spare, kid," he says. "You're not getting rid of me."

EIGHTEEN

Carter

The day started good. Great, even. Audrey had texted me a minute past midnight with Happy Birthday, and the gesture—I know she likes to go to bed early—had made me smile. It's been ages since someone did that.

My mother calls at breakfast and sings. She's done it every birthday morning for as long as I can remember, even during the college years when I asked her not to. I put her on speaker in the car to work and catch Tom's smile from the front seat.

So it's a great day, all in all. Even better is the prospect of Audrey spending the night at mine tonight. She's going for drinks with her colleagues first, and I'm having dinner with Mom. Couldn't ask for a better Wednesday, not to mention birthday.

But then I see the text on my phone.

It was from an unknown number. Just a few innocent lines that fall like a cannonball through my day.

Happy birthday, son. Hard to believe it's already been thirty-three years since you blessed your mother and me by arriving. If you ever want to talk, on the phone or in person, I'm here. Would love the chance to catch up. Dad.

The main question I have is how he found my number. Not what he wants, no, because I'm not a fool. He wants money. He wants to hustle me like he has so many other people, to nestle himself into my life. And he'll say whatever he has to to get there.

My mood is suddenly black. Pitch-dark, a night without sun. And I hate that too. That he still has the ability to anger me after all these years. I'd pushed him to the very bottom of my mind for a reason, because I fucking hate feeling like this. I hate feeling anything at all where he's concerned.

There's a timid knock on my door. "What?" I bark. If it's Wesley again, with an obsequious smile, I swear to God I'll—

"It's Tim," my assistant says. "There's a journalist here from Investigative for a meeting. She says it's been scheduled?"

It has to be Audrey.

I run a hand through my hair, forcing my voice to relax. Battle it back into the charming, smooth mannerisms I've perfected over the years. Even that's a remnant of my father.

"Send her in!"

The door opens and there she is, stepping in with a giant box in her hands. "The files you asked for," she says. Her eyes widen with meaning.

Urging me to play along.

"That's right," I tell Tim. "Thank you. Push my meeting after this by ten."

"Yes, of course," he says, shutting the door behind us.

I stand. "Kid?"

"Happy Birthday." She's grinning as she crosses the space to me. "I brought you something."

"I can see that. Files, apparently."

She chuckles and puts the box down on my desk. Right on top of the documents I'd been reviewing. "It took me *a lot* of sneakiness to get this up to you. Even now, I'm sure someone's going to bust me for it. Ask why I'm on the executive floor."

"I'll cover for you," I say. It will be easy to add this to my calendar retroactively.

Her smile flashes again. "I hoped you would. Look... ta-da!" She pulls off the top piece of cardboard to reveal a tiny pastry box. Inside is a single cupcake with a candle. "It's not lit. I was planning to, but setting off the fire alarm would *not* be particularly sneaky."

"Good call." I look at the cupcake, and her wide, expectant smile, and reach for her. She fits into my arms like she belongs there. Because she does. I kiss her thoroughly, as if I can forget the text on my phone and the feelings whirling inside of me. *Disappear,* I tell them. *Not here.*

She looks dazed when I lift my head. "Well," she whispers. "Happy birthday indeed."

I chuckle and reach for the cupcake. "You really brought this to work today for me?"

"I snuck out during my lunch break. Had to bring an extra-large bag to bring it back in without Declan noticing."

"Declan?"

"My deskmate," she says. "You spoke to him, remember? He notices everything."

"Right." I vaguely recall a lanky man in glasses. There had been a lot of names that day.

"It's a carrot cake muffin," she says, and she looks so proud of herself that I kiss her again.

"You remembered?"

"I did. It's your favorite type." She looks over her shoulder at the closed office door, her cheeks rosy with excitement. "Gosh, I feel like I'm doing something I shouldn't."

I lean against my desk. She fits in between my legs, her hands resting on my chest. "A crime against humanity," I say. "Visiting the man you're dating."

"Who's also my boss," she reminds me, smiling.

Second by second with her in my arms, tension leaks out of me. "Thank you."

"You're welcome. Just sending a text wasn't enough." She rises up on her tiptoes and presses her lips to mine in a quick kiss. "Can I ask about your bad mood, too, or will that set it off?"

I rest my head atop hers. "You noticed?"

"Yes," she says, "but you made a valiant effort to hide it."

"You just helped a lot."

"Mhm. I'm glad." But Audrey doesn't leave it at that. She leans back, her hair lightly tousled from my touch, and meets my gaze. There's kind curiosity there. "Did Wesley upset you?"

I snort. "No. He's as meek as a lamb."

She frowns. "He is?"

"Yes. No, it's not him. Or the *Globe* at all."

"Then what? Do you not-so-secretly hate your birthday?"

"No." I run a finger over her jaw and find the edge of her bottom lip. She's soft, but deceptively so. There's strength beneath it. "My dad sent me a text."

"Oh?"

"It's the first time we've had contact in years."

Her mouth parts beneath my finger. "I'm sorry, Carter."

"Sorry," I repeat. Perhaps that is something to be sorry about, but I can't find the emotion. "There's a good reason we haven't spoken."

Audrey's hands find the collar of my shirt, fingers curving around the fabric to rest against my skin. "Want to tell me about it?"

The smart answer is no. Especially not here, in my office, and not when I've barely leashed the irritation flaring up inside me.

But apparently I'm not smart today.

"He recently got out of prison."

Audrey's eyes widen, and there's such shock on her beautiful face that I gently pull her hands away from my shirt. Grip the edge of my desk instead and put some distance between us.

"In prison?" she says. "You've never mentioned him before. Is that why?"

I think of her descriptions of her family. Of dentists and chiropractors and a brother she worries about. Retirement parties and vanilla ice cream. How different my story must seem to her.

"It's one of the reasons, yes. He's not a good man," I say. Audrey says nothing, just looks at me with those big eyes of hers. My teeth grind together. "He travelled a lot for business when I was a kid. Only later did we realize, my mother and I, that he had another family. And that most of his business dealings were illegal."

"Oh my God," Audrey says quietly.

I run a hand through my hair. Of all the things I thought I'd be doing today, explaining my father's sordid past was low on the list. "We haven't met in almost a decade. Spoken only once, during his time in jail. And now he's out."

"Did he wish you a happy birthday?"

I snort. "Yeah. Probably the first step in his master plan of getting back in my good graces."

"Hmm," Audrey says. Her eyes are troubled, and there's more on her tongue, but we're not going into more detail here. I pull her close and kiss her instead.

"Thanks for the cupcake," I tell her. "You should head back downstairs before my next meeting."

Her smile widens. "Right, I should. I'll have to sneak again."

"Felt naughty, did you? Coming up to this floor."

"Wildly so." She looks over her shoulder toward the door, but it remains closed. "At first I planned a different surprise."

"Did you?"

She nods and reaches for the neckline of her blouse, tugging it down to reveal the red, lacy detailing of her bra. "It's a matching set," she whispers.

I close my eyes and take a deep breath. "Go," I say.

She laughs and heads to the door. "I'll see you tonight," she says. "And happy birthday again."

The door closes behind her and leaves me alone in the

office, but with a gift on my desk. A cupcake. I push back my meeting another five minutes so I can eat the entire thing before they arrive, the memory of her smile and red lace bra burning behind my eyes.

"No," I say. "Please tell me that's a joke."

"It's not," Audrey insists. Her hair is a beautiful mess around her head, her eyes glowing. "I went a full ten minutes thinking he was the owner."

"And you asked him questions like he was, too?"

"Yes! How long have you had this business, *sir.*" She groans, but she's grinning. "How will this affect your family, sir?"

I laugh and put my arm beneath my head. There's no looking away from her stretched out on my bed, naked and laughing. "When did you realize you were talking to the son?"

"Embarrassingly late. He made a remark about college, and I thought that was odd, and then I saw his shoes. They were the kind of sneakers I've seen my brother wear. By the time his *actual* father walked in, the man I'd come there to interview, I'd manoeuvred my way out of the conversation."

"Very slick," I say. "But how could you confuse a twenty-one-year-old with a forty-five-year-old?"

She raises a finger my way. "Oh, you would have too, my sarcastic friend. He had a moustache and was at least your height. Plus, they had the same name!"

"He didn't mention the Junior when he introduced himself, did he?"

"Nope," she says. "He very conveniently left it out."

I can imagine the young guy had seen Audrey come into his shop, beautiful and incandescent with curiosity about their struggling bodega, and seized the opportunity.

Couldn't blame the guy, really.

"Did you get what you needed for the story?"

She nods and reaches for the edge of my comforter, letting the fabric run through her fingers. "Yes. I'm going to send it to Booker next week."

"Nervous?"

"Terribly. It'll be my first solo piece for the *Globe*, one where I've pitched the topic myself." She buries her face against the comforter. "It's good. I know it's good. So why am I so nervous?"

"Because it matters to you. Because you're secretly hoping that Booker will read it, think you're a genius, and promote you to senior reporter instead."

She laughs, the sound muffled. "Yes. How do you know what I'm secretly hoping for?"

"Because we all do it when we're starting out. You think I didn't hope the first company I worked on would join the Fortune 500 listing as a big cap?"

"Did it?"

"It did not," I say with a grin. "It turned a profit, but only barely, and then I sold it on. I was sweating through the whole negotiations. If the other investment firm hadn't taken it on, I had no backup plan. I was several millions of dollars in and had no other buyers."

"Jesus," she says. "How do you handle the pressure?"

"You get used to it. I couldn't imagine interviewing strangers every day for a living."

"Well, that part can be nerve-wracking, I admit. But it's not every day. And most people *want* to tell their story. All I have to do is get the ball rolling and they supply the rest." She rests her head on her hand, watching me just like I'm watching her. The best evenings are the ones she spends at mine. We still haven't been out much, and I know it's because she's afraid of someone from the paper seeing us. "Would it be a conflict of interest if I ask you to read it?"

"Your article?"

She nods. "Yes, before I send it to Booker. I want another set of eyes on it, you know."

"I'll read it," I say. "Just send it over."

"You're sure?"

I raise an eyebrow at her. "Yes, I'm absolutely sure."

Audrey smiles and shifts closer on the bed. I can see the soft curve of her breasts, her cleavage made deeper by the angle. The stunning view is made even better by her free hand moving over my chest. She traces patterns across the skin. "Thank you," she says.

"Wait to thank me until after you've seen my notes."

"Think you'll have many?"

I pretend to consider that. "Probably none, but I can't let you think I'd go easy on you, so I'll have to manufacture some. Tell you off for not using an Oxford comma or recommend a stronger synonym."

Her fingers play with my chest hair. "You always have notes," she says. "Especially about my place."

"They're entirely justified when it comes to your living situation."

"So bringing a new lock to my place wasn't heavy-handed?"

"It was," I say, entirely without remorse. "But it's to stop heavy-handed people from getting in, you know. Including me. Did you talk to your landlord about installing it on your door?"

"I mentioned it, yeah. I think he pretended not to hear me."

"Tell him we'll handle the installation. I can have a guy there within the hour to put it up on your door."

"You worry too much," she says.

"You worry too little," I say.

She smiles and looks down at my chest. Traces her name on my skin. "Something did happen just yesterday, actually."

"Tell me about it."

"I know what you'll say."

"I promise I'll say something entirely different. I'll surprise you, kid."

She sighs. "I saw a rat in my kitchen."

"In your kitchen," I repeat quietly. "So… by your microwave in the corner."

Her nails dig into my skin. "Be nice. We can't all be multi-millionaires."

"But a *rat*. Did you tell Pierce?"

"He's not going to do anything about it. But I've bought poison."

I close my eyes. The idea of her in a place like that bothers me more than I'd imagined. It's like needles beneath my skin, knowing that when I say goodbye to her she's going back there. Living in a house with two people who are practically strangers, and she can't even lock her door.

"You're not saying anything," she says. "That's good."

"I'm trying very hard to respect your independence and not sound like a multi-millionaire," I say, eyes still closed.

"Excellent!"

"And I'm also considering how it would look if I singled you out in the newsroom for a massive raise."

Her hand slaps at my chest. "Absolutely not."

"I know. It would be impossible. Think of the HR nightmare." I shake my head sadly and capture her hand. "I'll have to give them all raises."

"If you had the budget allowances for that, you wouldn't have made all those buyouts and layoffs." She shakes her head. "No, you'll just have to endure me living in a place fit for my budget."

"You'll give me an ulcer."

"And you're exaggerating." She rests her head on my chest, her cheek warm. I reach down and pull her more squarely along my own body, skin against skin, her leg between mine.

"Cold?" I ask.

She shakes her head. "You grew up in Queens. Surely you didn't have a perfectly maintained loft apartment then."

"No," I say, smoothing my hand down her back. Her skin is like velvet. "But we didn't have rats and there was most certainly a lock on our door. It's a good neighborhood. You just happened to find the worst room."

"Such bragging," she says. "Did your dad live with you then?"

My hand falters on her back, stutters, before I resume the slow, rhythmic sweeps. "Are you treating me like one of your interview subjects? Getting the ball rolling and all that?"

She smiles against my skin. "Is it working?"

It's been a week since my birthday, since the text I didn't answer. He hasn't tried contacting me again. "Maybe," I admit. "I haven't spoken about that part of my life in a very long time."

"You and your mom don't talk about it?"

"No," I say. "We both tried to forget he existed, honestly. After we learned about all the lies."

"With his other family?"

"And his *profession*," I say, the word sarcastic. "He had been embezzling, evading taxes, funneling money offshore. There was no one he wouldn't manipulate to get what he wanted. Of course, when I was a kid, I thought he was the coolest. Travelling for work two or three weeks out of the month, with his briefcase."

Audrey makes a soft, humming sound. "Was he a good dad?"

"When he was home, yeah," I say reluctantly. "We played Monopoly a lot. That was his favorite game, ironically enough. He shared the apartment with my mother, and the weeks he was home, it was like Christmas. She'd make all of his favorite dishes and I'd get to stay up late to watch TV with him." The idiocy of it makes me shake my head. "Now we know he was putting us up in a flat far away so his real family wouldn't notice."

"I can't imagine," she whispers.

"I couldn't either, when I realized. The worst part is that he hadn't married my mother legally. His real wife was his only legal wife."

"But he... pretended?"

"Yeah. He got a buddy to perform the ceremony, and not an ordained one. Mom didn't know until the cops showed up, after he'd been arrested." I snort. "Turns out it was a pretty good thing, too. Their assets were separate. One of his worst deeds turned out to be one of the best."

"Do you have... I mean, did he have other kids?"

"Yeah."

"So you have—"

"I don't think of them like that," I say. Then I take a deep breath and force my voice to soften. "I can't, really. Maybe one day. But not yet. Besides, I don't even know if they're aware of my mother and me."

"Do you know their names?"

It takes me a long time to answer. "Yes. I had a PI find out all of that a few years ago. It's on a file in my computer, but I've only opened it once."

Two girls and one boy. Women, now, really, and a man. One older than me and two younger. In the family Christmas card the PI had dug up, they're all sitting in front of a beautiful Christmas tree. Five stockings hang over the fireplace with all their names on. Including my father's.

No wonder he so often had to work holidays, too. He spent it with them.

"What did he go to prison for?"

"Tax evasion and fraud. I'm sure there's more they couldn't get him for, but apparently they'd been on his tail for some time. He got a fifteen-year sentence and only served ten for good behavior." I shake my head. "He's a charmer, kid. Could sell snake oil to anyone."

She's quiet, and I wonder if she hears the same thing I do. She's called me a charmer plenty of times too. Suddenly I hate that part of myself. The one that mimics what I'd seen my father do plenty of times, with waitresses and cab drivers and our landlord. The smile I use that's not mine.

But that's not what she asks. "Do you miss him?"

"No," I say immediately.

Her hand smooths over my chest. "Carter..."

"I don't. Not after what he did. To me, sure, but mostly to my mother. He's a... villain. A compulsive liar. Wouldn't surprise me if he's a psychopath or a sociopath, clinically speaking."

"Would you want to tell him all of this?"

I shake my head. "Don't tell me I should meet him just to get this off my chest."

"Let me guess. Your mom already told you the same?"

She's too intuitive. "Yes," I admit. "But I'm not going to. He's out of my life and that's where he belongs."

My tone is final, because if there's one place he *certainly* doesn't belong, it's in bed with Audrey. I wrap my hand around her waist and flip us over. She gasps, but it quickly turns to laughter as I bury my hand against her neck.

"Okay," she says breathlessly. "I guess that conversation's over."

I kiss down her collarbone, her chest, to the soft rounds of her breasts. They're just the right size for my hands, fitting into my palm like they're made for each other. "Yes," I say, and bend to her nipple. It rises rosy and pink beneath my tongue. "Come with me to a dinner this Friday."

"Where would we—oh. Jesus." Her voice turns shaky as I add my teeth to her nipple. She's sensitive here, I've learned, and it happens to be one of my favorite spots. "Where would we go?"

I let my fingers take over the teasing. "It's with my business partners and their girlfriends. Or spouses, really."

"Business partners? Like... the other members of your venture capitalist firm?"

I grin at her. "Yeah, in Acture Capital. And you're not allowed to interview anyone on the record."

She smiles back at me. "Not what I was thinking. But... what would you introduce me as?"

"My girlfriend," I say.

Her breath catches, and this time it has nothing to do with my hands or lips. "Oh," she says. "I'd like that."

I raise an eyebrow. "Good. Because if you really insisted, I could introduce you as the junior reporter from the newspaper we co-own, but I think that could be awkward."

She laughs, fond exasperation in her eyes. "No, I don't want to be introduced that way."

"Good. It's a mouthful."

"We won't tell them, will we? Where I work?"

"Not if you don't want to," I say, raising myself up on an elbow. I run a finger around her nipple. "But in full disclosure, not a single one of them would mind. They shouldn't, at any rate. The others all met their partners at work, too."

"They did?"

"Yeah. Outrageous, really."

"You're all walking HR violations."

I grin at her. "Yes. But one's just married, one's engaged, and the third are renewing their vows soon."

"I'll come to the dinner," Audrey says, her fingers sliding into my hair. "And I'll tell them all I met my boyfriend at a bar."

"While on a date with someone else," I say, clucking my tongue. "This man of yours must be quite special."

Her eyes glow with happiness. "He definitely is."

NINETEEN

Audrey

Carter is sitting on my bed. He didn't need to come up, but he'd insisted, and now he's being decidedly unhelpful while I search for an appropriate outfit.

"You look beautiful," he says.

"You said that about the last dress."

"The clothes change, but the woman stays the same," he says with a grin. "And she's the one I'm complimenting."

I roll my eyes, but I'm smiling too. It's impossible to be in a bad mood when he's around. "Not helpful, but thank you."

"I've liked every outfit."

I turn back to my closet. Everything's either practical or office wear, down to my sensible black pumps. "You're in a suit," I say. "What about the others? Will it be fancy?"

I don't have to see him to know he's shrugging. He looks comfortable in a suit with no tie, gray Italian fabric and a white shirt beneath. I wish I'd had an option as easy.

"Go with the prom dress," he says. "The one you wore to the ball."

I pull it out of the closet. It's too long, for one, but the memory makes me smile. "I still can't believe I spoke to Dean Allen."

"It was a great night."

"You drove me home," I say, running my hand over the fabric.

"So I did," he says. "You were still on the fence about me then."

"I wasn't on the fence."

"But you didn't trust me fully."

I smile at him. "No, perhaps not. But it never stopped me from enjoying your company."

He joins me by my closet. True to his word, he hasn't said a word about the lock still uninstalled next to my door, or the little bowl of rat poison in the hallway outside. He hasn't even commented on the relentless EDM music my student neighbor is blasting across the hall.

He puts a hand on my bare waist and kisses my temple. "Yours was the best date-crashing I've ever done," he says softly. "You'll look good in anything, but I liked the red."

"Oh." I reach for the blouse, the fabric silky against my skin. I'll wear it with a skirt and nice shoes. "Good choice."

"Don't worry about meeting my business partners or their girlfriends," he says.

I kiss him on the cheek, but my nerves don't disappear. How could they? These are people who buy and transform—or bankrupt—entire companies. It's exhilarating and absolutely frightening.

We leave my apartment and Carter gives my door one last irritated glance when he thinks I can't see him. I hide my smile. His concern over my apartment is sweet, but it's a great place for my budget, and Pierce is a hands-off landlord.

The car smells of the same leather as always, and I say hello to Michael the driver. I've learned that Carter employs a service, and two drivers alternate. Michael and Tom.

We really live in different worlds.

"I read your article today," Carter says.

"You did? I only sent it to you around lunch."

"I made time."

"It's pretty long," I say apologetically. "I think Booker might cut at least half if she decides to run it."

Carter surprises me by shaking his head. His eyes are serious on mine. "It's a great piece. You connect it to construction in the city, faulty policies protecting tenants, and a business practice that's legally gray at best. It's local, investigative journalism."

I release the breath I'd been holding. "You're not just saying that because I'm sleeping with you?"

He laughs, surprised and delighted, and reaches for my hand. "No. Although it helped ensure I made time to read it, I'll admit. But no. I made some notes and will send it back to you, but they're marginal. You overuse the word 'therefore' a bit."

I groan. "I cut out three therefores already."

"Well, there are about eight too many left." He squeezes my hand. "Pitch it to Booker. I have no doubt she'll run it."

"God, I hope so. She's terrifying in the best of ways. I'm so glad to be working for her."

Carter's smile is genuine. Like he understands. "I had a mentor like that once. And when I'd finally spent years building up my fortune, my knowledge and my own investment company, he invited me to join him and his partners. I've learned a lot from him."

"Really? Who was he?"

"Tristan Conway," he says. "Our host for tonight."

We arrive at the beautiful Upper West Side building with little to no time to spare. The traffic had been heavy, and with every slow-moving jam, nerves ratcheted up in my stomach.

Carter says thanks to Michael and gives me his hand. The building's lobby is all marble and doormen and a smartly dressed receptionist, like we're here to check into a hotel.

"Through here," Carter says softly at my side. "And remember, they're—"

"No interviewing them for an expose on venture capitalists," I whisper. "I remember."

He grins at me. "Right."

"Let's do this." I stand on my tiptoes and kiss him. His free hand drifts to my hip and pulls me closer. It's a delicious kiss, comforting and deep, and I don't want to let go when the elevator doors open.

Someone clears a throat.

Carter lifts his head from mine and chuckles. "Hey, man. Thanks for having us."

"Glad you're making yourself comfortable," a man drawls. He's standing in a beautifully decorated hallway, navy slacks and a deep-blue shirt on with the shirtsleeves rolled up. He looks a few years older than Carter, with laugh lines fanning out by his eyes.

The elevator opened straight into this man's apartment… and not in a hallway.

My cheeks flare with heat. "I'm sorry."

"You have nothing to apologize for. I'm Tristan." He extends a hand, a smile softening his features.

"Audrey," I say, and shake his hand.

"A pleasure. Come in, both of you. Carter, you know where the wine is."

"I'll grab a glass for us both," Carter says. "You're in the living room?"

"Yes."

Carter moves through the place like he knows it, pouring us a glass each. The sound of laughter draws us through the space, beneath ceilings with crown molding and art on the walls. The view from the living room stops me in my tracks.

It's Central Park, and on the other side, the Upper East Side.

It's breathtaking.

"Nice, huh?" Carter says at my side.

I nod. "Uh-huh."

He nudges me forward to the group of people sitting around a designer coffee table. Behind them is an entire wall of framed black and white photos.

"Hey," Carter says. "Room for two more?"

"Of course," a woman says. Her hair is the color of wheat, and she smiles at me as she moves to the side. "Have a seat."

They all introduce themselves, with Summer being the smiling blonde. Next to her is a dark-haired man named Anthony, who gives me a firm handshake and looks at me for a long time. Tristan's wife is named Frederica, a diminutive woman with long, luscious black hair and clever eyes. She looks between me and Carter like she's analyzing us. I like her immediately.

The last two arrive about half an hour after us, putting a halt to the pleasant small talk. The dark-blond man keeps his suit jacket on, and he gives everyone a curt nod hello. The woman at his side smiles wide. "Hi! Sorry we're late!"

"Another fifteen minutes and we'd have put out a missing person's ad," Carter says.

The newcomers are Victor and Cecilia, and with them, all guests have arrived. There's obvious familiarity, more in the way of friends than just business partners. Summer and Cecilia pull me into a discussion of running, a pastime I've never enjoyed, and I learn they run in the park a few times a week.

"Join us," Cecilia says. "We usually run in the mornings."

I think of my apartment in Queens, the subway ride, my job. "Thank you," I say, smiling. "Maybe one day."

Carter sits next to me, and when we move to the dinner table, he takes the seat by my side. It's a comfort to have him here, even when he's engaged in a discussion with Victor about the merits of a new pharmaceutical company Tristan's considering.

His hand finds my leg beneath the table and squeezes softly. I smooth my hand over his in quiet reply. *All good.*

Halfway through dinner, Tristan makes a toast. He thanks us all for being here. "And thank you, Carter, for finally bringing along a date. Audrey, you're very welcome here."

"Thank you," I say, conscious of the eyes turning my way. *Finally?* The conversation doesn't drift away from that topic, either. Freddie asks how we met.

I cut through the asparagus on my plate to avoid the curious looks. "Well, I was about to go on a blind date... and I was a bit nervous."

"She came to the bar for a glass of water," Carter says. "I tried to steady her nerves."

"Drove me half-insane, was more like it."

"Settled the nerves, though," he says.

I laugh. "Yes. Definitely. He promised to help me escape, too, in case the date was bad. Which it was."

"Terrible," Carter says with emphasis, draping an arm around the back of my chair. "I could see from the bar how awful it was. So she took me up on the offer halfway through."

Summer looks delighted across the table. "Really?"

"Yes. I came over and told her to come right away. Her mother needed her. There wasn't much time left."

"That's diabolical," Victor says. He sounds pleased.

I shrug. "It worked, at any rate. I would have felt worse if the man I was on a date with wasn't being so rude."

"So you stole someone else's date," Tristan says, eyes on Carter. "I don't know if I'm impressed or horrified."

"Saved," I say, correcting him with a smile. "Not stole. Thanks for getting me out of there, Carter."

He smiles down at me. "My pleasure, spitfire."

The conversation flows smoothly from there, just like it does with people who know each other well and meet often. They discuss business meetings, trips, and conferences before jumping effortlessly to the topic of Victor and Cecilia's vow renewal. They'd only been married a year, but from what I gather, their first wedding had been a quick City Hall affair.

"Do you have everything prepared?" Freddie asks the pair. They're beautiful together, the put-together brunette and Victor's stoicism.

"I think we do," Cecilia says. "It'll be small, with just a few friends and family. Great food and music."

"Great guests," Carter deadpans.

Cecilia grins. "Oh, the absolute best. You're more than welcome to come too, Audrey."

"Thank you, that's really kind," I say, and I mean it. The flow of conversation is fun to listen to, and only occasionally terrifying, as when Summer and Anthony mention their Montauk beach house. I can't imagine the dizzying wealth some of these people have. Not to mention that Acture Capital, the owners of the newspaper I work at and arbiter of its fate, are all seated around the same dinner table. With me.

It's heady stuff. It makes me feel like an investigative reporter, and at the same time, an insider. I'll never use what I hear here, but... wow. Pinch me.

After dinner, I join Freddie in the kitchen as she pours herself a glass of sparkling water. The men have moved back into the living room. "So," she says. "You're not too overwhelmed?"

I chuckle. "A little, perhaps, but in a good way."

"I remember the feeling," she says, leaning against the counter. "Although when Tristan and I first started dating, the others were all single."

"Acture was a bachelor's club?"

She laughs. "Gosh, yes. I'm glad that's changed."

"Have you joined the team now?" I ask. She gives off the impression of a woman with ambition, and from what I overheard at the dinner table, she's working with Tristan now on Acture's latest acquisition.

Freddie gives a half-shake of her head. "In a way, I suppose. I was always interested in business strategy, and I spent the past two years at Exciteur—that's the company Victor's the CEO of, now—working on Strategy. Now I'm a consultant, really, for Acture. Tristan and I work well together."

"That's impressive," I say. "Working with your husband?"

She smiles crookedly. "Some days it's the best decision I've ever made, and others we both consider it a grave error. But overall... yes, it's been great. Wouldn't change it for the world."

Summer and Cecilia join us, then, and the kitchen island shrinks. "Talking business?" Summer asks. "Please tell me you weren't. The guys are, too, and I've already told them off twice."

Freddie laughs. I twist my wineglass around in my hand, smiling at the other women. "That must be a common thing when you all meet?"

"It's constant," Cecilia says. "Sometimes I wonder if I married an Excel spreadsheet or a man."

We all laugh at that. Summer reaches for a lime from the fruit bowl and searches through a drawer for a knife. "Time for more drinks," she declares. "Audrey, what do you do?"

"I'm a journalist, actually."

"Wow. Really?"

"Yeah."

Freddie's intelligent eyes meet mine. "What a coincidence," she says, "considering Carter's current project within Acture."

I laugh weakly and look down at my hands. "Yeah. It's funny."

"Do you guys talk shop?"

"Sometimes we do, yes. I'm a big believer in traditional print media, in local journalism. The value it has for our cities and our country."

She nods thoughtfully. "I agree with you on that, actually. I also think owning a newspaper long-term is a great move for Acture."

A surprise ally! But before I can ask her why that is, Cecilia ushers us all back to the living room to, as she so lovingly puts it, halt the men's workaholic tendencies. When they come within earshot, she looks over her shoulder at us with a meaningful expression. *Listen to them*, it says.

Snippets reach me too. "... the latest numbers were better, but still abysmal."

"It's turning a profit," Carter says. "Slim, perhaps, but still."

My feet slow on the hardwood floor. They're discussing the *Globe*.

"Slim isn't good enough," Victor says. "Not long term. Traditional print media is an opportunity, sure, but also a huge liability."

Anthony now. "Only two months left before the second quarter check-in. I'm still voting for selling it if the numbers aren't better."

"Seconded," Victor says.

The voice I hear then is familiar. Achingly so. "I agree," Carter says. "But I'm not ready to give up before then."

Freddie walks around the room and comes to sit next to Tristan. He takes his wife's hand absently and continues the conversation. "We could still sell it without a loss. Rosen Investing has made their interests clear."

Carter sighs. "I know. Jacob Finch has been in contact. I'm keeping as much as I can intact, to keep the sale value high, just in case."

Which means he's keeping the profitable areas afloat. The ones a vulture fund like Rosen will strip and sell, dismantling the entire organization until there's only a lonely reporter left in a newsroom to cover all story beats and subscribers facing ever-higher prices. Driving it into bankruptcy and skipping away into the sunset with the profitable corpse.

The exact thing he'd promised he wouldn't do, would never do. But they're discussing it like it's a possibility.

More than a possibility.

A likelihood.

A sickness claws its way up my throat. Carter hadn't told

me everything, it seems. Only what I wanted to hear, back when he convinced me he wasn't like this. Anger rushes through me. At him, and at me, for thinking this would be an exception.

That *he* would be an exception.

"Audrey," Summer calls. "Come join us."

I force my feet to move. Carter looks over his shoulder, eyes meeting mine, and there's an apology there. He knows I overheard. I sit down next to him on wooden legs, focusing on the drink in my hand.

Victor had called stealing another man's date diabolical, but it's not. This is. They're considering stripping this city of one of its oldest and finest newspapers.

I'd defended Carter and his executive team's vision to Declan over lunch, just yesterday.

"Audrey," Carter whispers at my side. His hand reaches for my leg, as if to rest it there. I cross them out of his reach.

"I know I've already thanked you all for coming," Tristan says. He has a hand on Freddie's shoulder, but the smile on his face gives me pause. Something's happening, and I wish I could take it in, but all I hear are Carter's words on repeat. *It's a possibility.*

He'd told me it wasn't.

"You're getting your vows renewed, too," Carter guesses. "Is this a new trend?" His voice is as charming as ever, dry and joking, and the others laugh.

I wonder if they can hear the tension beneath it too.

"Not quite," Freddie says. "We just wanted to... ah shoot, now this is a big thing. I suppose it is, but we just wanted to tell you that, if all goes well, the Conways will go from three to four in a few months."

"Oh my God," Cecilia whispers.

Summer bounds out of her chair to wrap her arms around Freddie. "You're pregnant!"

Freddie laughs. "Yes."

In the flurry of excitement and hugs, masculine claps on

the back and Tristan's proud smile, I feel like a sudden imposter. Not alienated from them... but from the man at my side.

We don't talk about it until we leave Tristan's. Carter is quiet by my side. That's unusual, like he's testing the waters. But when the car rolls through Midtown, I speak up.

"Could we go to Queens first, please?"

"Audrey," he says quietly.

"I'd prefer to sleep at home tonight." *Alone*, I think, though I don't add it. My chest feels tight. Like I'm about to cry, and I don't know why. Because of my own foolishness, perhaps, or for the dream that cracked at his words. The future I'd imagined.

"You won't let me explain myself," he murmurs, "or our business plan?"

"I thought I had. Many times before, and gotten the truth."

Carter sighs. He's quiet for a long time. Even as Michael changes lanes and starts heading toward Queens. "It's not the outcome I want," he says.

"But it's not an impossible outcome."

"No," he says, "even if I wanted it to be."

"Wanting something doesn't make it happen."

He runs a hand through his hair, the trademark smile nowhere to be seen. "Thought I'd already learned that lesson," he mutters. "Look, kid, it's a business. You know it is. At the end of the day, the four of us answer to the shareholders in Acture Capital as much as to our own wallets."

"Right."

"If the *Globe* isn't doing what we want it to do..."

"If you're not willing to give it enough time, you mean. Or investment."

"Print media is dying."

I turn to him, hands balling into fists. "Yes, and you told me you wanted to fix it! To modernize! Not butcher it."

"We wouldn't do that," he says.

"No, but you'd sell it to someone who would. How is that different?"

He closes his eyes. "I'm twenty-five percent of Acture. I have one vote."

He could have been honest about that too, I think. Or maybe I shouldn't have been so naive. "Right. Well, tonight was very enlightening."

"Audrey…"

"They're lovely people. Well, some of them, when they're not discussing stripping an entire workplace of its resources and personnel."

His voice rises. "That's my job. Part of it, at least. You know that."

"I never knew you intended that for the *Globe*. You were the one who convinced me it wasn't! You took me to that dive bar, and you told me… you told me you were different." I bury my head in my hands. He charmed me, I think. Got what he wanted, and I bought all of it, hook line and sinker.

"Come back to mine," he says. "We can talk about it. I'll tell you anything you want to know, and tomorrow—"

I shake my head. "No."

His hand tightens on the door handle. "Fine."

We don't speak for the rest of the trip. I'm acutely aware of Michael in the front seat, overhearing our entire argument, and my own stupid tears hiding in my throat. The wine is not helping the roil of emotions inside.

Carter speaks again when we drive onto my street. "I never wanted you to hear the *Globe* spoken about that way."

"We should have stayed in the kitchen five minutes longer, you mean?"

"No. Fuck, that's not what I meant." His hand catches my arm, and he stares out at the brownstone. "Please don't make me drop you here."

"It's a perfectly good apartment."

"It's an unsafe, vermin-infested shithole," he says darkly. "Come home with me."

I jerk my arm free, and he releases me immediately. "It's all I can afford on my salary, boss," I say acidly. "And this is my home."

"Kid, I—"

"I'll talk to you tomorrow," I say, and close the car door behind me. I make it halfway up the stoop before the tears start falling.

TWENTY

Audrey

The article is ready. Arguably, it's past ready. Booker had asked for the first draft three days ago. "That thing you were working on," she'd said, snapping her fingers. "What was it? Evictions, right?"

"Yeah, in Queens. A construction company has put it into practice."

"That's the one. I think it could work for a Sunday issue. Have it on my desk soon, yeah?"

I'd nodded, and inside, I'd almost passed out. The Sunday issue is the biggest of the week. If you want a story to get read widely, you put it in the Sunday issue.

Now my article is lying on my desk, printed and ready. The changes Carter had suggested were good. Minor, but good. They made it stronger.

Even if it was hard to incorporate them after the other night.

"You're done," Declan says by my side. "Come on, you just have to submit it."

"Yeah. Will do."

He leans back in his chair. His hair is artfully tousled today, but in a different direction than usual. It looks good. "She cut half of mine and asked Johnson to add it to his beat," he says dryly. "We can't be precious about our first stories."

He's right, of course. I know it too. The term I was student editor of my college newspaper, I'd made countless decisions like that. Not as high stakes, though. Not at all. I see the faces of the family being evicted in front of me, their bodega, the metaphorical wrecking ball coming closer.

I grab the papers. "You're right."

"Grab her by the balls, tiger," Declan says.

I look at him, and he gives me a sheepish shrug. "Sounded better in my head."

I laugh. "Thanks, though. I appreciate it."

Booker is having two conversations at the same time. Firing off story beats at a rapid pace. When she turns to me, her eyes are feverish. "Spitfire," she says. "Thank God. Want to do me another favor?"

I lower my article. "Sure."

"Tyrell is sick and Johnson just told me we have to push the epilepsy story for tonight's print. Which means we're several articles short for Friday's edition."

"Shoot. What can I—"

"I have two half-baked articles banked. They're approved already, but they need filler, better research, and all their facts checked. Can you stay late and do that?"

"Yes, absolutely."

"Great. I was thinking about your article, too—is that it?"

"Oh, yes, it is." I hand over the document. "It's long, but for a Sunday piece it could work."

Those are bold words for a junior reporter.

Booker meets my gaze with a shrewd one of her own. "I'll look it over. I promise I'll give it a fair shake, too. You're a good writer. But right now I want you focused on the articles for tonight. I'll email you the details."

"Will do."

Another late night at the newsroom, then. I return to my desk with a grin.

"That good?" Declan asks.

"She asked me to stay late," I say. It's grunt work, of course, for a junior reporter. But it also means she trusts me to deliver.

Declan gives as noncommittal sound. He'd had to stay late just a few days ago, and he's smugly complained about it the whole day.

Working is good. Working is what I love to do, what I've fought to do, and it's a great way to keep my mind off other things. Like the owner of the very newspaper I work at.

Carter's words had played over and over in my head the last couple of days. They were impossible to forget, even if I've tried to look at the situation objectively from every angle. To separate my own emotions from it.

Yes, he's a businessman. He didn't buy the *Globe* as a philanthropic move. And yes, print media is struggling. But I had so wanted to believe him when he'd explained his vision for revamping the paper.

And maybe that's what hurts the most. Not the truth itself, but the pain of discovering my own beliefs were always naively impossible.

One after one, the newsroom empties out. A stressed Booker gives me a nod on the way out, telling me she'll continue working from home after she's picked up her son. *I'm available on email,* she tells me before ducking out, walking like a warrior to battle.

An empty newsroom. It happens rarely, and during one of my five-minute breaks, I stretch my legs by walking through the space. It's not fancy. Just an office and rows and rows of desks. But this is where scandals broke. Where the *Globe* risked everything for a meeting with a whistleblower during the seventies. Where Isaac Mason exposed corrupt cops in the eighties. History has been made here.

On one of the walls are some of the *Globe*'s most important front pages framed. The Kennedy assassination, the moon landing, when the Berlin Wall fell. Back then the *Globe* had foreign correspondents. That was a different era.

"I wondered if I'd find you here," a voice says.

I take a deep breath before I turn around, but I'm still not prepared for the sight of him. Tall and suited, the thick hair pushed back. He feels like an extension of myself, one I can no longer access. Like the argument has put up a wall between us. The anger is gone, and left is only my own disappointment, irrational as it might be.

"Hey," I say.

Carter inclines his head. "Hi. Staying late?"

"Two reporters were sick and couldn't deliver for Friday's edition. Booker asked me to stay late."

His voice softens. "And you don't mind?"

"Not at all." I fiddle with the sleeve of my shirt, not knowing what to say. It's not the first time we've spoken in the four days since Tristan's dinner, but the texts had been dry. *Let's talk. Yes, soon. Just a few more days. What are you thinking? I don't know, really.*

Carter taps his hands against the cheap wood laminate of a desk. "Need help?"

There are articles he could proofread. Facts to be checked.

And conversations to be had.

So I nod. "Yeah. It shouldn't take long if we're two."

"Good. Just give me the beats, boss."

That makes me smile a bit. "If you want me to play Booker, you'll be disappointed. I'm not even a poor man's version."

"Yet," he says. "But there's time."

He pulls out a chair and joins me by my desk. It's just the two of us, side by side, in a room that's usually filled with his employees. I try not to let that thought bother me.

"These are the articles?"

"Yes. Booker wants them print-worthy by the morning, ready for her to approve."

"Right. Walk me through the process."

I do, and he listens patiently, nodding or asking questions occasionally. When I'm done, he starts fact-checking right away. "I'll leave the wordsmithing to you," he says with a crooked smile.

I've missed him these past days. Missed his voice, his jokes, his way of turning a sentence on its head. Maybe he feels the same way, because over the next forty-five minutes, his chair gets closer and closer to mine until our thighs touch beneath the table.

"Johnson's piece is almost done."

"It *is* done," Carter says. "The ending quote you added is killer."

I dig my teeth into my lower lip. "I don't know. One of my college professors always told me to be selective when you cede the last word to someone."

"But using a quote by the veteran who was interviewed earlier? Excellent way to end it." Carter shakes his head. "You're done with this article. It's perfect."

"If only you were my editor," I tease, and his face lights up with a smile.

"If only," he agrees. I reach for the mouse at the same time as he does. He lets me get it, but keeps his hand there, brushing against mine.

He takes a deep breath. "Audrey, I want to apologize."

I close my eyes. "You do?"

"Yes. Not for my words, and not for you overhearing them. But for not being more truthful with you from the start."

"Oh."

"The truth is that I... well, I knew if I admitted that Acture considered selling the *Globe* to a vulture fund, or breaking it up ourselves, you would have run from me. It would have confirmed all your worst suspicions."

"I might've," I murmur. "Back then."

"But not now?"

I take a deep breath. "It's hard for me to understand the

thinking. Actually, that's not true. I can understand it all too well, and wish I couldn't. I care so much about this newspaper and the industry, and I hate, like truly *hate* those vulture funds. You know what they've already done to newspapers around the country."

"I know," he says quietly.

"But I also know that you don't share that. I mean, you and your business partners are part of the ecosystem. You keep things that work alive, and make them better, and things that don't…"

Carter's hand covers mine. "I want to keep the *Globe* running. I've wanted that from the start. Selling it to another hedge fund has always been a backup option, and one that helped convince my business partners it was a good investment."

"I know," I say. And the worst part is, I do. Because if it wouldn't be Acture, it would be someone else. Someone worse.

"But I shouldn't have pretended that wasn't an option at all."

I look down at our hands, his long fingers curling around mine. Broad, short nails rest next to my almond ones. "Carter… I really like you."

His hand tightens around mine. "Not what I expected you to say," he murmurs. "But I really like you too."

"I want this to work. Despite our odd working relationship, and despite the Acture and *Globe* thing. But it only will if we're honest with one another, even about the hard things."

He's quiet for a long time, the odd, golden color of his eyes more serious than I've ever seen them. "Audrey, it's been a long time since I was honest and open with someone. Since I trusted them with the hard things."

"I don't know if I ever have," I whisper, and he gives a half-smile. But I know he's talking about deeper things. About not running from the pain, from the arguments, from the difficulty.

"But you've been open to it from the start. You're yourself, kid. Always, and I admire you for it." His thumb sweeps over the back of my hand.

"You were the one who took the first step. Asking me out, and all."

He grins. "Back when you hated dating."

"I still hate dates. First dates, that is."

"Good thing we've already had our first, then."

I reach for him, wrapping my hands around his neck. "I want to apologize too."

"For what?"

"For being judgemental about this," I say. "Like you said in the car, you've never hidden the fact that you're here to make money."

He looks down at our bodies, now angled toward one another. His voice is low. "Not at the expense of people, though. And never at the expense of your affection. We'll talk more about this from here on out."

"I could talk to you forever," I admit. "Never met anyone I wanted to talk to from sunrise to sundown."

"How odd," he murmurs, lowering his face to mine. "Because I feel the same."

The kiss is soft and sweet, and laced with emotions that make my chest ache. Maybe this little argument was for the best... made us stronger. I wrap my arms around his neck. "I missed you," I say.

His hands settle on my hips. "Kid, every day this week has been torture."

"You're right, by the way."

"Mmm. Thanks." He kisses along my jaw, slow, teasing touches. "About what?"

"My place is a shithole."

He pauses at my neck, quiet laughter rocking through him. "Wow. Are you sure you're in your right mind?"

"Fully," I say. I can't stop smiling. "It's awful. But it's mine, and it's what I can afford right now."

"Please let me help you look for something else."

"We can look, yeah. But I'd very much like to cook something at yours this weekend. Maybe we can watch another movie?"

"Stay at mine tonight," he says. "I'm not above begging, you know."

"I didn't pack anything today. I don't have my toothbrush, or clean underwear, or—"

"So we'll stop by a supermarket on our way. Come on, let's go."

"I have to get this article done!"

"It's good enough."

I laugh and lean back, out of reach from his roving lips. "As the owner of this newspaper, you should crave perfection."

"Perfection is the enemy of efficiency," he counters. "If what I craved was perfection, I'd have gone into a different field."

"You have an answer to everything, don't you?"

"Most things," he says, grinning wide. "But not all. Audrey Ford, light of my life, will you *please* come home with me tonight?"

I roll my eyes, but I'm chuckling. "Yes, I will. But only if you help me finish this article."

"I've never been more committed to anything," he says.

TWENTY-ONE

Carter

Audrey: I think I found a winner. Look at this one.

I click the apartment link she's sent me. It's a fourteen-room penthouse on the Upper East Side with a price tag in the hundreds of millions. It's also godawful, decorated with all-gold furniture and the tackiest of fountains in the hallway. I zoom in. Yes, that's a cherub in the center.

Great views, though.

Carter: Please tell me you're considering buying it furnished.

Audrey: Oh, of course. I wouldn't change a thing. I can see you lounging on the seashell-shaped sofa.

Carter: Naked, right?

Audrey: When I picture you it's always nude.

I laugh outright at that. The conversation devolves, like it often does, and I love it. The past week with Audrey has been one of the best of my life. She's stayed at mine nearly every night.

On Tuesday she had us cook fajitas together in my kitchen. From scratch, including making tortillas. Turned out she'd only done it once before, and the place was a battlefield by the time we were done, flour everywhere. I'd mostly focused on getting flour on the tip of her upturned nose, but all jobs are equally important.

Then we'd let a movie play while I fucked her slowly on the couch, my hand working her clit, until she shook in my arms with her orgasm.

Again, all jobs are equally important.

On Wednesday we'd both had to work late from home. She'd made us popcorn and coffee, and beneath the table, I'd had my hand on her bare knee. It had been intoxicating in how comfortable it was, how happy she made me. It was the true kind, not the fleeting exhilaration of winning a business deal or seeing my name in print.

She'd left my apartment earlier than me this morning, bashful about travelling in my car without me. As if she feared it was a nuisance instead of pleasing on a deep, molecular level, the same way I felt when I saw her wearing one of my T-shirts to bed or the scent of my shampoo in her hair.

Audrey: Good luck with your meeting today, by the way.

I answer her in the elevator on my way down.

Carter: Thanks. Let me know as soon as Booker gives you proper feedback on your article, okay?

Audrey: Promise. See you tonight.

Carter: Can't wait, kid.

It's the truth, too. Most of my waking hours spent apart from her feel wasted. I nod at John in the lobby and he gives me a grin back. They've noticed my new girlfriend, too, although none of the staff in the building have mentioned it.

I make it a few strides out of my building before I stop dead.

He's standing on the sidewalk. His hair is grayer than I'd seen it last, and the lines marking his face have deepened. He looks distinguished, but smaller than I remember.

His eyes are locked on mine. "Carter," he says. "It's good to see you."

I consider walking in the other direction. Leaving him and the past behind, where it can't hurt me or anyone anymore.

But my feet won't let me. "You're here," I say. Accusation makes my voice dark.

"Yes. Sorry for ambushing you like this, son. But you didn't leave me with many options."

"Not ambushing someone outside their house is always an option."

My father smiles, like we're old friends. "You're right. But I so wanted to see you. Will you let me buy you a coffee?"

I want to say *fuck no*. The words dance on my tongue in burning motions. But I also hear my mother's voice in my head, and Audrey's. *It's a chance to say your piece.*

And a chance to tell him to stay away from me and my mother.

"Yeah. Okay. There's a place up the street," I say.

"Won't take long," he says, falling into step beside me. "I know you're a busy man now. Big company and all."

A sour taste rises in my throat. "You've read about me?"

"It was one of my favorite things in prison," he says. "You know, they give us computer access. I'd read everything published about you. Your first deal, and when you merged Kingsley Investment with Acture Capital. Smart move, that. Did it sting to lose your name in the company title?"

Damn him.

"Yes," I admit.

"Figured it did." He chuckles, his voice pleased. "I know

my son. But it was necessary. Gave you the leverage you needed. You're making bank now."

So often, I'd heard him use terms like this, and as a kid I'd thought him the smartest man on Earth. Now I wonder if he really understands most of them at all. He was never interested in building businesses.

Only in stealing their assets.

"You're out of prison," I say. We've reached the coffee shop up the street, and I hold the door open for him. He steps inside and tugs off his leather gloves. How long had he waited outside my building?

"Yes," he says. "Six months now."

"Your wife must be glad."

He gives me a shrewd look. "She is," he admits, "and she isn't. It makes divorce proceedings a bit simpler."

We order two coffees, both black, and take a seat near the front. I don't take off my coat and beneath the table, I keep my leg bouncing to work off the adrenaline coursing through me. The anger is hot and heavy behind it.

Dad smiles widely. "So? How have you been?"

"You know how I've been if you've been following the news." I take a sip of the coffee. It burns. "Why did you want this meeting?"

He looks down into his cup. The edges of his mouth soften, like he's frowning. It's a look of contrition.

I don't trust it one bit.

"I did a lot of things I'm not proud of. More than you know, more than I'd mention. But one of the things I hate myself most for is what I did to your mother and you."

"Pretending to be married to her when you weren't," I say. "Pretending to work on holidays when you didn't."

He doesn't seem surprised by the acid in my voice. "Yes. All of that. And for going to prison, for disappearing from your life. For ever doing anything illegal to begin with."

"Mhm." I take another deep sip of my coffee. It feels like the only thing keeping me sane.

"I'm still your father," he says, "even if I screwed things up. And I did. But I'll be your father until the day I die, and I want... very much, Carter, to get a chance to prove to you that I'm a changed man."

I level him with a stare. I'm not nineteen anymore, green-eyed and naive. Not even twenty-five and hopeful. "You will never get a cent of my money," I say. "I will never invest in one of your start-ups, I will never call a high-powered friend on your behalf. Do you understand?"

"Yes. God, yes, that's not what I'm here for."

"I don't care if that's not what you're here for today. But one day, you'll think that thought, if you haven't in the past. And I need you to know that door is closed forever. It's fucking welded shut. Got it?"

"Closed door. Got it," he says, nodding slowly. His expression doesn't change. "You're right to say that to me. You're cleverer, you know, than your siblings."

I narrow my eyes. This isn't the path I wanted this conversation to take. Hell, I never wanted this conversation at all.

"They visited me in prison, did you know that? All three of them. They were angry too, of course, but they let me explain. You never did." Dad sounds almost proud of that fact, giving me a crooked grin. "We're the same, you and I, Carter."

"No. We are nothing alike."

He chuckles. "Think your drive is a coincidence? You have my ambition, kid, but the smarts to do it the legal way. You got those from your mother."

I shake my head. "I don't want to hear this."

He looks out at the line of smartly-clad people waiting for the cashier. All ready to go to work. "Jenny just got married. Did you know that? She waited until I was out, so I could walk her down the aisle."

Not what I want to hear. Not at all. Fury, mixed with sympathy, for that other family. How could they forgive him?

"Do they know about me? And Mom?"

Dad nods. "I told them everything a few years back. No more lies, Carter. Not to them and not to you. Never again."

"You're the best liar I've ever met."

"I am," he says. There's no shame or regret on his face. "But it's not worth it. It ruined my life, and hurt too many people I love."

Love. The thing he's never been capable of, I think, but I don't say it.

"William is a doctor now. He's two years older than you."

I put my cup down hard enough to rattle the table. "I don't want to know."

"All right, noted. In your own time," he says. "They're curious about you, though."

"You texted Mom," I say, my voice granite. Enough of this. "I never want you to contact her again."

Dad gives a slow nod. "I understand that. But we had a relationship aside from you, you know. She might want to—"

"Then you wait for her to reach out. She has your number. But you will never fucking wait outside her apartment like you did with me today. Do you get that? You do that, and I will never speak to you again until the day I die. And I fucking mean that. You don't mess with Mom again."

He leans back, eyes widening slightly. But he nods. "Understood," he says. "You're good to her."

"Not something I learned from you." I drain the rest of my coffee. This has already gone on for too long. "Look, I get that you're out of prison and ready to pick up the pieces of your old life. But we haven't been sitting around waiting for that. I have a life. Mom has a life. And we're both better without you in them."

Dad is still, eyes unreadable. "Okay. I understand."

"You lied to us every single day you were with us in New York. If not by your words, then by your actions," I say. "I thought my father was a brilliant travelling businessman. Turns out he was a cheat, and a liar, and a con artist."

"I was all of those things," he says. "And a father. I always treasured that role the most."

"I don't believe you." The word I don't add is *yet*. Maybe I will, one day. But opening myself up to this man again is so far in the future I'd need binoculars to see it.

"Thanks for speaking to me," Dad says. "Do you want me to—"

"Wait for me to contact you."

"Okay. I can do that."

I stand, ready to leave, when something strikes me. William and Jenny. He'd said the names of my half-siblings, the names I'd only seen once in a PI's file and been unable to forget. William, Jenny, and Sarah.

And me, Carter.

A terrible suspicion threads its way through me. I know so little of what he did when he was away... but none of it was good.

"Were you ever in Alrich? Around ten years ago? Must have been right before you went to prison."

His eyebrows rise, but he nods. "Yes."

"A dentist," I say quietly. "Two teenage kids. He trusted you with his pension and his kid's college funds."

Dad looks out the window for a moment. "Now that you mention it... yes. I met them. He's one of the many I need to make penance for. I had a scheme at the time, for dentists. Met a number of them upstate."

"You could give them their money back."

"I wish I could," he says. "But I have nothing left."

That, at least, I believe. His money management skills were always terrible.

I feel sick. "Will C. Jenner."

"Was that the alias I used in Alrich?"

He doesn't even remember. I nod, my breath coming fast. I want to punch him. I want to weep. Dad was the man who ruined Audrey's family, who forced her into student debt,

214

who rolled like a wrecking ball through her safe and loving home life with lies and deceit.

Dad chuckles a little. "That was a foolish, arrogant habit. I used to name myself after you kids. Different combinations, you know. That name had Will, for William, of course. C for Carter. Jenner for Jenny."

"You," I tell him, "are the worst man I've ever known."

He looks at me with eyes that are bottomless. They're as wise and ancient as they'd been when I was a kid, when I'd thought he knew everything. I wonder when he learned that trick. "I've been in prison, Carter," he says, "and I know there are men far worse than me."

"I'm sure," I say, "but none are my father. Don't contact me again."

"Carter..." he says, but I'm already reaching for the door. The New York air is cold and fresh, and I take deep breaths as I walk.

Audrey had always wanted to find the man who swindled her father. It makes me laugh, humorless and mad, to think I've found him for her. But if I tell her the truth, it might make me lose her altogether.

TWENTY-TWO

Audrey

"Look at it," Carter says, spreading out the newspaper on the kitchen table. "You're right there on the front page."

I push the pitcher of orange juice far out of reach. Nothing is allowed to spill on this Sunday edition. "Wow. Just... oh my God. I'll remember this moment forever."

Carter rests his head atop mine and we both stare down at the front page. "Your first lead article in the *Globe*."

The headline is printed in bold, serif letters, and below it is a picture of the bodega. The photographer had gotten down on his knees to get a shot of the construction cranes behind it. They're not related, but it paints a stark picture, especially with the accompanying headline. **City does nothing to stop illegal evictions of businesses.**

And beneath it: Written by Audrey Ford.

"It's a great piece," Carter says. "I read it last night before it went to print."

"Booker's additions made it stronger."

"They did. She knows what she's doing."

I lean back against him. He hasn't put on a shirt from his shower and his skin is warm. "No wonder she pushed it two weeks. Johnson's source from within the construction company really came through."

"It's a stronger piece for it," Carter says. "I also expect I'll get a call from the CEO of that construction company in about fifteen minutes."

My hand tightens around his wrist. "I didn't think about that."

He chuckles. "I don't mind. I've gotten a few calls since Acture bought the *Globe*, actually. Most are fun to fend off."

"Aren't people... angry?"

"Most who bother calling are," he says matter-of-factly. "When they thank us it's usually by email. But I like to remind those who are upset—and their lawyers—about the First Amendment."

I look up at him. From this angle, the tips of his eyelashes look almost golden. "Do they enjoy that?"

"No," he says, grinning. "But I do. Now, you and I have to go buy a dozen of these."

I nod, looking back down at the paper. "My parents will want one, and my grandparents too. I need to send a picture to my best friend. God, the longer I look at it, the crazier it seems."

"You've worked hard for it."

"Yes, but still... And I know I have a long way left to go. Booker said my writing style was solid, but too melodramatic." I shake my head. "She's probably right, too."

"So you'll continue to refine. That's life." He kisses the top of my head. "What solo investigative piece will be your next?"

I dig my teeth into my lower lip. "Maybe it's a long shot, but I was thinking of finally doing that piece on con artists."

"Oh," Carter says. "Do you mean... trying to find the man who swindled your dad?"

His concern, the tentative note in his voice, makes me smile. The memory doesn't hurt me anymore. It angers me instead, on my parents' behalf, and all the others who were affected. "Yes," I say, "but I realize that's a long shot. I'll keep trying, though. But the personal connection would be an inroad to a larger piece on con artists in the state, or across the country. Their methods, their victims, that sort of thing."

"Right." Carter slides his hands off my waist and heads to the coffee machine. "A refill?"

"Yes, please. Thanks." I sit down at his kitchen table and smooth a hand over the newspaper. It still doesn't feel real. "Do you know, I think this is one of the best days of my life."

"Let's see if we can keep it going," he says. But he doesn't rejoin me at the table. He's leaning against the counter instead, hand gripping the coffee cup.

I pull my legs up beneath his large T-shirt. "Carter?"

"Yes?"

"I spoke to my parents last night," I say, trying not to smile. "And I might have told them about you."

He looks down into his coffee, his lips curving. "Did you now?"

"Yes."

"What did you say?"

"That I have a boyfriend. That it's very early yet, but that he's great to me. He treats me really well."

Carter's smiling fully now. "He attempts to, you know. Always."

"He succeeds most of the time." I untangle my legs and cross the space to him, forcing him to put down his coffee. My hands curl around his neck. "I told them he's smart, and capable, and funny. And one of the most infuriating men I've ever met."

"Infuriating?" Carter repeats. He's gripping my waist, a thumb smoothing over my hipbone.

"Yes, but that's okay, because I love arguing with him over what movie to watch or the best way to drink coffee."

"I'm right about the coffee thing."

"I'll let you think you're right about the coffee thing," I say. My heart feels light inside my chest, so airy it might float away. "They were very happy about it."

"Were they?" he murmurs. His eyes are locked on my hip,

where his hand is smoothing its way beneath the cotton of the T-shirt.

"Mhm."

"They asked how we met."

His voice is low. "What did you tell them?"

"The truth. Dad laughed, and Mom said you were heroic."

"Heroic," Carter repeats softly. "I'd like the chance to meet them one day. They must be pretty amazing, if they raised you."

"Open with that line and they'll love you."

He smiles crookedly. "I'll take your word for it."

"You're a charmer, and you'll charm them just as thoroughly as you've charmed me."

Carter looks back down at my body. "It's what I do best," he says.

I frown at the tone in his voice. "Well, not only, of course. You're also sweet, and intelligent, and funny, and strong, and capable, and—"

He stops me with a kiss. "Are you trying to tell me you like me, kid?"

"Yes. Glad you got that."

"Message received loud and clear." He pulls me in closer, my hips against his. But I still have one more question.

"What are we going to do about work?"

He rests his head against my shoulder, soft hair tickling my neck. "What about it?"

"Since you and I are in a relationship…"

"We very much are," he confirms against my skin. His hands tighten on my hips. "I'm never letting you go."

I smile against his cheek. "So we're in a committed relationship. But you're also my boss's boss's boss, and we can't have people at work knowing. Does that mean we'll be sneaking around indefinitely?"

It seems like an impossible riddle to answer.

"Not forever," Carter says. His voice is confident.

"Okay," I murmur, "but how will that work? I really like

my job, and I happen to really like my boyfriend too. I don't want to give either of them up."

"Happy to hear it," he says, grinning crookedly.

I laugh. "You're enjoying this."

"Hearing you say over and over again that you like me? Yeah, I am."

"Carter," I complain.

His hands settle more firmly around my waist. "We'll figure it out, kid. I'll never do anything to jeopardize your job."

"I know that. But you just took over the newspaper. And you have grand plans for it, and I definitely *don't* want you to sell it."

"I might have gathered that, too, yes."

"So we're at an impasse."

Carter's arms flex beneath my hands and he lifts me up, depositing me on the kitchen counter. Leisurely, as befits the Sunday morning we're enjoying, he reaches for the hem of my T-shirt. I let him peel it off me—his own shirt, really—and toss it behind him. It lands halfway in the sink.

"I don't see an impasse," he says, eyes moving in heated circles across my face, hair, stomach, chest. "I only see perfection."

"Carter…"

He steps closer between my splayed thighs and I lock them at his hips. A problem we may have, but I'm not ready to give either of my two passions up. Nothing will stop me from having him—or my career.

"I won't be running the *Globe* forever," he says. "You know, Tristan stepped down from running Exciteur when he met Freddie."

"She worked at the company?"

"She was a trainee when they met."

I grimace. "Ouch."

"It was tough, but they're perfect for one another. She's

got a great head for business too. Anyway, he stepped down when they got serious."

I trace the outline of his bare abs. "He stepped down? From the position of CEO?"

Carter nods. His hands are moving over my bare back, down to the lace edge of my panties and up again. The man is a damn fine multitasker, I'll give him that.

"Yes. It's an option here too," he says.

I shake my head. "You worked for years to buy the *Globe*. Didn't you tell me about all the preparation you did, to learn about the industry?"

"You're more important."

"You're not giving up your career," I say, "and neither am I."

His lip quirks. "I could step down nominally."

"Nominally," I repeat.

"Yes. Let's say we sneak around for a year. After that, I could hand over the reins to a board. Acture would still be the owner. But my face wouldn't be visible in day-to-day operations."

"Could work," I murmur, "but you know those investigative reporters…"

"They'll be investigating. I know," he agrees. "Ultimately, I'll do whatever you want, kid. But I will let you know right now that I can't wait for the day you'll be my date to all those boring events I'm forced to endure. I want you on my arm, always."

"If we go to the Reporters' Balls," I say, "then it's a deal."

He groans, but he's smiling. "I can't compete with the Dean Allens of this world, can I?

"Spend a year in a war zone or win a Pulitzer, and you might."

"I'll forever be in his illustrious shadow." His gaze drops to my breasts, where a large hand is teasing my nipple. "But he doesn't get to do this, and I do, so he can keep all his damn Pulitzers."

He tweaks it hard and my breath catches. The pleasure-pain radiates out through my body, and I grip his hips tighter with my thighs. "I'm all yours," I say.

"I contacted him, actually. About freelancing for the *Globe*."

I grip his shoulders. "What?!"

Carter half-smiles. "Yes. Remember this, too, the next time you're angry at me."

"You're *hiring?*"

"I'm pouring more funds into Investigative, yes. The newsroom is what'll sell papers. That and the damn news app with the advertising algorithm."

"Oh my God." I hug Carter tight, and he laughs, the sound rumbling through his bare chest. "I like you, I like you, I like you so so so much…"

He laughs again and finds the backs of my knees. With a faint grunt, he lifts me boldly off the counter and strides in the direction of his bedroom. "My beautiful, front-page featuring, Dean Allen-fangirling, award-winning girlfriend," he says. "Your parents aren't the only ones curious about this new relationship."

He tosses me on his bed, still unmade from last night. I crawl backwards up toward the pillows. "They're not?"

"No." He climbs after me. "I'm meeting my mother for lunch next weekend. Come with me."

"To meet her?"

"No, to take notes. *Yes*, of course to meet her."

I laugh again, but it's quickly stopped by his heavy weight on top of me. He feels delicious, and so right, fitting between my thighs. The fabric of our underwear does nothing to hide the hard length of him.

"Will you?" he asks, mouth at my neck.

I run my hands down his broad back. Weights, I've learned, and swimming. I've seen him lift now.

This is important for him, just like telling my parents

about him was important for me. My entire body feels like it's a live wire. *I think I love him.*

"I'd love to meet her."

His mouth trails across my chest and toward the hard peak of my nipple. We have breakfast prepared in his kitchen. Orange juice, coffee, bagels. And I couldn't care less. The wonder of him, I've found, is that he does exactly what he wants, when he wants, and always expects me to do the same.

It's liberating.

"You drive me insane," he whispers against the lace edge of my panties. His hands have already hooked around the fabric, and his golden eyes are locked on the skin he's slowly unveiling.

I know what he's planning... and he's gotten dangerously good at it. Perhaps it's knowing how much he enjoys it that lets me give in entirely.

"Carter," I murmur.

He grins up at me and bends his auburn head to the spot between my thighs. It's a long time later, and one slow, trembling orgasm, when he finally eases inside of me. He's hard and thick and when he's fully seated, I can feel him throbbing inside.

He mutters against my neck. "Christ," he says, and I can feel him shaking.

"You don't have to go slow."

He groans and speeds up, hips thrusting in deep strokes that send the padded headboard of his bed against the wall in rhythmic beats. I brace a hand against it and keep the other on his broad back.

Nothing is like this. Feeling him inside me, on top of me, holding me. Breathless kisses and heady pleasure, feeling his heart beat and knowing there is no way, never could be, to be closer to another person than this.

I love you, I think with every roll of his hips. *I love you I love you I love you.*

I wrap my hands around his biceps, hard as stone from holding up his body weight, and find the curve of his ear with my lips. "I'm so happy I met you," I whisper. "You're everything I wanted, and so much more I didn't know I did."

He groans. It's a low and hoarse sound, deep from his chest. I feel the spasms inside as he orgasms and I clasp him close to me the entire time. Legs and arms and heart, all holding him.

"Fuck," he says weakly and buries his head against my neck. "I don't know what I'd do if you ever left me."

I smile, too dazed and tired to think, and run my nails up his back. "Luckily I have no plans to do that."

I expect his laughter to rumble through his chest and into me. He loves joking in bed. Once, he said having sex with me felt even better while I was laughing, because of the tremors. But that might have been a joke, too. It had definitely made me laugh, at any rate.

Carter doesn't, though. He kisses me instead, languid and lazy. He's still moving gently inside me, and I can feel him in every cell of my body. "Promise me you never will," he murmurs.

That's easy. "Never," I say.

TWENTY-THREE

Audrey

"He thought he could talk his way out of anything," Susan says fondly. She's searching through a drawer in a closet, tucked into the corner of the room that was once Carter's. It's a guest room and sewing room now, for when her sister visits or—as she tells me—when the muse strikes.

I smile at the back of her head. In some ways she's much like Carter, but she's different, too. Quieter, but with a strength that's clear in her eyes. She keeps working as a teacher because she loves it. 'Not,' as she'd said, 'because my son is too stingy to help me retire early.'

"Mom," he'd protested. Seeing them together was fascinating. Watching him interact with someone who saw right through the bluster and the jokes.

"I don't want Audrey to think you don't take care of me," she'd fired right back. "Because he does."

Now she's searching for old photo albums, and the son and boyfriend in question is downstairs hunting for the super. The water pressure is off, apparently.

It looked okay to me. Weak, perhaps, but normal. But Carter had been decisive. Susan had agreed, in the tone of someone who'll cede the battle to win the war, and had sent me a little wink.

He's overprotective of her too, it seems.

"He was too clever for his own good," she continues, head inside the closet. "There were times, in school, where my colleagues asked me if I'd given him the answers in advance for tests. He didn't like to study, you know, but he'd get it right anyway."

"That sounds like him. Irritatingly good at a lot of things."

Susan laughs. "Yes, that's the best way to describe it. Oh, here we are. I have to show you… he was the cutest kid."

"I'd love to see," I say honestly. Because I can't imagine Carter ever as a kid, without the air of supreme confidence he carries around him like a shield now.

She carries a heavy, bound album to the guest bed and gestures for me to join her. The first page she opens to has pictures of the Bronx Zoo… and Carter as an eight-year-old.

"He wanted pictures in front of all the animal exhibits," she says. "That's him and the chimps, him and the meerkats, him and the tigers. They wouldn't show themselves, so I had to take a picture of him next to the sign."

I smile down at the image of my boyfriend, so much younger, with a wide grin at the camera. It looks entirely unguarded. A thick mop of hair, a lighter shade of auburn than it is now, hangs down over his eyes. He looks gangly, legs just starting to shoot up.

"He loved animals?"

"Back then, yeah, he sure did." She flips a few pages forward. "There's one where he's fallen asleep in front of Animal Planet… let me find it. Oh, no. Look at this one. His tenth birthday."

I look down at a picture of a group of people, all watching Carter on the ground. He's sitting behind a mountain of gifts in bright colors. I spot a younger Susan standing behind him. Other adults mill around, and a group of children run in the background, their forms blurry.

But it's the man in the corner my eyes land on.

He's wearing a well-pressed suit. Thick, dark hair is swept back over heavy brows. The charming smile is familiar. Too familiar. He looks down at Carter with a proud expression. Even in the picture, he frightens me.

There's something too *clean* about him.

It's a younger image of Will C. Jenner. The man I've been looking for over a decade for.

Susan has noticed my zeroed-in attention. "Ah," she says softly. "That's Carter's dad. Has he told you about him?"

I can't find my voice, so I nod instead. It's a tiny movement.

The man who ruined my father's life is my boyfriend's dad. It would be funny, if this was a sitcom, a farce, a romantic comedy. Now it just makes me want to cry and scream at the same time.

Susan sighs. "It's not a pretty story. But it is our story, and I'm not afraid to tell it anymore. He was a complicated man. Brilliant, in some ways, and he gave me my son. But I can't say that he was good."

"No," I say quietly. "Carter told me about him."

"He's always been harsher on his father than I have been. Not that I wasn't angry too," she says. "But it's faded. I don't think Carter's has. He's reached out now, and I've told him it might be a good idea to meet him... just to clear the air, you know? To have the chance to say his piece." The smile she gives me is soft. A bit shy, perhaps, and encouraging. "My son told me you'd said the same thing."

I feel sick. "Yeah, I did."

"We'll see if he listens," Susan says, turning the page, taking the image of Will Jenner away with it. "But Carter isn't quick to forgive when someone wrongs him."

The revelation shakes the ground beneath me. The truth, at last. And it's not at all what I wanted and miles from what I expected.

Carter returns to the apartment like a conquering hero,

water pressure sorted. *The super told me he'll fix it within the hour.* No problem is too small or too large for him to solve, it seems. Had he charmed the super too? Used that wide, crooked smile, his powers of persuasion, or promises of money or bribes? I'd seen him do it before. I'd watched his father use it in a different way.

I can't stop seeing the two of them. The similarities.

When we leave Susan's, the unease has settled into a pit of despair in my stomach. I can't keep this a secret. I have to talk about it, but I have no idea what to say or where to start.

Carter takes my hand in his. He lifts it to his lips and presses a kiss to the back. "Thank you for coming with me."

"My pleasure," I say.

"Remember our first non-date? The pizza place across the street?"

"Yes. After my date stood me up."

"Worst mistake of his life, but I'm eternally grateful," Carter says. "Let's get pizza again. Eat it on your fire escape. Who knows how long you'll have the place?"

My chest feels tight, and breathing is difficult. Thinking is difficult. I shake my head slowly. "I can't. Carter..."

"Yes?"

"Oh my God. I don't know where to start. I..."

Troubled, golden eyes meet mine. There's concern in them. "No pizza," he says firmly. "Come, let's go to yours. Do you feel faint?"

"Yes," I say, but not in the way he means. *Will C. Jenner,* I think. *I love the son of the man who took everything from my family.*

Carter keeps a hand on my back, and he's the one who unlocks the door to Old Man Pierce's house. The familiar smell of mildew and mold hits us. We walk the creaky steps in silence. The words feel heavy on my tongue. I don't know how he'll react. Will it make him hate his father even more? Feel... shame, anger, hurt? It's not his favorite topic.

It's never been mine either.

"Honey, what's wrong?" Carter says. He closes the door to my room behind us. He's never called me *honey* before. It's always been kid or spitfire or sometimes Audrey, and to my surprise, the endearment make my eyes tear up.

There's alarm in his eyes now. "Did something happen?"

"Yes. I don't know how to tell you this."

"You can tell me anything. Don't cry, kid. Please. Come here." He locks his arms around me and I bury my face in his chest. "Tell me," he says softly.

My words come out muffled. "Your mother showed me old pictures of you when you were a kid."

His arms tense around me. "The old photo albums?"

"Yes. And I saw… I saw…" My breath is spiralling out of control.

"Shit," he says quietly, troubled eyes meeting mine. "Tell me what you saw."

But it's there in his eyes. The suspicion. The knowledge. "You already know?"

"Tell me what you saw," he repeats.

I shake my head and step back. "You know. Don't you? I saw a picture of your father."

Carter's eyes drift closed, like he can't look at me. There's pain on his face. "Fuck," he mutters.

"He's Will C. Jenner. The man who swindled my father, who sat at our dinner table, who joked with my brother and asked me about my college plans. Who made my dad feel two inches tall after he left with all the money he'd charmed his way into." I feel like sobbing, and I feel like screaming. "Why aren't you surprised? Did you know?"

"Yes. Audrey, I never—"

"How long?"

He looks pained. "Don't focus on that."

"How long did you know he was the same man? The man I've been looking for for years?"

"About a month," he says.

The admission goes off like a bomb in my head. A month. *A month.* He'd known, when I'd pitched him my con-artist investigative piece. He'd known, and he'd taken me out to dinner, and laughed at my jokes, and made love to me all the same.

He hadn't trusted me with the truth.

I back away until I hit the wall, feeling like I can't breathe. Good thing there's solid plaster behind me, or I wouldn't be upright.

Carter steps closer, and all I can make out are the sudden similarities. The heavy brows. The wide, charming mouth. The thick hair.

"Were you ever going to tell me?" I ask.

He falters, and in the pause, I hear the reply loud enough to rattle my bones. *No.* "I was planning to," he says.

"No," I whisper. "You weren't. Not really. Can't you at least admit that?"

"Audrey," he says, and there's heartbreak in his eyes. Like I'm the one hurting him.

"Oh my God. I can't believe you wouldn't tell me the second you found out."

His voice strengthens. Snaps into business-mode, solution-mode. "How much did my father swindle off yours?"

"What?"

"How much? I'll pay it all back. Every last cent."

I stare at him. "This isn't something you can fix with money. Especially not your money," I say. If there's *one* person who shouldn't pay for Will C. Jenner's mistakes, it's his son.

But Carter steps back like I've insulted him. "Audrey," he says, voice hoarse. "I can't have my father's dealings ruin this. Ruin us."

I close my eyes. I don't want that either, but right now, the only thing I can think is that he wasn't going to tell me. He was planning on going his whole life knowing, and not telling me.

"I want you to leave," I whisper. "Please, Carter. I need to be alone."

He doesn't say another word. He just closes the door softly on the way out, footsteps disappearing down the steps beyond, and I sink slowly to the floor.

TWENTY-FOUR

Audrey

It's been a week.

One long week since I learned the truth, since Carter walked out of my apartment. Since I *asked* him to leave me alone. A week since the funny, annoying, sweet, soft texts stopped.

He'd known. It's difficult to wrap my head around. He'd known and not told me, even after we'd had the discussion about honesty. The betrayal stings like salt in a wound.

Booker's voice booms through the newsroom. "Decker, Johnson, Peters and Kim. I want your stories on my desk by the end of the day. Feel free to use the juniors if needed!"

"Yes, boss!" someone calls back.

Declan snickers beside me. "Use the juniors," he repeats.

Grunt work is exactly what it sounds like, but I don't mind it. Working with the seasoned journalists is sometimes a pain in the ass. Decker is especially finicky, and Peters doesn't tolerate criticism from a junior colleague, but I'm learning a lot.

I'm still loving my job… even if I've hated coming here every single day this week. The knowledge that Carter is only a few floors above me feels like torture. A part of me wishes I'd never found out. Which means his plan of never telling me wasn't the worst one, and I hate that part of me, too.

I hate that I don't know my own mind where I've always been able to trust it before. And I also hate that he knew and didn't tell me. It makes me feel sidestepped. Neglected. Patronized.

But most of all, I miss him so much it hurts.

The only thing that helps is focusing on work, even when my focus drifts in and out of view. The paper I'm researching for now is about the rise of remote work. Interesting enough, even if my mind is filled with Carter.

Kim stops by Declan's desk. I catch snippets of their hushed conversation, until I'm fully eavesdropping.

"…going on for over half a year."

"Not that long?"

"Started at the Christmas party, apparently."

"That's insane. I understand why he did it, but why would she risk her position?"

Declan's voice is filled with glee at the gossip. "Nate's hot. She probably gambled no one would find out."

"HR is involved, last I heard," Kim says. "Nate could lose his job."

"So much for sleeping with a superior. Didn't land him the promotion, did it?"

Kim and Declan both chuckle. They fall quiet as Booker breezes past and quickly disperse. It's not the first I've heard of this particular piece of company gossip, and I'm sure it won't be the last.

But it's the first time it sends a shiver of fear down my spine.

Didn't land him the promotion, did it?

That's what Declan would say about me and Carter, if he knew. What everyone would say. I put my head in my hands, and for the first time since I started at the *Globe*, I feel like crying.

I love him, I think. *And it hurts so much.*

By afternoon the newsroom is half-empty, and I'm at my wit's end. I grab a bunch of files at random and head toward the stairs. No one uses them, and luck of all luck, I don't meet anyone.

Tim is sitting at his desk outside the executive offices. I pray Carter's in. "Dropping off some more papers from the newsroom," I say. "As requested."

He doesn't even bat an eye. We must have sold it well the last time I snuck up here, for Carter's birthday.

"Head on in," Tim says.

Carter is not expecting me, that much is clear from his gaze, widening with surprise before it settles into a golden wariness. He doesn't know what I'm here to say.

That makes two of us.

"Hey," he says, and steps past me to close the door to his office. "Everything okay?"

"Yeah. Yes, I mean. How have you been?"

"This past week?" He leans against his desk, crossing strong arms over his chest. The need to touch him aches in my fingertips. "Not great, kid."

"Me neither," I say. My throat is thick and words come out shaky. "What are we really doing here, you know?"

His eyes are those of a hawk. "What do you mean?"

"It'll only be a matter of time before people at work find out. And if we can't trust one another... if I can't trust you..." I shake my head, eyes blurring. "Maybe it's better if we stop this now. We'll never figure things out with the work situation, will we?"

He's so still he might as well be a statue. Frozen to ice before me, Carter's grin is nowhere to be seen. His eyes are so cold they burn. "Okay," he says slowly. "If that's what you want."

No, I think. *That's not what I want at all.* My heart feels like it's frosting over, something fracturing deep within. But I don't know if I can trust him... and I need this pain to go away.

"I don't know why you didn't tell me," I whisper.

He closes his eyes. "You're giving up on us. You haven't sent me a single text this week, kid. Not one."

"I needed time to think."

"And this is what you've settled on." His eyes open, and there's nothing detached about them now. They blaze. "If you think it's easier to just end this, then fine. Let's end it."

A tear spills over and races down my cheek. Carter walks around his desk and sits down. Like I'm not here, like I'm not hurting. Like he's not hurting.

I love you, I think again. *Don't you care at all?*

Where is the man I've come to care for? Who held me on a fire escape, who asked me for permission to ask me out, who is funny and intelligent and never backs down from an argument?

"Okay," I say. "All right. I… well. Here are some papers from the copy machine downstairs." I set them down on the edge of his desk, feeling worthless. "It was just an excuse to come up here, but I can't leave…"

Without dropping them off. But the words are caught in my throat, stuck in the ball of tears.

"Got it. Just leave them here."

Right. I retreat to the door, my hand shaking at my side. Why is he like this? "Can I call you in a week or two?" I manage. "After we've both had time to think?"

Because this can't be the last time we talk about this.

"Sure," he says. His gaze flows from me to his screen, like I'm nothing. "Sounds good."

I leave his office without looking at Tim, and in the stairwell, my tears turn into muffled sobs.

TWENTY-FIVE

Carter

Another week passes without a text or call from Audrey. Another week, in other words, with time to mull over her fucking words. She'd used *we might as well* and *how about we* like it was some sort of mutual decision. Like she hadn't already made it and was now forcing me to live with the consequences.

I was furious with her at first, for focusing on what my father did, when that was never my crime. How long can I pay for what he did? Then I was furious at my father, again, and for an entirely new reason. For *still*, almost a decade later, fucking up my life and ruining one of the best things I've ever had.

For changing the way she looked at me.

And finally… me. I swirl the brandy around in my glass and keep my gaze on the amber liquid, away from the eyes of anyone who might want to small talk. Now I'm finally furious with myself for letting her walk out of that office.

For not taking the fight.

But it had hurt like a damn freight train to hear her give up. To hear the pain in her voice, and *still* have her make that decision. Lead me toward it like she was a guidance counselor. Like it wasn't even worth an argument.

People claim to love me, and then they leave.

The brandy burns going down and I enjoy every painful second of it.

"You look happy," a voice says at my side. Calm, collected, an undertone of concerned sarcasm. He's using his dad voice on me.

I turn to Tristan. "My drink's empty."

He gives a thoughtful nod and leans against the wall beside me. We both look out at the mingling group of people filling the inn. Anthony and Summer, Cecilia and Victor, mother-in-laws and aunts and uncles. Freddie is sitting in the center, holding court. There's no sign of a bump yet.

Tristan must be ecstatic. For the first time, I hate him a little bit for it. For the unconditional love she gives him.

"You're staring," he says softly. "Want to tell me what you're thinking about?"

Fuck it. I throw my pride to the wind. "How did you get her to love you? Without leaving when she found out about your flaws?"

Tristan's lips quirk. "You're assuming I have flaws, Kingsley."

"Be straight with me."

He raises an eyebrow. "Is this about Audrey and why she's not here?"

"I asked you a question first."

"So that's a yes," he says. "Okay then. I have tons of flaws, as does my wife, you know. Everyone does. But if you love someone, that's insignificant in contrast."

"Yes, but how did she overlook yours?"

"She loves me too," he says. "For some goddamn reason, and I'll never stop being grateful for it, or trying to deserve her. But why don't we start at the root of this? Tell me what happened with Audrey first."

I narrow my eyes at him, but he just gazes serenely back at me. Unshakeable, this man. Always has been.

So I set down my glass and turn to him. "Fine. So, my

dad's a piece of shit."

"Not where I expected you to start," Tristan says. "But go on."

I tell him the whole story in a few abbreviated sentences. About my father, about her family, and my own decision to keep it from her. It sounds ugly spoken out loud, and I know even without admitting it that I don't come off good. Not in any part of it.

"And then she left," I finish. "She decided it would be easier if we just ended it."

Tristan nods. "I see. And did you want her to run?"

"What? No."

"Maybe not consciously, but did it feel safer when she did? Rather than telling her the honest-to-God-truth."

"The truth," I say. "And what would that be?"

"That you were terrified of telling her the truth because you suspected she'd leave you," he says. "Like your father did. So you didn't, but she found out, and now she's left you anyway. Just like you secretly predicted. Confirms your story, doesn't it?"

"Fuck you," I say quietly, and mean it.

Tristan's eyes soften. "It's not easy to hear any of this stuff. I know, Kingsley. Trust me. But from the look on your face... you want her back."

I look out the window at the falling leaves outside. This is a charming little city. I wish Audrey would be here to see it, too. "Yes," I admit. "More than anything."

"Perhaps she came up to your office hoping you would convince her to stay, you know. Hoping you'd tell her that everything would be okay? Perhaps even wanting you to apologize?"

I groan. "I didn't do any of those things."

"No." Tristan's voice is tinged with faint hesitation when he speaks again, like he knows he might be overstepping but won't stop. "You were already protecting yourself, I'm guessing. Had your wall all the way up?"

I close my eyes. *Idiot*, I think. She was right there, and with her soft eyes on mine, asking me to reassure, to apologize, to fight. And I'd been too busy wallowing in my own feelings to see any of it.

"I'll never forgive myself," I say.

"Well, that's a bit harsh," Tristan says. "I saw how the two of you looked at the dinner a few weeks ago. Do you really think it's too late?"

"It better not be," I say. "God, when can I leave this thing?"

He laughs. "I think you have to stay until after the ceremony, at least."

"Fuck the ceremony. They're already married."

"Get out of here first thing tomorrow morning," Tristan says, putting a hand on my shoulder. "Be honest with her about why you reacted the way you did. That's the secret, you know. To me and Freddie. We're honest, even when it's terrible."

"Couldn't the secret just be to have a lot of really great fucking sex?" I mutter. "Because I could work with that."

Tristan chuckles again, looking over his shoulder. But we're out of earshot. "That helps too," he tells me.

It feels like an age later until we're finally all seated outdoors, beneath the shade of an oak with rapidly falling leaves. The water across the pond ripples gently with the wind. A sunny day, as opposed to yesterday's rain. They've chosen well.

Audrey would have enjoyed it. She'd comment on things I don't notice, like the silkiness of the chair coverings or how pretty the sunlight is through the leaves. I'd take her hand, and look at Victor standing there, waiting for Cecilia to join him.

Wondering how I'd feel in his place. Waiting for the woman next to me to promise to love me forever.

But she's not here, and the absence is like a lost limb, a disease, an ache. Beside me is Summer, and Anthony to her right. From the corner of my eye I can see their tightly clasped hands.

Their wedding is coming up, too.

I used to roll my eyes at my friends' obsession with marital bliss. The joke doesn't seem quite as funny now, when I'd rather be the punchline than the joker.

A single violinist starts to play, a soft, warm sound. Everyone turns in their seats to watch Cecilia... but I look at Victor. He's in a tux, hands relaxed at his side. Watching his wife walk down the aisle to him.

And beneath his composure, he's burning with emotion.

I see it in his eyes. They're locked on her. We might as well not be here for all he cares. It's not even that he'd prefer it... but he doesn't care. Because he's focused on her and her alone. We don't exist.

This man, who I've argued with time and time again. The competitive bastard who loves to find weaknesses and exploit them, who has never seen a business he couldn't make more efficient, who is a far bigger proponent of layoffs than I've ever been.

He's standing here with love shining in his eyes.

If Victor St. Clair can change for Cecilia and embrace vulnerability, then I can't do anything less for Audrey. I'll be nothing short of what she deserves.

I watch them renew their vows. Eyes locked on one another, a silent conversation flowing beneath their softly spoken words. Audrey might not be mine, but by God am I hers. The need to talk to her is a bone-deep ache. For so many years, convincing people had been my job. I'd used my charm in more ways than I care to count. Some I'm proud of and many I'm not.

This time is different.

I'm going to have to be one hundred percent myself, and even that might not be enough. But I'm not going to run anymore.

TWENTY-SIX

Audrey

The landscape flashes outside the train window, mile after mile of distance added between me and my family. Returning to the city is always a mixed bag. Exciting, with the lure of New York and my life there. The job I've dreamed of forever. And sad, because it's a renunciation of my home, my past, my little hometown and the street I spent the first eighteen years of my life on. Safety and adventure, and always the balance between the two.

I feel it more acutely now than I have in years.

It's been a week since I heard from Carter. The disastrous conversation in his office has been on replay in my head. I've tried to analyze every angle. To find the point where it derailed. He'd been impossible to talk to. Shut off somehow.

And in my head, the only thing in my mind had been how he'd kept the truth from me. *He didn't tell me, he didn't tell me, he didn't tell me.*

But in the week since, that refrain has changed, the words shifted around. I miss him so much he's like a song beneath my own singing. *I love him, I love him, I love him.*

And I never got a chance to tell him that.

The conversation I'd had with my dad helped, soothing the jagged edges of my hurt. He'd been the true victim of Will

C. Jenner, after all, him and my mother. Just money, sure, but it had always been his pride and self-esteem that took the worst hit.

Maybe that's why I've had such a tough time wrapping my head around Carter's father being the same person who hurt my dad, the best man I've ever known.

We took a walk in the woods behind our neighborhood with my parents' black Labrador patrolling the leaves beside us. "Is a person more than their parents?" I'd asked.

Dad answered immediately. "Of course they are, sweetie. You're more than Mom and me."

"But what I mean is… are they more than their parents' worst actions?"

He'd laughed. "God, yes. What's all this?"

I'd taken a deep breath. Wondered if this was wise, and then throwing caution to the wind, trusting him the same way I had when he taught me to swim, to ride a bike, I told him the entire story.

I told him who Carter's dad was.

Dad had listened with patience. He'd asked a few cautious questions here and there, about the timeline. *No, I haven't met him. Never, ever want to.*

"Poor boy," he said finally, when my words ran out, and we both watched Nibbles dig industrially behind a tree stump. "I can't imagine having that man in my life permanently. Being his son… Christ."

"They have virtually no contact, at Carter's insistence."

"Good decision," Dad had said. He looked over at me with a half-smile. "This has thrown you for a loop, hasn't it?"

"Yes. How could it not have? I mean, what he did—what happened—I don't know if… How could I?"

It was half-coherent at best, but Dad's smile had only grown deeper. Like he heard the real issue immediately. "If you're worried about me, don't be. This man is not his father. You wouldn't be with him if he was. All I care about is that he makes you happy, and treats you well."

"He has, and he does. He just didn't tell me about this."

"Have you asked him why?"

"He shut down."

Dad made a hmming noise and whistled for Nibbles, who'd followed a scent trail nearly out of view. "I'm guessing he was scared. He's been defined by his dad's actions all his life, hasn't he? And now it has once again interfered."

"You're wise," I said.

He'd laughed. "I don't know about that, but I've been around the block a few times, sweetheart."

"How can you be so... forgiving about this? We've never spoken much about what happened in the years since. Have you gotten over it? What the con man did?"

He paused, and when he spoke again, his voice was quiet. "I won't tell you that I've stopped regretting it," he said. "I don't think I ever will. But, sweetheart... Will Jenner came to me with nothing but cynicism and greed, masked in charm. I met him with hope. Naively, perhaps. Foolheartedly. What he was selling me was too good to be true. But I'd rather be too hopeful than too cynical, and if I know you, you would be too."

The words had lodged like a hot stone beneath my breastbone. I carry them even now, a day after, on the train transporting me back to New York. *I'd rather be too hopeful than too cynical.* Maybe I'd lost that thinking for a while, stuck in my dream of investigating corruption and fraud, righting wrongs and exposing secrets with my journalism.

Too hopeful than too cynical.

I don't know what'll happen. If Carter even wants to talk to me again, if that bridge is burned, if I'm back to bad first dates and nursing a broken heart. But I carry Dad's words with me like a token.

The city is cold and empty when I arrive at the station. I lug my too-heavy bag with me on the subway. Mom had insisted on baking bread, two whole loaves, and packing them in with my clothes.

I round the street to mine. The familiar stoop beckons, and I can't wait to collapse on my too-small bed in my too-small shithole of an apartment. Work starts tomorrow again, and the idea of seeing Carter from a distance is painful.

Something I'll have to get used to, I suppose.

There's a figure sitting on my stoop. I slow down. There are plenty of weirdos in the city. Should I just keep walking and circle back? No, that coat looks nice... and the hair is familiar.

Carter is sitting outside my house.

My bag slips through my fingers, landing with a soft thud on the wet sidewalk.

Carter notices. He rises fluidly off the steps, lengthening to his full height. He stretches out a leg like he's been sitting there for a long time.

"Hi," I whisper.

"Hey, kid," he says quietly. "Sorry to ambush you like this. I'll leave if you don't want to see me."

My hair is unwashed and in a low ponytail, and I don't have a drop of makeup on. My feet hurt and I'm tired. And there's absolutely no way I'd tell him to go.

"Don't," I say. "How long have you been sitting here?"

"Too long," he admits. "Pierce came outside and asked me if I wanted to wait up in your room. Which, by the way, is another reason why—no. Never mind."

A slow smile spreads across my face. "Were you about to tell me to install that lock you got me?"

"No," he says, looking sheepish. "Move out, actually."

"Going for the throat immediately."

He shakes his head. "No. I'm sorry. Not what I'm here for."

I swallow. "What are you here for?"

"I was wondering... would you be okay if I asked you to go to the pizza place with me? To talk to me? Please, kid, let me explain myself."

"Will I get a week to think about it, like last time?" I ask with a smile. Back when he'd asked me out on that almost-date, giving me ample time to back out, to consider how wise it is—or isn't—to date my boss.

Carter shoves his hands in his pockets. It's so good to see him, the familiar face, the sharp cut of his jaw, the sudden hesitation in his eyes. He doesn't want to say yes. But he does. "Of course," he says. "Whatever time you need."

"Just let me drop off my bag upstairs, okay? I'll be right down."

"Of course, yeah. I'll wait."

My heart is beating fast as I burst into my room, and it's not just from running up the stairs. I pull a brush through my hair and change my top before rushing back down.

He's where I left him. No change, and no longer the distant, cold figure he'd been in his office. We walk toward the restaurant in silence.

"I'm nervous," I admit.

"Yeah. Hell, Audrey, so am I."

"I didn't... know you'd be here."

"I should have texted. Somehow I just started walking, and thinking about what I wanted to say to you... and I ended up here."

"You walked here all the way from your place?"

"I had a lot of thinking to do."

Hope is a fragile thing in my chest, dancing about to the sound of his words. "I've done a lot of thinking, too," I say.

We don't speak until we reach the restaurant. Maybe neither of us want to dive into it until we're sitting down, or maybe it's nice to delay it. Prolong the time spent in each other's company.

I've missed just being near him.

We're given a table near the front.

"How was the vow renewal?" I ask. "That was this weekend, right?"

He nods. "Got back this morning. It was nice."

"Nice?"

"I had trouble concentrating," he admits. A longer finger smooths over the edge of the menu he's not reading. "Audrey, I…"

The waitress cuts us off. We order the same as last time. A full pizza, even though I'm not hungry, my stomach filled with nerves and hope.

"I've missed you," he says quietly. The gold in his eyes is molten, locked on mine. "So much. Watching you walk out of my office was the worst thing I've ever seen."

"Really?" I whisper.

He gives a single nod. "I regret a lot of things, but I'm the most sorry for making you think it was easy to hear. For thinking I didn't care."

"You were so cold," I say. "It seemed like you agreed with what I was saying. That… breaking up would be easier."

"Maybe I did think that," he says. "But not in the way you think. Audrey, for so long, I have… damn." He runs a hand through his hair, clearly agitated. "It hurt to hear you say that you figured it would be easier to just end it."

Oh. "I didn't realize."

"I didn't let on," he says. "That's what I've done for years. Not being honest about when something's painful. When someone leaves."

I realize it, then. The connection. It's deeply internalized for him… and I'd left. Not in the same way, of course. But it had triggered the same feelings.

"I should have told you to stay," he says. "Told you that we'd figure it out. But most of all, I should have asked you to forgive me."

"For not telling me sooner?"

"Yes. God, yes. I should have told you the same day I found out, when he ambushed me, when we met for coffee. Christ, I would have been a mess about it. But I should have fallen apart in front of you instead of hiding it from you."

"I can handle the ugly," I say. "That's a relationship."

"I'm realizing that." Carter reaches across the table and

grips my hand in his, so tight I can feel the sharp edges of his knuckles. "I love you, kid."

Everything slows down. The spinning of the Earth, my breathing. "Sorry?"

"I love you," he repeats. "And I was terrified of losing you."

I swallow thickly, my brain moving through syrup. He loves me. "I noticed," I say. "Not telling me about the plan B for the *Globe*, about your father's connection with mine, the insistence I have a lock on my door..."

"I hate the the idea that one day you'll disappear, and not have meant anything you said. Or that I can't protect you from someone who means to hurt you." He shakes his head, short, rough movements. "I'm sure someone could psychoanalyze the hell out of that."

I give him a teasing smile. "The *Globe* has a therapist column, you know."

He chuckles. "God, do I love you. And I wish I had made a hundred different decisions. I should have told you about my father. I should have trusted you with that information, instead of withholding it. I'm sorry I'm related to him. If I could change that too, believe me, I would."

I look down at his hand covering mine. Slowly, I cover it with my other one too. "Honesty," I say. "It has to be the cornerstone going forward."

"I'll tell you everything. So much, kid, you'll ask me to shut up."

I laugh. "I don't think I'll ever do that."

"You will. Just wait." His free hand comes up beneath my chin, tipping my head back. "Does this mean you forgive me? It's okay if it takes time. If you never do. What I did was unforgivable."

I look into the hesitant, loving, vulnerable eyes across from mine. He's never said these words to anyone, I realize. It's a kick to my soul, reverberating in tune to his across the table.

"Not unforgivable," I say. "It wasn't your fault that your dad did what he did, you know."

"I know," he answers.

A bit too quickly.

"It wasn't. Not any of it."

"Well, he didn't care enough to stay out of prison for his children," Carter says. "Felt pretty personal."

"That was a reflection on him, not you."

He shakes his head slowly, and I know this is a conversation for another time. But I'm not going to forget about his answer.

"I'm sorry," he says again. "If I keep saying it, I worry it'll come off as insincere. But I know I have a hundred times left to say it before I come close to making up for it."

I shake my head. "You don't."

"Finding my father is one of your life missions. I remember. And I hid that from you." He reaches into the pocket of his jacket and pulls out a neatly folded wad of papers. "Here."

"What's this?"

"Ammunition," he says.

I unfold the pieces of paper. Pictures of his father. His prison sentence. Documents from the court case. Lists of the crimes he committed. And beneath it, a list of possible aliases he used. I see Carter's name several times amongst them.

"Carter..." I whisper.

"Expose him," he says. "Use him as the leading example in your article. I don't care. His real name is Mark Fischer."

Tears come to my eyes. "He's your father."

"He stopped being that a long time ago. I changed my last name to my mother's six months after he went to prison."

"But he's your sibling's father. Your mother's ex-husband. I'm not going to do this." I push the papers to the side and reach for him. The table is narrow enough to let me, my hands settling on the sides of his face. The stubble tickles my skin. "Carter," I say. "You don't have to atone for his crimes."

He gives a tiny nod.

There's more to talk about. But in this moment, there's only one thing left to say.

"So you love me?"

His lips curl into the smile I love the most. The genuine one, lighting up his eyes. It makes my insides flutter. "Yes," he says. "More than I know what to do with."

"I love you too," I tell him. "But don't worry, I have a few ideas."

His smile widens. "You'll have to show me."

He kisses me for longer than is appropriate in public. At some point, we notice the appearance of mozzarella-oozing pizzas beneath us on the table, but neither of us reacted when they were put down.

And surprise, surprise… it's the best pizza I've ever had.

TWENTY-SEVEN

Carter

"*Essential Reporting: A Guide for Journalists,*" I say, putting the frayed book into her brand-new bookcase. I pull another from the box. "*The Count of Monte Cristo.* There are some highs and lows here, kid."

"A classic!" she calls from the kitchen. It's an actual kitchen, too. When we first visited the rental, she'd swooned when she saw the full-sized fridge.

Thats when I knew I had her.

I pick up another book. "*A Narrative History of the Free Press,*" I read. "God, I'm dating a nerd, aren't I?"

Audrey laughs in the kitchen. It's my favorite sound. I've tried to lure it out over and over in the past three weeks, as many times as I can, to make up for the time when I didn't have it in my life.

"You're a nerd too! I caught you reading expense reports before bed last night."

I smile down at the books I'm unboxing. She'd insisted I didn't have to help her move, and I'd told her, in all honesty, that doing anything at all is better than not being with her.

"It's happy reading now," I call back. "I fall asleep with a smile on my face."

She sticks her head out of the doorway, curls falling in

bouncy patterns around her head. "So that smile had nothing to do with me last night, did it?"

I give her a slow grin back. "Oh, it certainly did."

Her cheeks color and she looks so adorably proud of herself that I can't help myself. "I love you," I say.

She laughs and ducks back into the kitchen. "You said that yesterday night too! After you finished."

I reach for another book, still smiling. Oh, I'd finished all right. Or more aptly—she'd finished me off. In her mouth. It had been surprising and amazing and she'd looked up at me with delighted surprise afterwards.

"You know what my favorite thing about this place is?" she says. There's the rustle of cutlery as she pours it into a drawer.

"The lock?"

"No, but that's a close second."

"The kitchen," I say.

"Wrong again. But that's... a close third? No, I revise my list. The lock is number three, kitchen number two."

"How close it is to mine, then," I say, and put the final book in place on her shelf. Another moving box empty. She hadn't had many, and moving her stuff from Pierce's to the new apartment had only taken half a day.

She returns to the living room, wearing a smile and a striped apron. "Yes," she says.

"Got it on my third try."

"It's close to yours *and* work." She reaches up, fitting her arms around my neck, and I find her waist. I love holding her like this.

"Me *and* work," I say. "Good to know we get one abbreviated point."

"You happen to be at both places."

"I'm a clever man." I kiss her, a brief brush of the lips that turns lingering and sweet. "Are you happy, kid?"

Her smile is blinding. Something hurts, physically hurts in my chest. *I would kill anyone who harmed her*—the thought is crystal clear in my head. It doesn't even bother me.

"I'm happier than I can ever remember being," she says. "This place is gorgeous… and I know you pulled some strings. Don't try to hide it from me."

I look up at the ceiling, pretending to consider. "I promised honesty, right?"

"Carter," she warns, but there's laughter in her voice.

"Yes," I say, "I pulled some strings. But they were minor. The owner of this building is a family friend of Conway's. I asked if they had any rent-controlled properties."

"And they just happened to have this one free?"

"As a matter of fact, yes. They were searching for a tenant who would likely stay only for a year or two."

"And you thought of me?" she says. Her fingers drift up into my hair, nails scraping softly against my scalp. It becomes hard to keep my train of thought.

"Yes," I say. "Who knows where we'll be in a year or two?"

"Carter Kingsley," she murmurs. "Have you been thinking about the future?"

"I've been called a visionary in the past, you know. Forward-thinking. Strategic. A brilliant young face in the business industry. A—"

She pulls me across the hardwood floor of her new apartment, toward the couch I'd gotten for her as a moving-in present. It's a smaller replica of mine, the one she'd complimented often.

We fall down on the soft cushions. I have just enough time to reach out and support myself on an arm before crushing her.

"You think highly of yourself, don't you?" she teases.

I find the curve of her ear with my lips. "Can I tell you a secret?"

She nods, her legs coming up to grip my hips.

"The most brilliant woman on earth loves me," I whisper. "So yeah, I think pretty highly of myself. How can I not?"

Audrey laughs and pulls me down for a kiss. It's sweet, and soft, and I never thought I'd be here. Play this part. Love so openly that it feels like I'm carrying around a wound I never want to heal. She can break me, and I wouldn't have it any other way.

"You have to go soon," she murmurs a long while later. Her hands are running through my hair, back and forth, the way she likes to do at night.

"Nothing could make me leave this spot," I say. "Right here is where I want to live and die."

"On top of me? Your business partners won't like that."

"They don't have to like it."

"You accepted this invitation a long time ago. All the important people from the paper will be there. Booker, by the way. She even got a babysitter for tonight, just for this event."

"Yes, but you won't be there. Come with me," I tell her. "Be my date. Please." The desire to be with her in public is overwhelming. Maybe it's my pride, but I can't wait for the day she'll accompany me to these events. They're boring at best, and yet... I want others to see us together.

I want others to see her with me.

Audrey sighs, her hands tightening in my hair. "I want to. You know I want to."

"Then do it, kid."

"You know I'll say no. We have a deal."

"One year," I say against her skin. "Yes. I know."

One more year of me being her boss. Twelve months, fifty-two weeks, and no dating in public. Going on trips out of state, evenings in our apartments, and being nothing to each other at work.

"You wore the red blouse to work yesterday," I say.

Her fingers still in my hair. "Yes. You noticed?"

"Of course I did. I had to go down to the newsroom, and I

couldn't look at you twice, because no one is allowed to suspect a thing. But I wanted to."

"You know, I might start wearing sexier outfits to work just to taunt you."

"You're the devil."

"Yes, and you're stuck with me," she says, locking her legs around me. "For eternity."

"Go ahead and torment me." I find her lips again, and God, I can't wait until this year is over. For all of the *Globe*'s allure—and there's plenty, especially as the newspaper has started to slowly increase its subscriber count—I want to stop hiding us.

And I never want her to worry about what her colleagues might say if they find out.

So in a year, I'm going to change jobs. I'd offered to do it sooner, but Audrey had been adamant. It has to be fair to both of us, she'd said, and the *Globe* needed me too much to step down.

It's a compromise we both benefit from.

"Go," she tells me, another ten minutes later.

"I wish I could cancel," I say, watching her sprawl on the couch. She's in her pajama shorts, bare legs stretched out, feet on an overturned moving box.

"You can't," she says. "You won't be gone for long, and you'll get all those tasty mini quiches."

"You're tastier."

She blushes, but doesn't look away. My girl doesn't faze easily anymore. "You can taste me when you get back," she says. "How does that sound?"

I reach down to adjust myself through the fabric of my suit pants. "Fuck, kid."

She laughs. "Go. I'll be here when you get back."

"I can't wait."

"Oh, I remembered something. I can't come for lunch tomorrow."

"Not a problem. What came up?" I shrug into my suit

jacket and tuck my shirt more firmly into my pants. I'm going to have to be charming. It used to be so easy. Fun, even. A game for a bachelor to play. Now the only person I want to charm is in this apartment, and I'm leaving it.

"Freddie asked me to have lunch with her and I very much want to say yes."

"Second choice to my colleague's wife," I say morosely. "It's a sad day."

Audrey grins and pushes off the couch. She reaches up to fix my hair, smoothing out the mussing she'd done earlier. "You're always my first choice," she says. "I love you."

"I love you too," I say. "I'll be back as soon as I can."

"I'll be here," she says, and I think those might be the sweetest words I've ever heard. She's not going anywhere.

And neither am I.

Audrey

EPILOGUE

Two years later

"Kid, you look beautiful!" Carter calls from the living room. "You always do!"

I turn around in front of the full-length mirror and inspect the dress for the fourteenth time. It fits great, but it's tighter than I'm used to. Floor length and sweeping. My hair's up, curls hanging down along my back. That part I like. The dress?

I still haven't quite gotten used to wearing clothes like this. The fabric falls like liquid silk around my legs. I'll have to be careful when I walk.

"Sure I don't look too fancy?" I call back. The dress is art on the hanger. But on me? I don't want to look like I'm playing dress-up.

Carter comes into our bedroom. He's in a tux, wearing it like he wears everything. Naturally and comfortably. "You look beautiful," he says, "and delicious, and expensive, and intelligent, and mine, and—"

"Yours?" But I grin as I reach up to wrap my arms around his neck. "That was a mighty list of compliments."

He bends to kiss me, remembering last second that I have

lipstick on, diverting to my cheek. "All true. Now, please, light of my life, can we leave?"

"You're eager?"

"The sooner we get there the sooner we can leave," Carter says.

I laugh. "Don't let the Winters hear you say that."

Carter looks over his shoulder. "Are they here?"

I roll my eyes. "No."

"Then come on. There's something waiting for you in the kitchen, too." His hand slides down to capture mine, and he leads me out into the living room. Our living room, now. He'd been right about me renting my apartment for a short period. I'd been in that beautiful little space for a year and a half until the conversation about extending the lease came up.

We'd both decided it would be better if I moved in.

His apartment is ours now, with new art on the walls and plants I'd insisted on brightening the space. It's home.

"Something waiting?" I ask. "Should I be worried?"

"No. You'll like this."

"Oh, I'm intrigued now."

There's a bouquet of flowers on the kitchen counter. It's a simple thing, two slender white lilies in the center surrounded by leaves of deep green. Attached is a card.

"Read it," Carter says. His eyes are trained on me.

"Did this just arrive?"

"Yes."

I frown, reaching for the envelope. "Do you know who it's from?"

"The porter said who it was, yes."

I open the envelope. My eyes scan the simple sentence and the name beneath.

"Oh my God," I say.

Carter grins. "It's from your lover?"

"Yes. I mean, my instinct is to say no, but you won't stop calling him that."

"What did he write?"

I turn the card over to show Carter the scrawled words. *Good writing, kid.*

- Dean Allen.

"Kid," Carter repeats. "He knows about my nickname for you?"

I laugh. "Might also be because he's in his seventies. Everyone under the age of forty is a kid to him."

"And sending my girlfriend flowers? I need to be on the lookout."

I laugh, feeling giddy with happiness. "He read the article."

"He sure must have," Carter says. "How couldn't he? Everyone who's anyone has read Audrey Ford's latest piece. Besides, he would be a poor mentor if he didn't." Carter comes closer, hugging me against him. "I'm happy for you."

I relax against his chest. "The response has been incredible. I didn't expect it."

"I did," he says quietly, a hand smoothing over my back. "The piece is strong."

"It's personal," I say. "Maybe that's why. It feels odd when people comment on it. I know it shouldn't. We put it out there, after all."

"We did. All of us."

"Does it still feel okay?" I ask. "Having the story told publicly?"

He's quiet. I lean closer, listening to the beat of his heart. The article had come out last week, but it had been months, if not years, in the making. It's so much more than the piece on con artists I'd always wanted to write.

It's an exploration of all sides of the story. The people who lie… and the people whose lives are ruined by it. Carter and I became a focal point in it. A way into the story.

My dad is interviewed. Carter's dad is interviewed.

Not to sensationalize, but to humanize.

"It feels good," he says finally, hand still stroking over my back. "We read it a dozen times before sending it off. I know every word by heart."

"And yet...?"

He snorts. "Nothing, really. It's a good piece. I'll admit, I was terrified about introducing you to my father, but you were brilliant, kid. Didn't buy any of his bullshit."

"You coached me beforehand," I say. Not to mention that it would take a great deal for me to forget who the man was—what he'd done not only to my father, but to my boyfriend. He'd hurt the people I love most.

Carter had explained to his father what we wanted over email, about the road to reconciliation, taking responsibility. His dad had been more open to it than either of us had expected.

My father had been, too, answering my questions with candor. *If it can make others aware of these schemes,* he'd said, *then my mistake won't feel quite so huge.*

The two men still haven't met, and I don't think it's a meeting either of them want, nor their children. Carter had sat next to me the entire time while I spoke to his father. He'd been strung taut like a bow. Tension had radiated through his flexed arm and into me.

Oddly enough, I'd snapped into professional mode. In front of me had been a man. The man I remembered, yes, and yet... not. Older. Grayer. Softer around the eyes, sharp as a tack, but his manner felt sheathed. His weapons put away.

He didn't remember me, but he'd apologized nonetheless. It had been profuse and, in Carter's opinion, insincere. I don't know what I believe yet.

"You're thinking," Carter says above me. "I can feel it."

I laugh against his chest. "Sorry. I was thinking about our dads."

"Well, I care a great deal for one of them," he says. That makes me smile. Carter had fit into my family with surprising ease, winning my parents over with his steadiness. His charm had been hidden away, instead all genuine smiles and calm conversation. It mattered a great deal to him, he'd told me afterwards, that they like him, because he's planning on being in their daughter's life for as long as she'd let him.

"I love you," I tell him. "And you're already my parents' favorite. The chocolates you brought my mom last weekend sealed the deal."

He laughs. "It was nothing."

"It was everything, and you know it. She loves pralines."

"Well, I have a great deal to be grateful to them for." He presses his lips to my hair. "Think they'll react well to the article?"

"They know what's in it," I say. "And at the end of the day, it's not an incriminating piece. It's telling a much bigger story, about fraud and con men in America, and using our family to ground it. Declan called it 'accomplished' the other day."

Carter laughs. "I swear to God, you two have the weirdest friendship."

I grin at that. My deskmate has been promoted, as have I, but our old rivalry lives on. It's one of the best parts of my work at the *Globe*. "Well, weird friendships are kind of my specialty," I say. "You and I were weird in the beginning."

Things are different now, in a good way. Wesley is gone. It hadn't taken Carter long to see what the rest of us saw. Booker is editor-in-chief now, presiding over the entire newspaper instead of just the Investigative newsroom.

She's still my idol.

"We were never weird," Carter says. "We were... unorthodox."

"Isn't that just a fancier word for weird?"

He kisses my cheek again, avoiding the lipstick. "Smart-ass."

I laugh. "You have a point, though. We didn't exactly start out very conventionally."

"Not at all."

"Did you usually chat with women at bars? Like you did with me?"

He smiles, golden eyes warm. "This feels like a trick question, honey."

"It's not. I swear."

"Sometimes," he says. "But I'd stopped that kind of thing years before I met you."

"So why did you speak to me?"

He raises an eyebrow. "You looked like you needed help. An escape from your thoughts, you know? Plus, you were stunning. I thought that from the beginning."

"I thought you were attractive from the first time we met."

He grins. "I suspected, kid, even when you pretended not to notice. Come on. We'll be late."

We're late.

But no one cares.

The Winter Hotel is an imposing feature in New York, old and storied, with marble floors in the giant atrium. Security is tight tonight, a testament to the kind of people Isaac and Anthony Winter had invited. The night is beautiful. Our friends are there, and try as we all should to mingle with the other guests, it's always more fun when we talk to one another.

Freddie steals me away as soon as she can. She's no longer breastfeeding and drinks a glass of champagne with obvious relish. "Julie was asleep when we left," she tells me. "She's an angel most of the time, except when she's not, of course."

Tristan and Freddie had bought a townhouse not far from Anthony and Summer. It's a beautiful place, family-oriented, and I'm there at least twice a month to visit Freddie. She's become the sister I never had.

An ambitious, intelligent, endlessly supportive sister.

"The sweetheart," I say. Julie is the cutest little baby.

"I saw your article. Brilliant, Audrey," she says. "Absolutely brilliant. I had tears in my eyes halfway through."

I'd cried several times while writing it, putting my family's pain to paper, and I squeeze her arm. "Thank you."

Carter is talking to the other men in the distance. All three of them are married now, Anthony and Summer tying the knot just last summer. We're the last couple left.

I smile at his tall form. I'm not in a rush, and I don't think he is either. What we have is the best thing in my life.

"I wonder why he's still single," Freddie murmurs at my side. Summer and Cecilia are close by, but neither overhear.

"Who?" I ask.

"Isaac? Isn't that who you're looking at?"

My gaze travels up to the twin grand staircases in the lobby. Isaac Winter is there, standing at the top with his hand on the railing. His suit looks sharp. Edges crisp, eyes expressionless as he looks out over the crowd. He's Anthony's older brother and heir to the Winter hotel fortune. He must be in his late thirties or early forties now.

"Oh. You're right. I've never seen him with anyone. He didn't even bring a date tonight?"

Freddie shakes her head. "Summer says he's married to the hotel."

"Oh. That's a shame," I say. "Have you ever heard—oh, sorry."

The room quiets down as Isaac takes the mic. He welcomes us all here and gives a short overview of the history of the hotel. The Winter Hotel in New York is the original one, over a century old, the head to the many offshoots worldwide. Summer and Anthony's honeymoon had been to one of their newly opened resorts internationally.

A strong arm slides around my waist. Carter's found me, the scent of his cologne subtle and delicious. I'd bought it for his birthday. "Hey," he whispers.

"Hi," I whisper back.

"Let's get out of here."

"You're sure?"

"Yes." And then, his lips to my ear, "I have a surprise."

It doesn't take us long to leave the event. Our friends don't look surprised at our early departure, either, which is unusual. We usually end the night with a nightcap together. Less often now, perhaps, when Tristan and Freddie have a newborn. But still. Not a single raised eyebrow?

Michael is waiting for us by the curb. He gives us both a smile. It's uncharacteristically wide.

I start getting suspicious. "Carter," I say. "Exactly what kind of surprise is this?"

He reaches for my hand. "A good one."

"Your surprises vary a great deal."

He laughs. "Yes, well, I promise I've learned. This will be something you like. I think."

"Do the others know?"

He glances at me, still smiling. "Stop asking questions."

"I can't *not*."

"You can. No need to interview me." His hand tightens on mine. "We're almost there."

I peer out the window of the car. It looks like a normal street at nightfall, people going about their business, shops closing just as restaurants pick up steam.

Michael pulls us to a stop at the curb. "We're here," he says. Is that excitement in his voice?

Nerves take up residence in my stomach, and a tiny, sneaky suspicion forms in my mind. Where is he taking me…?

Carter opens my door for me. He looks brilliant in his tux, thick hair swept back from his forehead. He gives me a crooked smile. "My lady," he says.

I laugh. "Wow."

His hand rests on the small of my back. People on the sidewalk watch us as we pass, both dressed to the nines. My ballgown is more than a little out of place.

"Patience," he murmurs at my side. The arm beside me is taut.

That's when I recognize the place. It's the bar where we first met. Where we had our first date.

"Oh," I say.

Carter holds the door open for me. "After you, kid."

I step inside. There's no one here. It's empty, and on every single table is a single lit candle. It looks magical.

My throat starts to close up. The suspicion grows stronger, and anticipation rushes through me. Oh my God.

"It's a bit different," he says quietly at my side. "The place was bought a while ago. I asked the management to make it look like it did our first night."

"It's beautiful," I whisper.

"Now… where were we? Here, right?" Carter walks us toward the bar counter. He leans against it, eyes serious on mine. There's something vulnerable in them. He's nervous, I realize.

Sweet Jesus.

"Yes," I say. "I think this is where we were. I was… standing like this."

"Asking the bartender for water."

I nod and look around. "Are we really alone in here?"

"Yes," he says. "Though I can't tell you the staff room is empty."

I give a hoarse chuckle. "Wow."

"You were nervous back then," he says quietly. "Are you nervous now?"

"Yes. A little. There are no peanuts."

His lips curve into a small smile. The flickering candlelight sets off the auburn notes in his hair. "No, I forgot that detail."

I shake my head. "Not necessary."

"I'll tell you a secret. I'm nervous too."

"Oh."

"Audrey," he says.

I take a deep breath. "Yes?"

"Meeting you here was the greatest coincidence in my life.

I can't imagine where I'd be if I hadn't gone to this bar that night, over two years ago."

"Me neither," I whisper.

He smiles, a brief tug of his lips. "When we came here the second time, it was on our first proper date. Do you remember?"

"Yes."

"You'd said yes to me. I was ecstatic, and oddly… grateful. That you'd take the risk you did. We worked together and you didn't entirely trust me. I wanted to prove your courage right."

"You did, and you have. These two years have been the best in my life," I say. He doesn't seem to mind me interrupting his speech. Nerves make it hard to talk, but this is important. Important that he knows.

Carter reaches for my hand. His skin is warm. "You are the greatest thing in my life, kid. I can't imagine living without you. So here, in the place where we first met…"

He drops down to one knee. Time slows down. I watch his open expression, the hand reaching into his pocket. The glittering stone on a platinum band. "Audrey Ford," he says. "I love you more than I ever thought possible. Will you marry me?"

Tears make it hard to see, but I nod. "Yes. Yes, Carter, of course. Oh my God."

He laughs and wraps his arms around me. I hold on tight as he spins me around, the bar becoming blurry. The others had known. He'd planned this, coordinated with the staff, but kept it small and intimate. Just the two of us.

And now it always will be.

GET THE BONUS SHORT

Want more Carter and Audrey?

Join my newsletter at www.oliviahayle.com to read a 5000-word bonus scene, set after their wedding…

OTHER BOOKS BY OLIVIA
LISTED IN READING ORDER

New York Billionaires Series

Think Outside the Boss
Tristan and Freddie

Saved by the Boss
Anthony and Summer

Say Yes to the Boss
Victor and Cecilia

A Ticking Time Boss
Carter and Audrey

Seattle Billionaires Series

Billion Dollar Enemy
Cole and Skye

Billion Dollar Beast
Nick and Blair

Billion Dollar Catch
Ethan and Bella

Billion Dollar Fiancé
Liam and Maddie

Brothers of Paradise Series

Rogue
Lily and Hayden

Ice Cold Boss
Faye and Henry

Red Hot Rebel
Ivy and Rhys

Small Town Hero
Jamie and Parker

Standalones

Arrogant Boss
Julian and Emily

Look But Don't Touch
Grant and Ada

The Billionaire Scrooge Next Door
Adam and Holly

ABOUT OLIVIA

Olivia loves billionaire heroes despite never having met one in person. Taking matters into her own hands, she creates them on the page instead. Stern, charming, cold or brooding, so far she's never met a (fictional) billionaire she didn't like.

Her favorite things include wide-shouldered heroes, late-night conversations, too-expensive wine and romances that lift you up.

Smart and sexy romance—those are her lead themes!

Join her newsletter for updates and bonus content.
www.oliviahayle.com.
Connect with Olivia

- facebook.com/authoroliviahayle
- instagram.com/oliviahayle
- goodreads.com/oliviahayle
- amazon.com/author/oliviahayle
- bookbub.com/profile/olivia-hayle